THE CENTAUR

ALGERNON BLACKWOOD

SANAGE
PUBLISHING HOUSE

Paperback: 9789362052735
Hardback: 9789362053497
eBook: 9789362057105

Printed by: Manipal Technologies Limited, India

Sanage Publishing House LLP
Mumbai, India

sanagepublishing@gmail.com

Algernon Blackwood (1869-1951) was an English journalist, novelist, and short-story writer, remembered as one of the most prolific and most celebrated writers of ghost, horror, and "weird" stories during the early 20th century. Among his most popular works are the novellas The Wendigo, The Willows, the novel The Centaur, the John Silence stories, and his collection Incredible Adventures, considered by some critics to be the "premier weird collection of" all time.

CONTENTS

I

"We may be in the Universe as dogs and cats are in our libraries, seeing the books and hearing the conversation, but having no inkling of the meaning of it all."

—WILLIAM JAMES, A Pluralistic Universe

"... A man's vision is the great fact about him. Who cares for Carlyle's reasons, or Schopenhauer's, or Spencer's? A philosophy is the expression of a man's intimate character, and all definitions of the Universe are but the deliberately adopted reactions of human characters upon it."

—Ibid

"There are certain persons who, independently of sex or comeliness, arouse an instant curiosity concerning themselves. The tribe is small, but its members unmistakable. They may possess neither fortune, good looks, nor that adroitness of advance-vision which the stupid name good luck; yet there is about them this inciting quality which proclaims that they have overtaken Fate, set a harness about its neck of violence, and hold bit and bridle in steady hands.

"Most of us, arrested a moment by their presence to snatch the definition their peculiarity exacts, are aware that on the heels of curiosity follows—envy. They know the very things that we forever seek in vain. And this diagnosis, achieved as if it were en passant, comes near to the truth, for the hallmark of such persons is that they have found, and come into, their own. There is a sign upon the face and in the eyes. Having somehow discovered the 'piece' that makes them free of the whole amazing puzzle, they know where they belong and, therefore, whither they are bound more, they are definitely en route. The littleness's of existence that plague the majority pass them by.

"For this reason, if for no other," continued O'Malley, "I count my experience with that man as memorable beyond ordinary. 'If for no other,' because from the very beginning there was another. Indeed, it was probably his air of unusual bigness, massiveness rather,—head, face, eyes, shoulders, especially back and shoulders,—that struck me first when I caught sight of him lounging there hugely upon my steamer deck at Marseilles, winning my instant attention before he turned and the expression on his great face woke more—woke curiosity, interest, envy. He wore this very look of certainty that knows, yet with a tinge of mild surprise as though he had only recently known. It was less than perplexity. A faint astonishment as of a happy child—almost of an animal—shone in the large brown eyes—"

"You mean that the physical quality caught you first, then the psychical?" I asked, keeping him to the point, for his Irish imagination was ever apt to race away at a tangent.

He laughed good-naturedly, acknowledging the check. "I believe that to be the truth," he replied, his face instantly grave again. "It was the impression of uncommon bulk that heated my intuition—blessed if I know how—leading me to the other. The size of his body did not smother, as so often is the case with big people: rather, it revealed. At the moment I could conceive no possible connection, of course. Only this overwhelming attraction of the man's personality caught me, and I longed to make friends. That's the way with me, as you know," he added, tossing the hair back from his forehead impatiently,"—pretty often. First impressions. Old man, I tell you, it was like a possession."

"I believe you," I said. For Terence O'Malley all his life had never understood half measures.

II

"The friendly and flowing savage, who is he? Is he waiting for civilization, or is he past it, and mastering it?"

—WHITMAN

"We find ourselves today in the midst of a somewhat peculiar state of society, which we call Civilization, but which even to the most optimistic among us does not seem altogether desirable. Some of us, indeed, are inclined to think that it is a kind of disease which the various races of man have to pass through....

"While History tells us of many nations that have been attacked by it, of many that have succumbed to it, and of some that are still in the throes of it, we know of no single case in which a nation has fairly recovered from and passed through it to a more normal and healthy condition. In other words, the development of human society has never yet (that we know of) passed beyond a certain definite and apparently final stage in the process we call Civilization; at that stage it has always succumbed or been arrested."

—EDWARD CARPENTER, Civilization: Its Cause and Cure

O'Malley himself is an individuality that invites consideration from the ruck of commonplace men. Of mingled Irish, Scotch, and English blood, the first predominated, and the Celtic element in him was strong. A man of vigorous health, careless of gain, a wanderer, and by his own choice something of an outcast, he led to the end the existence of a rolling stone. He lived from hand to mouth, never quite growing up. It seemed, indeed, that he never could grow up in the accepted sense of the term, for his motto was the reverse of nil admirari, and he found himself in a state of perpetual astonishment at the mystery of things. He was forever deciphering the huge horoscope of Life, yet getting no further than the House of Wonder, on whose cusp surely he had been born. Civilization, he loved to say, had blinded the eyes of men, filling them with dust instead of vision.

An ardent lover of wild outdoor life, he knew at times a high, passionate searching for things of the spirit, when the outer world fell away like dross, and he seemed to pass into a state resembling ecstasy. Never in cities or among his fellow men, struggling and herded, did these times come to him, but when he was abroad with the winds and stars in desolate places. Then, sometimes, he would be rapt away, caught up to see the tail-end of the great procession of the gods that had come near. He surprised Eternity in a running Moment.

For the moods of Nature flamed through him—in him—like presences, potently evocative as the presences of persons, and with meanings equally various: the woods with love and tenderness; the sea with reverence and magic; plains and wide horizons with the melancholy peace and silence as of wise and old companions; and mountains with a splendid terror due to some want of comprehension in himself, caused probably by a spiritual remoteness from their mood.

The Cosmos, in a word, for him was psychical, and Nature's moods were transcendental cosmic activities that induced in him these singular states of exaltation and expansion. She pushed wide the gateways of his deeper life. She entered, took possession, dipped his smaller self into her own enormous and enveloping personality.

He possessed a full experience, and at times a keen judgment, of modern life; while underneath, all the time, lay the moving sea of curiously wild primitive instincts. An insatiable longing for the wilderness was in his blood, a craving vehement, unappeasable. Yet for something far greater than the wilderness alone—the wilderness was merely a symbol, a first step, indication of a way of escape. The hurry and invention of modern life were to him a fever and a torment. He loathed the million tricks of civilization. At the same time, being a man of some discrimination at least, he rarely let himself go completely. Of these wilder, simpler instincts he was afraid. They might flood all else. If he yielded entirely, something he dreaded, without being able to define, would happen; the structure of his being would suffer a nameless violence, so that he would have to break with the world. These cravings stood for that loot of the soul which he must deny himself. Complete surrender would involve somehow a disintegration, a dissociation of his personality that carried with it the loss of personal identity.

When the feeling of revolt became sometimes so urgent in him that it threatened to become unmanageable, he would go out into solitude, calling it to heel; but this attempt to restore order, while easing his nature, was never radical; the accumulation merely increased on the rebound; the yearnings grew and multiplied, and the point of saturation was often dangerously near. "Someday," his friends would say, "there'll be a bursting of the dam." And, though their meaning might be variously interpreted, they spoke the truth. O'Malley knew it, too.

A man he was, in a word, of deep and ever-shifting moods, and with more difficulty than most in recognizing the underlying self of which these outer aspects were projections masquerading as complete personalities.

The underlying ego that unified these projections was of the type touched with so sure a hand in the opening pages of an inspired little book: The Plea of Pan. O'Malley was useless as a citizen and knew it. Sometimes—he was ashamed of it as well.

Occasionally, and at the time of this particular "memorable adventure," aged thirty, he acted as foreign correspondent; but even as such he was the kind of newspaper man that not merely collects news, but discovers, reveals, creates it. Wise in their generation, the editors who commissioned him remembered when his copy came in that they were editors. A roving commission among the tribes of the Caucasus was his assignment at the moment, and a better man for the purpose would have been hard to find, since he knew beauty, had a keen eye for human nature, divined what was vital and picturesque, and had, further, the power to set it down in brief terms born directly of his vivid emotions.

When first I knew him he lived—nowhere being always on the move. He kept, however, a dingy little room near Paddington where his books and papers accumulated, undusted but safe, and where the manuscripts of his adventures were found when his death made me the executor of his few belongings. The key was in his pocket, carefully ticketed with a bone label. And this, the only evidence of practical forethought I ever discovered in him, was proof that something in that room was deemed by him of value—to others. It certainly was not the heterogeneous collection of second-hand books, nor the hundreds of unlabeled photographs and sketches. Can it have been the MSS. of stories, notes, and episodes I found, almost carefully piled and tabulated with titles, in a dirty kitbag of green Willesden canvas?

Some of these he had told me (with a greater vividness than he could command by pen); others were new; many unfinished. All were unusual, to say the least. All, too, had obviously happened to himself at some period of his roving career, though here and there he had disguised his own part in them by Hoffmann's device of throwing the action into the third person. Those told to me by word of mouth I could only feel were true, true for himself at least. In no sense were they mere inventions but arose in moments of vision upon a structure of solid events. Ten men will describe in as many different ways a snake crossing their path; but, besides these, there exists an eleventh man who sees more than the snake, the path, the movement. O'Malley was some such eleventh man. He saw the whole thing from some kind of inner bird's-eye view, while the ten saw only limited aspects of it from various angles. He was accused of adding details, therefore, because he had divined their presence while still below the horizon. Before they emerged the others had already left.

By which I mean that he saw in commonplace events the movement of greater tides than others saw. At one remove of time or distance—a minute or a mile—he perceived all. While the ten chattered volubly about the name of the snake, he was caught beyond by the beauty of the path, the glory of the running glide, the nature of the forces that drove, hindered, modified.

The others reasoned where the snake was going, its length in inches and its speed per second, while he, ignoring such superficial details, plunged as it were into the very nature of the creature's being. And in this idiosyncrasy, which he shared with all persons of mystical temperament, is exemplified a certain curious contempt for Reason that he had. For him, mere intellectuality, by which the modern world sets such a store, was a valley of dry bones. Its worship was a worship of the form. It missed the essential inner truth because such inner truth could be known only by being it, feeling it. The intellectual attitude of mind, in a word, was critical, not creative, and to be unimaginative seemed to him, therefore, the worst form of unintelligence.

"The arid, sterile minds!" he would cry in a burst of his Celtic enthusiasm. "Where, I ask ye, did the philosophies and sciences of the world assist the progress of any single soul a blessed inch?"

Any little Dreamer in his top-floor back, spinning by rushlight his web of beauty, was greater than the finest critical intelligence that ever lived. The one, for all his poor technique, was stammering over something God had whispered to him, the other merely destroying thoughts invented by the brain of man.

And this attitude of mind, because of its interpretative effect upon what follows, justifies mention. For to O'Malley, in some way difficult to explain, Reason and Intellect, as such, had come to be worshipped by men today out of all proportion to their real value. Consciousness, focused too exclusively upon them, had exalted them out of due proportion in the spiritual economy. To make a god of them was to make an empty and inadequate god. Reason should be the guardian of the soul's advance, but not the object. Its function was that of a great sandpaper which should clear the way of excrescences, but its worship was to allow a detail to assume a disproportionate importance.

Not that he was foolish enough to despise Reason in what he called its proper place, but that he was "wise" enough—not that he was "intellectual" enough!—to recognize its futility in measuring the things of the soul. For him there existed a more fundamental understanding than Reason, and it was, apparently, an inner and natural understanding.

"The greatest Teacher we ever had," I once heard him say, "ignored the intellect, and who, will ye tell me, can by searching find out God? And yet what else is worth finding out...? Isn't it only by becoming as a little child—a child that feels and never reasons things—that anyone shall enter the kingdom...? Where will the giant intellects be before the Great White Throne when a simple man with the heart of a child will top the lot of 'em?"

"Nature, I'm convinced," he said another time, though he said it with puzzled eyes and a mind obviously groping, "is our next step. Reason has done its best for centuries and gets no further. It can get no further, for it can do nothing for the inner life which is the sole reality. We must return to Nature and a purified intuition, to a greater reliance upon what is now subconscious, back to that sweet, grave guidance of the Universe which we've discarded with the primitive state—a spiritual intelligence, really, divorced from mere intellectuality."

And by Nature, he did not mean a return to savagery. There was no idea of going backwards in his wild words. Rather he looked forwards, in some way hard to understand, to a state when Man, with the best results of Reason in his pocket, might return to the instinctive life—to feeling with—to the sinking down of the modern, exaggerated intellectual personality into its rightful place as guide instead of leader. He called it a Return to Nature, but what he meant, I always felt, was back to a sense of kinship with the Universe which men, through worshipping the intellect alone, had lost. Men today prided themselves upon their superiority to Nature as beings separate and apart. O'Malley sought on the contrary, a development, if not a revival, of some faultless instinct, due to kinship with her, which—to take extremes—shall direct alike the animal and the inspired man, guiding the wild bee and the homing pigeon, and—the soul toward its God.

This clue, as he called it, crystallized so neatly and so conclusively his own mental struggles, that he had called a halt, as it were, to his own intellectual development.... The name and family of the snake, hence, meant to him the least important things about it. He caught, wildly yet consistently, at the psychic links that bound the snake and Nature and himself together with all creation. Troops of adventurous thoughts had all his life "gone west" to colonize this land of speculative dream. True to his idea, he "thought" with his emotions as much as with his brain, and in the broken record of the adventure that this book relates, this strange passion of his temperament remains the vital clue. For it happened in, as well as to, himself. His Being could include the Earth by feeling with her, whereas his intellect could merely criticize, and so belittle, the details of such inclusion.

Many a time, while he stretched credulity to a point, I have heard him apologize in some such way for his method. It was the splendor of his belief that made the thing so convincing in the telling, for later when I found the same tale written down it seemed somehow to have failed of an equal achievement. The truth was that no one language would convey the extraordinary freight that was carried so easily by his instinctive choice of gestures, tone, and glance. With him these were consummately interpretative.

* * * * *

Before the age of thirty he had written and published a volume or two of curious tales, all dealing with extensions of the personality, a subject that interested him deeply, and one he understood because he drew the material largely from himself. Psychology he simply devoured, even in its most fantastic and speculative forms; and though perhaps his vision was incalculably greater than his power of technique, these strange books had a certain value and formed a genuine contribution to the thought on that particular subject. In England naturally they fell dead, but their translation into German brought him a wider and more intelligent circle. The common public unfamiliar with Sally Beauchamp No. 4, with Hélène Smith, or with Dr. Hanna, found in these studies of divided personality, and these singular extensions of the human consciousness, only extravagance and imagination run to wildness. Yet, nonetheless, the substratum of truth upon which O'Malley had built them lay actually within his own personal experience. The books had brought him here and there acquaintances of value; and among these latter was a German doctor, Heinrich Stahl. With Dr. Stahl the Irishman crossed swords through months of somewhat irregular correspondence, until at length the two had met on board a steamer where the German held the position of ship's doctor. The acquaintanceship had grown into something approaching friendship, although the two men stood apparently at the opposite poles of thought. From time to time, they still met.

In appearance there was nothing unusual about O'Malley, unless it was the contrast of the light blue eyes with the dark hair. Never, I think, did I see him in anything but that old grey flannel suit, with the low collar and shabby glistening tie. He was of medium height, delicately built, his hands more like a girl's than a man's. In towns he shaved and looked fairly presentable, but once upon his travels he grew beard and moustache and would forget for weeks to have his hair cut, so that it fell in a tangle over forehead and eyes.

His manner changed with the abruptness of his moods. Sometimes active and alert, at others for days together he would become absent, dreamy, absorbed, half oblivious of the outer world, his movements and actions dictated by subconscious instinct rather than regulated by volition. And one cause of that loneliness of spirit which was undoubtedly a chief pain in life to him, was the fact that ordinary folk were puzzled how to take him, or to know which of these many extreme moods was the man himself. Uncomfortable, unsatisfactory, elusive, not to be counted upon, they deemed him: and from their point of view, they were undoubtedly right. The sympathy and above all the companionship he needed, genuinely craved too, were thus denied to him by the faults of his own temperament. With women his intercourse was of the slightest; in a sense he did not know the need of them much. For one thing, the feminine element in his own nature was too strong, and he was not conscious, as most men are, of the great gap of incompleteness women may so exquisitely fill; and, for another, its obvious corollary perhaps, when they did come into his life, they gave him more than he could comfortably deal with. They offered him more than he needed.

In this way, while he perhaps had never fallen in love, as the saying has it, he had certainly known that high splendor of devotion which means the losing of oneself in others, that exalted love which seeks not any reward of possession because it is itself so utterly possessed. He was pure, too; in the sense that it never occurred to him to be otherwise.

Chief cause of his loneliness—so far as I could judge his complex personality at all—seemed that he never found a sympathetic, truly understanding ear for those deeply primitive longings that fairly ravaged his heart. And this very isolation made him often afraid; it proved that the rest of the world, the sane majority at any rate, said No to them. I, who loved him and listened, yet never quite apprehended his full meaning. Far more than the common Call of the Wild, it was. He yearned, not so much for a world savage, uncivilized, as for a perfectly natural one that had never known, perhaps never needed civilization—a state of freedom in a life unstained.

He never wholly understood, I think, the reason why he found himself in such stern protest against the modern state of things, why people produced in him a state of death so that he turned from men to Nature—to find life. The things the nations exclusively troubled themselves about all seemed to him so obviously vain and worthless, and, though he never even in his highest moments felt the claims of sainthood, it puzzled and perplexed him deeply that the conquest over Nature in all its multifarious forms today should seem to them so infinitely more important than the conquest over self. What the world with common consent called Reality, seemed ever to him the most crude and obvious, the most transient, the most blatant un-Reality. His love of Nature was more than the mere joy of tumultuous pagan instincts. It was, in the kind of simple life he craved, the first step toward the recovery of noble, dignified, enfranchised living. In the denial of all this external flummery he hated, it would leave the soul disengaged and free, able to turn her activities within for spiritual development. Civilization now suffocated, smothered, killed the soul. Being in the hopeless minority, he felt he must be somewhere wrong, at fault, deceived. For all men, from a statesman to an engine-driver, agreed that the accumulation of external possessions had value, and that the importance of material gain was real.... Yet, for himself, he always turned for comfort to the Earth. The wise and wonderful Earth opened her mind and her deep heart to him in a way few other men seemed to know. Through Nature he could move blind-folded along yet find his way to strength and sympathy. A noble, gracious life stirred in him then, which the pettier human world denied. He often would compare the thin help or fellowship he gained from ordinary social intercourse, or from what had seemed at the time quite a successful gathering of his kind, with the power he gained from a visit to the woods or mountains. The former, as a rule, evaporated in a single day; the other stayed, with ever growing power, to bless whole weeks and months.

And hence it was, whether owing to the truth or ignorance of his attitude, that a sense of bleak loneliness spread through all his life, and more and more he turned from men to Nature.

Moreover, foolish as it must sound, I was sometimes aware that deep down in him hid some nameless, indefinable quality that proclaimed him fitted to live in conditions that had never known the restraints of modern conventions—a very different thing to doing without them once known. A kind of childlike, transcendental innocence he certainly possessed, naïf, most engaging, and—utterly impossible. It showed itself indirectly, I think, in this distress under modern conditions. The multifarious apparatus of the spirit of Today oppressed him; its rush and luxury and artificiality harassed him beyond belief. The terror of cities ran in his very blood.

When I describe him as something of an outcast, therefore, it will be seen that he was such both voluntarily and involuntarily.

"What the world has gained by brains is simply nothing to what it has lost by them—"

"A dream, my dear fellow, a mere dream," I stopped him, yet with sympathy because I knew he found relief this way. "Your constructive imagination is too active."

"By Gad," he replied warmly, "but there is a place somewhere, or a state of mind—the same thing—where it's more than a dream. And, what's more, bless your stodgy old heart, someday I'll get there."

"Not in England, at any rate," I suggested.

He stared at me a moment, his eyes suddenly charged with dreams. Then, characteristically, he snorted. He flung his hand out with a gesture that should push the present further from him.

"I've always liked the Eastern theory—old theory anyhow if not Eastern—that intense yearnings end by creating a place where they are fulfilled—"

"Subjectively—"

"Of course; objectively means incompletely. I mean a Heaven built up by desire and intense longing all your life. Your own thought makes it. Living idea, that!"

"Another dream, Terence O'Malley," I laughed, "but beautiful and seductive."

To argue bored him. He loved to state his matter, fill it with detail, blow the heated breath of life into it, and then leave it. Argument belittled without clarifying; criticism destroyed, sealing up the sources of life. Any fool could argue; the small, denying minds were always critics.

"A dream, but a damned foine one, let me tell you," he exclaimed, recovering his brogue in his enthusiasm. He glared at me a second, then burst out laughing. "This is better to have dreamed and waked," he added, "than never to have dreamed at all."

And then he poured out O'Shaughnessy's passionate ode to the Dreamers of the world:

We are the music-makers,
And we are the dreamers of dreams,
Wandering by lone sea-breakers,
And sitting by desolate streams;
World-losers and world-forsakers,
On whom the pale moon gleams;
Yet we are the movers and shakers
Of the world forever, it seems.

With wonderful deathless ditties
We build up the world's great cities,
And out of a fabulous story
We fashion an empire's glory;
One man with a dream, at pleasure,
Shall go forth and conquer a crown;
And three with a new song's measure
Can trample an empire down.

We, in the ages lying
In the buried past of the earth,
Built Nineveh with our sighing,
And Babel itself with our mirth;
And o'erthrew them with prophesying
To the old of the new world's worth;
For each age is a dream that is dying,
Or one that is coming to birth.

For this passion for some simple old-world innocence and beauty lay in his soul like a lust—self-feeding, and voracious.

III

"Lonely! Why should I feel lonely? Is our planet not in the Milky Way?"

—THOREAU

March had passed shouting away, and April was whispering deliciously among her scented showers when O'Malley went on board the coasting steamer at Marseilles for the Levant and the Black Sea. The mistral made the land unbearable, but herds of white horses ran galloping over the bay beneath a sky of childhood's blue. The ship started punctually—he came on board as usual with a bare minute's margin—and from his rapid survey of the thronged upper deck, it seems, he singled out on the instant this man and boy, wondering first vaguely at their uncommon air of bulk, secondly at the absence of detail which should confirm it. They appeared so much bigger than they actually were. The laughter, rising in his heart, however, did not get as far as his lips.

For this appearance of massive bulk, and of shoulders comely yet almost humped, was not borne out by a direct inspection. It was a mental impression. The man, though broad and well-proportioned, with heavy back and neck and uncommonly sturdy torso, was in no sense monstrous. It was upon the corner of the eye that the bulk and hugeness dawned, a false report that melted under direct vision. O'Malley took him in with attention merging in respect, searching in vain for the detail of the back and limbs and neck that suggested so curiously the sense of the gigantic. The boy beside him, obviously son, possessed the same elusive attributes—felt yet never positively seen.

Passing down to his cabin, wondering vaguely to what nationality they might belong, he was immediately behind them, elbowing French and German tourists, when the father abruptly turned and faced him. Their gaze met. O'Malley started.

"Whew…!" ran some silent expression like fire through his brain.

Out of a massive visage, placid for all its ruggedness, shone eyes large and timid as those of an animal or child bewildered among so many people. There was an expression in them not so much cowed or dismayed as "un-refuged"—the eyes of the hunted creature. That, at least, was the first thing they betrayed; for the same second the quick-blooded Celt caught another look: the look of a hunted creature that at last knows shelter and has found it. The first expression had emerged, then withdrawn again swiftly like an animal into its hole where safety lay. Before disappearing, it had flashed a wireless message of warning, of welcome, of explanation—he knew not what term to use—to another of its own kind, to himself.

O'Malley, utterly arrested, stood and stared. He would have spoken, for the invitation seemed obvious enough, but there came an odd catch in his breath, and words failed altogether. The boy, peering at him sideways, clung to his great parent's side. For perhaps ten seconds there was this interchange of staring, intimate staring, between the three of them ... and then the Irishman, confused, more than a little agitated, ended the silent introduction with an imperceptible bow and passed on slowly, knocking absent-mindedly through the crowd, down to his cabin on the lower deck.

In his heart, deep down, stirred an indescribable sympathy with something he divined in these two that was akin to himself, but that as yet he could not name. On the surface he felt an emotion he knew not whether to call uneasiness or surprise, but crowding past it, half smothering it, rose this other more profound emotion. Something enormously winning in the atmosphere of father and son called to him in the silence: it was significant, oddly buried; not yet had it emerged enough to be confessed and labeled. But each had recognized it in the other. Each knew. Each waited. And it was extraordinarily disturbing.

Before unpacking, he sat for a long time on his berth, thinking....trying in vain to catch through a thunder of surprising emotions the word that might bring explanation. That strange impression of giant bulk, unsupported by actual measurements; that look of startled security seeking shelter; that other look of being sure of knowing where to go and being actually en route,—all these, he felt, grew from the same hidden cause whereof they were symptoms.

It was this hidden thing in the man that had reached out invisibly and fired his own consciousness as their gaze met in that brief instant. And it had disturbed him so profoundly because the very same lost thing lay buried in himself. The man knew, whereas he anticipated merely—as yet. What was it? Why came there with both happiness and fear?

The word that kept chasing itself in a circle like a kitten after its own tail, yet bringing no explanation, was Loneliness—a loneliness that must be whispered. For it was loneliness on the verge of finding relief. And if proclaimed too loud, there might come those who would interfere and prevent relief. The man, and the boy too for that matter, were escaping. They had found the way back, were ready and eager, moreover, to show it to other prisoners.

And this was as near as O'Malley could come to explanation. He began to understand dimly—and with an extraordinary excitement of happiness.

"Well—and the bigness?" I asked, seizing on a practical point after listening to his dreaming, "what do you make of that? It must have had some definite cause surely?"

He turned and fixed his light blue eyes on mine as we paced beside the Serpentine that summer afternoon when I first heard the story told. He was half grave, half laughing.

"The size, the bulk, the bigness," he replied, "must have been in reality the expression of some mental quality that reached me psychically, producing its effect directly on my mind and not upon the eyes at all." In telling the story he used a simile omitted in the writing of it, because his sense of humor perceived that no possible turn of phrase could save it from grotesqueness when actually it was far from grotesque—extraordinarily pathetic rather: "As though," he said, "the great back and shoulders carried beneath the loose black cape—humps, projections at least; but projections not ugly in themselves, comely even in some perfectly natural way, that lent to his person this idea of giant size. His body, though large, was normal so far as its proportions were concerned. In his spirit, though, there hid another shape. An aspect of that other shape somehow reached my mind."

Then, seeing that I found nothing at the moment to reply, he added:

"As an angry man you may picture to yourself as red, or a jealous man as green!" He laughed aloud. "D'ye see, now? It was not really a physical business at all!"

IV

"We think with only a small part of the past, but it is with our entire past, including the original bent of our soul, that we desire, will, and act."

—HENRI BERGSON

The balance of his fellow-passengers were not distinguished. There was a company of French tourists gong to Naples, and another lot of Germans bound for Athens, some business folk for Smyrna and Constantinople, and a sprinkling of Russians going home via Odessa, Batoum, or Novorossisk.

In his own stateroom, occupying the upper berth, was a little round-bodied, red-faced Canadian drummer, "traveling" in harvest-machines. The name of the machine, its price, and the terms of purchase were his universe; he knew them in several languages; beyond them, nothing. He was good-natured, conceding anything to save trouble. "D'ye mind the light for a bit while I read in bed?" asked O'Malley. "Don't mind anything much," was the cheery reply. "I'm not particular; I'm easy-going and you needn't bother." He turned over to sleep. "Old traveler," he added, his voice muffled by sheets and blankets, "and take things as they come." And the only objection O'Malley found in him was that he took things as they came to the point of not taking baths at all, and not even taking all his garments off when he went to bed.

The Captain, whom he knew from previous voyages, a genial, rough-voiced sailor from Sassnitz, chided him for nearly missing the boat—"as usual."

"You're too late for a seat at my taple," he said with his laughing growl; "it's a pidy. You should have led me know py telegram, and I then kepd your place. Now you find room at the doctor's taple howefer berhaps...!"

"The steamer's very crowded this time," O'Malley replied, shrugging his shoulders; "but you'll let me come up sometimes for a smoke with you on the bridge?"

"Of course, of course."

"Anybody interesting on board?" he asked after a moment's pause.

The jolly Captain laughed. "'Pout the zame as usual, you know. Nothing to stop ze ship! Ask ze doctor; he knows zooner than me. But, anyway, the nice ones, they get zeazick always and dizappear. Going Trebizond this time?" he added.

"No; Batoum."

"Ach! Oil?"

"Caucasus generally—up in the mountains a bit."

"God blenty veapons then, I hope. They shoot you for two pfennig up there!" And he was off with his hearty deep laugh and rather ponderous briskness toward the bridge.

Thus O'Malley found himself placed for meals at the right hand of Dr. Stahl; opposite him, on the doctor's left, a talkative Moscow fur-merchant who, having come to definite conclusions of his own about things in general, was persuaded the rest of the world must share them, and who delivered verbose commonplaces with a kind of pontifical utterance sometimes amusing, but usually boring; on his right a gentle-eyed, brown-bearded Armenian priest from the Venice monastery that had sheltered Byron, a man who ate everything except soup with his knife, yet with a daintiness that made one marvel, and with hands so graceful they might almost have replaced the knife without off offence. Beyond the priest sat the rotund Canadian drummer. He kept silence, watched the dishes carefully lest anything should escape him, and—ate. Lower down on the opposite side, one or two nondescripts between, sat the big, blond, bearded stranger with his son. Diagonally across from himself and the doctor, they were in full view.

O'Malley talked to all and sundry whom his voice could reach, being easily forthcoming to people whom he was not likely to see again. But he was particularly pleased to find himself next to the ship's doctor, Dr. Heinrich Stahl, for the man both attracted and antagonized him, and they had crossed swords pleasantly on more voyages than one. There was a fundamental contradiction in his character due—O'Malley divined—to the fact that his experiences did not tally as he wished them to do with his beliefs, or vice versa. Affecting to believe in nothing he occasionally dropped remarks that betrayed a belief in all kinds of things, unorthodox things. Then, having led the Irishman into confessions of his own fairy faith, he would abruptly rule the whole subject out of order with some cynical phrase that closed discussion. In this sarcastic attitude O'Malley detected a pose assumed for his own protection. "No man of sense can possibly accept such a thing; it is incredible and foolish." Yet, the biting way he said the words betrayed him; the very thing his reason rejected, his soul believed....

These vivid impressions the Irishman had of people; one wonders how accurate they were! In this case, perhaps, he was not far from the truth. That a man with Dr. Stahl's knowledge and ability could be content to hide his light under the bushel of a mere Schiffsarzt required explanation. His own explanation was that he wanted leisure for thinking and writing. Bald-headed, slovenly, prematurely old, his beard stained with tobacco and snuff, under-sized, scientific in the imaginative sense that made him speculative beyond mere formulae, his was an individuality that inspired a respect one could never quite account for. He had keen dark eyes that twinkled, sometimes mockingly, sometimes, if the word may be allowed, bitterly, yet often too with a good-humored amusement which sympathy with human weaknesses could alone have caused. A warm heart he certainly had, as more than one forlorn passenger could testify.

Conversation at their table was slow at first. It began at the lower end where the French tourists chattered briskly over the soup, then crept upwards like a slow fire overleaping various individuals who would not catch. For instance, it passed the harvest-machine man; it passed the nondescripts; it also passed the big light-haired stranger and his son.

At the table behind, there was a steady roar and buzz of voices; the Captain was easy and genial, prophesying to the ladies on either side Of him a calm voyage. In the shelter of his big voice even the shy found it easy to make remarks to their neighbors. Listening to fragments of the talk O'Malley found that his own eyes kept wandering down the table—diagonally across—to the two strangers. Once or twice, he intercepted the doctor's glance traveling in the same direction, and on these occasions it was on the tip of his tongue to make a remark about them, or to ask a question. Yet the words did not come. Dr. Stahl, he felt, knew a similar hesitation. Each, wanting to speak yet kept silence, waiting for the other to break the ice.

"This mistral is tiresome," observed the doctor, as the tide of talk flowed up to his end and made a remark necessary. "It tries the nerves of some." He glanced at O'Malley, but it was the fur-merchant who replied, spreading a be-ringed hand over his plate to feel the warmth.

"I know it well," he said pompously in a tone of finality; "it lasts three, six, or nine days. But once across the Golfe de Lyons we shall be free of it."

"You think so? Ah, I am glad," ventured the priest with a timid smile while he adroitly balanced meat and bullet-like green peas upon his knife-blade. Tone, smile, and gesture were so gentle that the use of steel in any form seemed incongruous.

The voice of the fur-merchant came in domineeringly.

"Of course. I have made this trip so often, I know. St. Petersburg to Paris, a few weeks on the Riviera, then back by Constantinople and the Crimea. It is nothing. I remember last year—" He pushed a large pearl pin more deeply into his speckled tie and began a story that proved chiefly how luxuriously he traveled. His eyes tried to draw the whole end of the table into his circle, but while the Armenian listened politely, with smiles and bows, Dr. Stahl turned to the Irishman again. It Vas the year of Halley's comet and he began talking interestingly about it.

"... Three o'clock in the morning—any morning, yes—is the best time," the doctor concluded, "and I'll have you called. You must see it through my telescope. End of this week, say, after we leave Catania and turn eastwards..."

And at this instant, following a roar of laughter from the Captain's table, came one of those abrupt pauses that sometimes catch an entire room at once. All voices hushed. Even the merchant, setting down his champagne glass, fell silent. One heard only the beating of the steamer's screw, the rush of water below the port-holes, the soft scuffle of the stewards' feet. The conclusion of the doctor's inconsiderable sentence was sharply audible all over the room—

"... crossing the Ionian Sea toward the Isles of Greece."

It rang across the pause, and at the same moment O'Malley caught the eyes of the big stranger lifted suddenly and fixed upon the speaker's face as though the words had summoned him.

They shifted the same instant to his own, then dropped again to his plate. Again, the clatter of conversation drowned the room as before; the merchant resumed his self-description in terms of gold; the doctor discussed the gases of the comet's tail. But the swift-blooded Irishman felt himself caught away strangely and suddenly into another world. Out of the abyss of the subconscious there rose a prophetic and immense gesture. The trivial phrase and that intercepted look opened a great door of wonder in his heart. In a second he grew "absent-minded." Or, rather, something touched a button and the whole machinery of his personality shifted round noiselessly and instantaneously, presenting an immediate new facet to the world. His normal, puny self-consciousness slipped a moment into the majestic calm of some far larger state that the stranger also knew. The Universe lies in every human heart, and he plunged into that archetypal world that stands so close behind all sensible appearances. He could neither explain nor attempt to explain, but he sailed away into some giant swimming mood of beauty wherein steamer, passengers, talk, faded utterly, the stranger and his son remaining alone real and vital. He had seen; he could never forget. Chance prepared the setting, but immense powers had rushed in and availed themselves of it. Something deeply buried had flamed from the stranger's eyes and beckoned to him. The fire ran from the big man to himself and was gone.

"The Isles of Greece—" The words were simple enough, yet it seemed to O'Malley that the look they summoned to the stranger's eyes ensouled them, transfiguring them with the significance of vital clues. They touched the fringe of a mystery, magnificent and remote—some transcendent psychical drama in the 'life of this man whose "bigness" and whose "loneliness that must be whispered" were also in their way other vital clues. Moreover, remembering his first sight of these two upon the upper deck a few hours before, he understood that his own spirit, by virtue of its peculiar and primitive yearnings, was involved in the same mystery and included in the same hidden passion.

The little incident illustrates admirably O'Malley's idiosyncrasy of "seeing whole." In a lightning flash his inner sense had associated the words and the glance, divining that the one had caused the other. That pause provided the opportunity.... If Imagination, then it was creative imagination; if true, it was assuredly spiritual insight of a rare quality.

He became aware that the twinkling eyes of his neighbor were observing him keenly. For some moments evidently he had been absent-mindedly staring down the table. He turned quickly and looked at the doctor with frankness. This time it was impossible to avoid speech of some kind.

"Following those lights that do mislead the morn?" asked Dr. Stahl slyly. "Your thoughts have been traveling. You've heard none of my last remarks!"

Under the clamor of the merchant's voice O'Malley replied in a lowered tone:

"I was watching those two half-way down the table opposite. They interest you as well, I see." It was not a challenge exactly; if the tone was aggressive, it was merely that he felt the subject was one on which they would differ, and he scented an approaching discussion. The doctor's reply, indicating agreement, surprised him a good deal.

"They do; they interest me greatly." There was no trace of fight in the voice. "That should cause you no surprise."

"Me—they simply fascinate," said O'Malley, always easily drawn. "What is it? What do you see about them that is unusual? Do you, too, see them 'big'?" The doctor did not answer at once, and O'Malley added, "The father's a tremendous fellow, but it's not that—"

"Partly, though," said the other, "partly, I think."

"What else, then?" The fur-merchant, still talking, prevented their being overheard. "What is it marks them off so from the rest?"

"Of all people you should see," smiled the doctor quietly. "If a man of your imagination sees nothing, what shall a poor exact mind like myself, see?" He eyed him keenly a moment. "You really mean that you detect nothing?"

"A certain distinction, yes; a certain aloofness from others. Isolated, they seem in a way; rather a splendid isolation I should call it—"

And then he stopped abruptly. It was most curious, but he was aware that unwittingly in this way he had stumbled upon the truth, aware at the same time that he resented discussing it with his companion—because it meant at the same time discussing himself or something in himself he wished to hide. His entire mood shifted again with completeness and rapidity. He could not help it. It seemed suddenly as though he had been telling the doctor secrets about himself, secrets moreover he would not treat sympathetically. The doctor had been "at him," so to speak, searching the depths of him with a probing acuteness the casual language had disguised.

"What are they, do you suppose: Finns, Russians, Norwegians, or what?" the doctor asked. And the other replied briefly that he guessed they might be Russians perhaps, South Russians. His tone was different. He wished to avoid further discussion. At the first opportunity he neatly changed the conversation.

It was curious, the way proof came to him. Something in himself, wild as the desert, something to do with that love of primitive life he discussed only with the few who were intimately sympathetic toward it, this something in his soul was so akin to a similar passion in these strangers that to talk of it was to betray himself as well as them.

Further, he resented Dr. Stahl's interest in them, because he felt it was critical and scientific. Not far behind hid the analysis that would lay them bare, leading to their destruction. A profound instinctive sense of self-preservation had been stirred within him.

Already, mysteriously guided by secret affinities, he had ranged himself on the side of the strangers.

V

"Mythology contains the history of the archetypal world. It comprehends
Past, Present, and Future."

—NOVALIS, _Flower Pollen, Translated by U.C.B.

In this way there came between these two the slight barrier of a forbidden subject that grew because neither destroyed it. O'Malley had erected it; Dr. Stahl respected it. Neither referred again for a time to the big Russian and his son.

In his written account O'Malley, who was certainly no constructive literary craftsman, left out apparently countless little confirmatory details. By word of mouth, he made me feel at once that this mystery existed, however; and to weld the two together is a difficult task. There nevertheless was this something about the Russian and his boy that excited deep curiosity, accompanied by an aversion on the part of the other passengers that isolated them; also, there was this competition on the part of the two friends to solve it, from opposing motives.

Had either of the strangers fallen seasick, the advantage would have been easily with Dr. Stahl—professionally, but since they remained well, and the doctor was in constant demand by the other passengers, it was the Irishman who won the first move and came to close quarters by making a personal acquaintance. His strong desire helped matters of course; for he noticed with indignation that these two, quiet and inoffensive as they were and with no salient cause of offence, were yet rejected by the main body of passengers. They seemed to possess a quality that somehow insulated them from approach, sending them effectually "to Coventry," and in a small steamer where the travelers settle down into a kind of big family life, this isolation was unpleasantly noticeable.

It stood out in numerous little details that only a keen observer closely watching could have taken into account. Small advances, travelers' courtesies, and the like that ordinarily should have led to conversation, in their case led to nothing. The other passengers invariably moved away after a few moments, politely excusing themselves, as it were, from further intercourse. And although at first the sight of this stirred in him an instinct of revolt that was almost anger, he soon felt that the couple not merely failed to invite, but even emanated some definite atmosphere that repelled. And each time he witnessed these little scenes, there grew more strongly in him the original picture he had formed of them as beings rejected and alone, hunted by humanity as a whole, seeking escape from loneliness into a place of refuge that they knew of, definitely at last en route.

Only an imaginative mind, thus concentrated upon them, could have divined all this; yet to O'Malley it seemed plain as the day. With the certitude, moreover, came the feeling, ever stronger, that the refuge they sought would prove to be also the refuge he himself sought, the difference being that whereas they knew, he still hesitated.

Yet, in spite of this secret sympathy, imagined or discovered, he found it no easy matter to approach the big man for speech. For a day and a half, he merely watched; attraction so strong excited caution; he paused, waiting. His attention, however, was so keen that he seemed always to know where they were and what they were doing. By instinct he was aware in what part of the ship they would be found—for the most part leaning over the rail alone in the bows, staring down at the churned water together by the screws, pacing the after-deck in the dusk or early morning when no one was about, or hidden away in some corner of the upper deck, side by side, gazing at sea and sky. Their method of walking, too, made it easy to single them out from the rest—a free, swaying movement of the limbs, a swing of the shoulders, a gait that was lumbering, almost clumsy, half defiant, yet at the same time graceful, and curiously rapid. The body moved along swiftly for all its air of blundering—a motion which was a counterpart of that elusive appearance of great bulk, and equally difficult of exact determination. An air went with them of being ridiculously confined by the narrow little decks.

Thus, it was that Genoa had been made and the ship was already halfway on to Naples before the opportunity for closer acquaintance presented itself. Rather, O'Malley, unable longer to resist, forced it. It seemed, too, inevitable as sunrise.

Rain had followed the mistral and the sea was rough. A rich land-taste came about the ship like the smell of wet oaks when the wind sweeps their leaves after a sousing shower. In the hour before dinner, the decks slippery with moisture, only one or two wrapped-up passengers in deck-chairs below the awning, O'Malley, following a sure inner lead, came out of the stuffy smoking-room into the air. It was already dark, and the drive of mist-like rain somewhat obscured his vision after the glare. Only for a moment though—for almost the first thing he saw was the Russian and his boy moving in front of him toward the aft compasses. Like a single figure, huge and shadowy, they passed into the darkness beyond with a speed that seemed as usual out of proportion to their actual stride. They lumbered rapidly away. O'Malley caught that final swing of the man's great shoulders as they disappeared, and, leaving the covered deck, he made straight after them. And though neither gave any sign that they had seen him, he felt that they were aware of his coming—and even invited him.

As he drew close a roll of the vessel brought them almost into each other's arms, and the boy, half hidden beneath his parent's flowing cloak, looked up at once and smiled. The saloon light fell dimly upon his face. The Irishman saw that friendly smile of welcome and lurched forward with the roll of the deck. They brought up against the bulwarks, and the big man put out an arm to steady him. All three of them laughed together. At close quarters, as usual again, the impression of bulk had disappeared.

And then, at first, utterly unlike real life, they said—nothing. The boy moved round and stood close to his side so that he found himself placed between them, all three-leaning forward over the rails watching the phosphorescence of the foam-streaked Mediterranean.

Dusk lay over the sea; the shores of Italy not near enough to be visible; the mist, the hour, the loneliness of the deserted decks, and something else that was nameless, shut them in, these three, in a little world of their own. A sentence or two rose in O'Malley's mind, but without finding utterance, for he felt that no spoken words were necessary. He was accepted without more ado. A deep natural sympathy existed between them, recognized intuitively from that moment of the first mutual inspection at Marseilles. It was instinctive, almost as with animals. The action of the boy in coming round to his side, unhindered by the father, was the symbol of utter confidence and welcome.

There came, then, one of those splendid and significant moments that occasionally, for some, burst into life, flooding all barriers, breaking down as with a flaming light the thousand erections of shadow that close one in. Something imprisoned in himself swept outwards, rising like a wave, bringing an expansion of life that "explained." It vanished, of course, instantly again, but not before he had caught a flying remnant that lit the broken puzzles of his heart and left things clearer. Before thought, and therefore words, could overtake, it was gone; but there remained at least this glimpse. The fire had flashed a light down subterranean passages of his being and made visible for a passing second some clue to his buried primitive yearnings. He partly understood.

Standing there between these two this thing came over him with a degree of intelligibility scarcely captured by his words. The man's qualities—his quietness, peace, slowness, silence—betrayed somehow that his inner life dwelt in a region vast and simple, shaping even his exterior presentment with its own huge characteristics, a region wherein the distress of the modern world's vulgar, futile strife could not exist—more, could never have existed. The Irishman, who had never realized exactly why the life of Today to him was dreadful, now understood it in the presence of this simple being with his atmosphere of stately power. He was like a child, but a child of some pre-existence utterly primitive and utterly forgotten; of no particular age, but of some state that antedates all ages; simple in some noble, concentrated sense that was prodigious, almost terrific. To stand beside him was to stand beside a mighty silent fire, steadily glowing, a fire that fed all lesser flames, because itself close to the central source of fire. He felt warmed, lighted, vivified—made whole. The presence of this stranger took him at a single gulp, as it were, straight into Nature—a Nature that was alive. The man was part of her. Never before had he stood so close and intimate. Cities and civilization fled away like transient dreams, ashamed. The sun and moon and stars moved up and touched him.

This word of lightning explanation, at least, came to him as he breathed the other's atmosphere and presence. The region where this man's spirit fed was at the center, whereas today men were active with a scattered, superficial cleverness, at the periphery. He even understood that his giant gait and movements were small outer evidences of this inner fact, wholly in keeping. That blundering stupidity, half glorious, half pathetic, with which he moved among his fellows was a physical expression of this psychic fact that his spirit had never learned the skillful tricks taught by civilization to lesser men. It was, in a way, awe-inspiring, for he was now at last driving back full speed for his own region and—escape.

O'Malley knew himself caught, swept off his feet, momentarily driving with him....

The singular deep satisfaction of it, standing there with these two in the first moment, he describes as an entirely new sensation in his life—an awareness that he was "complete." The boy touched his side, and he let an arm steal round to shelter him. The huge, bearded parent rose in his massiveness against his other shoulder, hemming him in. For a second he knew a swift and curious alarm, passing however almost at once into the thrill of a rare happiness. In that moment, it was not the passengers or the temper of Today who rejected them; it was they who rejected the world: because they knew another and superior one—more, they were in it.

Then, without turning, the big man spoke, the words in heavy accented English coming out laboriously and with slow, exceeding difficulty as though utterance was a supreme effort.

"You ... come ... with ... us?" It was like stammering almost. Still more was it like essential inarticulateness struggling into an utterance foreign to it—unsuited. The voice was a deep and windy bass, merging with the noise of the sea below.

"I'm going to the Caucasus," O'Malley replied, "up into the old, old mountains, to—see things—to look about—to search—" He really wanted to say much more, but the words lay dead or beyond reach.

The big man nodded slowly. The boy listened.

"And yourself—?" asked the Irishman, hardly knowing why he faltered and trembled.

The other smiled; a beauty that was beyond all language passed with that smile across the great face in the dusk.

"Some of us ... of ours ..." he spoke very slowly, very brokenly, quarrying out the words with real labor, "... still survive... out there.... We ... now go back. So very ... few ... remain.... And you—come with us ..."

VI

"In the spiritual Nature-Kingdom, man must everywhere seek his peculiar territory and climate, his best occupation, his particular neighborhood, in order to cultivate a Paradise in idea; this is the right system.... Paradise is scattered over the whole earth, and that is why it has become so unrecognizable."

—NOVALIS, Translated by U.C.B.

"Man began in instinct and will end in instinct. Instinct is genius in Paradise, before the period of self-abstraction (self-knowledge)."

—Ibid

"Look here, old man," he said to me, "I'll just tell you what it was, because I know you won't laugh."

We were lying under the big trees behind the Round Pond when he reached this point, and his direct speech was so much more graphic than the written account that I use it. He was in one of his rare moments of confidence, excited, hat off, his shabby tie escaping from the shabbier grey waistcoat. One sock lay untidily over his boot, showing bare leg.

Children's voices floated to us from the waterside as though from very far away, the nursemaids and perambulators seemed tinged with unreality, the London towers were clouds, its roar the roar of waves. I saw only the ship's deck, the grey and misty sea, the uncouth figures of the two who leaned with him over the bulwarks.

"Go on," I said encouragingly; "out with it!"

"It must seem incredible to most men, but, by Gad, I swear to you, it lifted me off my feet, and I've never known anything like it. The mind of that great fellow got hold of me, included me. He made the inanimate world—sea, stars, wind, woods, and mountains—seem all alive. The entire blessed universe was conscious—and he came straight out of it to get me. I understood things about myself I've never understood before—and always funked rather;—especially that feeling of being out of touch with my kind, of finding no one in the world today who speaks my language quite—that, and the utter, God-forsaken loneliness it makes me suffer—"

"You always have been a lonely beggar really," I said, noting the hesitation that thus on the very threshold checked his enthusiasm, quenching the fire in those light-blue eyes. "Tell me. I shall understand right enough—or try to."

"God bless you," he answered, leaping to the sympathy, "I believe you will. There's always been this primitive, savage thing in me that keeps others away—puts them off, and so on. I've tried to smother it a bit sometimes—"

"Have you?" I laughed.

"'Tried to,' I said, because I've always been afraid of its getting out too much and busting my life all to pieces:—something lonely and untamed and sort of outcast from cities and money and all the thick suffocating civilization of today; and I've only saved myself by getting off into wildernesses and free places where I could give it a breathing chance without running the risk of being locked up as a crazy man." He laughed as he said it, but his heart was in the words. "You know all that; haven't I told you often enough? It's not a morbid egoism, or what their precious academic books so stupidly call 'degenerate,' for in me it's damned vital and terrific, and moves always to action. It's made me an alien and—and—"

"Something far stronger than the Call of the Wild, isn't it?"

He fairly snorted. "Sure, as we're both alive here sitting on this sooty London grass," he cried. "This Call of the Wild they prate about is just the call a fellow hears to go on 'the bust' when he's had too much town and's got bored—a call to a little bit of license and excess to safety-valve him down. What I feel," his voice turned grave and quiet again, "is quite a different affair. It's the call of real hunger—the call of food. They want to let off steam, but I want to take in stuff to prevent—starvation." He whispered the word, putting his lips close to my face.

A pause fell between us, which was the first to break.

"This is not your century! That's what you really mean," I suggested patiently.

"Not my century!" he caught me up, flinging handfuls of faded grass in the air between us and watching it fall; "why, it's not even my world! And I loathe, loathe the spirit of today with its cheap-jack inventions, and smother of sham universal culture, its murderous superfluities and sordid vulgarity, without enough real sense of beauty left to see that a daisy is nearer heaven than an airship—"

"Especially when the airship falls," I laughed. "Steady, steady, old boy; don't spoil your righteous case by overstatement."

"Well, well, you know what I mean," he laughed with me, though his face at once turned earnest again, "and all that, and all that, and all that.... And so, this savagery that has burned in me all these years unexplained, these Russian strangers made clear. I can't tell you how because I don't know myself. The father did it—his proximity, his silence stuffed with sympathy, his great vital personality unclipped by contact with these little folk who left him alone. His presence alone made me long for the earth and Nature. He seemed a living part of it all. He was magnificent and enormous, but the devil take me if I know how."

"He said nothing—that referred to it directly?"

"Nothing but what I've told you,—blundering awkwardly with those few modern words. But he had it in him a thousand to my one. He made me feel I was right and natural, untrue to myself to suppress it and a coward to fear it. The speech-center in the brain, you know, is anyhow a comparatively recent thing in evolution. They say that—"

"It wasn't his century either," I checked him again.

"No, and he didn't pretend it was, as I've tried to," he cried, sitting bolt upright beside me. "The fellow was genuine, never dreamed of compromise. D'ye see what I mean? Only somehow he'd found out where his world and century were and was off to take possession. And that's what caught me. I felt it by some instinct in me stronger than all else; only we couldn't talk about it definitely because—because—I hardly know how to put it—for the same reason," he added suddenly, "that I can't talk about it to you now! There are no words.... What we both sought was a state that passed away before words came into use and is therefore beyond intelligible description. No one spoke to them on the ship for the same reason, I felt sure, that no one spoke to them in the whole world—because no one could manage even the alphabet of their language.

"And this was so strange and beautiful," he went on, "that standing there beside him, in his splendid atmosphere, the currents of wind and sea reached me through him first, filtered by his spirit so that I assimilated them, and they fed me, because he somehow stood in such close and direct relation to Nature. I slipped into my own region, made happy and alive, knowing at last what I wanted, though still unable to phrase it. This modern world I've so long tried to adjust myself to became a thing of pale remembrance and a dream...."

"All in your mind and imagination, of course, this," I ventured, seeing that his poetry was luring him beyond where I could follow.

"Of course," he answered without impatience, grown suddenly thoughtful, less excited again, "and that's why it was true. No chance of clumsy senses deceiving one. It was direct vision. What is Reality, in the last resort," he asked, "but the thing a man's vision brings to him—to believe? There's no other criterion. The criticism of opposite types of mind is merely a confession of their own limitations."

Being myself of the "opposite type of mind," I naturally did not argue, but suffered myself to accept his half-truth for the whole—temporarily. I checked him from time to time merely lest he should go too fast for me to follow what seemed a very wonderful tale of faerie.

"So, this wild thing in me the world today has beggared and denied," he went on, swept by his Celtic enthusiasm, "woke in its full strength. Calling to me like some flying spirit in a storm, it claimed me. The man's being summoned me back to the earth and Nature, as it were, automatically. I understood that look on his face, that sign in his eyes. The 'Isles of Greece' furnished some faint clue, but as yet I knew no more—only that he and I were in the same region and that I meant to go with him and that he accepted me with delight that was joy. It drew me as empty space draws a giddy man to the precipice's edge. Thoughts from another's mind," he added by way of explanation, turning round, "come far more completely to me when I stand in a man's atmosphere, silent and receptive, than when by speech he tries to place them there. Ah! And that helps me to get at what I mean, perhaps. The man, you see, hardly thought; he felt."

"As an animal, you mean? Instinctively—?"

"In a sense, yes," he replied after a momentary hesitation. "Like some very early, very primitive form of life."

"With the best will in the world, Terence, I don't quite follow you—

"I don't quite follow myself," he cried, "because I'm trying to lead and follow at the same time. You know that idea—I came across it somewhere—that in ancient peoples the senses were much less specialized than they are now; that perception came to them in general, massive sensations rather than divided up neatly into five channels:—that they felt all over so to speak, and that all the senses, as in an overdose of hashish, become one single sense? The centralizing of perception in the brain is a recent thing, and it might equally well have occurred in any other nervous headquarters of the body, say, the solar plexus; or, perhaps, never have been localized at all! In hysteria patients have been known to read with the finger-tips and smell with the heel. Touch is still all over; it's only the other four that have got fixed in definite organs. There are systems of thought today that still would make the solar plexus the main center, and not the brain. The word 'brain,' you know, never once occurs in the ancient Scriptures of the world. You will not find it in the Bible—the reins, the heart, and so forth were what men felt with then. They felt all over—well," he concluded abruptly, "I think this fellow was like that. D'ye see now?"

I stared at him, greatly wondering. A nursemaid passed close, balancing a child in a spring-perambulator, saying in a foolish voice, "Wupsey up, wupsey down! Wupsey there!" O'Malley, in the full stream of his mood, waited impatiently till she had gone by. Then, rolling over on his side, he came closer, talking in a lowered tone. I think I never saw him so deeply stirred, nor understood, perhaps, so little of the extreme passion working in him. Yet it was incredible that he could have caught so much from mere interviews with a semi-articulate stranger, unless what he said was strictly true, and this Russian had positively touched latent fires in his soul by a kind of sympathetic magic.

"You know," he went on almost under his breath, "every man who thinks for himself and feels vividly finds he lives in a world of his own, apart, and believes that one day he'll come across, either in a book or in a person, the Priest who shall make it clear to him. Well—I'd found mine, that's all. I can't prove it to you with a pair of scales or a butcher's meat-axe, but it's true."

"And you mean his mere presence conveyed all this without speech almost?"

"Because there was no speech possible," he replied, dropping his voice to a whisper and thrusting his face yet closer into mine. "We were solitary survivors of a world whose language was either uncreated or"—he italicized the word—"forgotten...."

"An elaborate and detailed thought-transference, then?"

"Why not?" he murmured. "It's one of the commonest facts of daily life."

"And you had never fully realized it before, this loneliness and its possible explanation—that there might exist, I mean, a way of satisfying it—till you met this stranger?"

He answered with deep earnestness. "Always, old man, always, but suffered under it atrociously because I'd never understood it. I had been afraid to face it. This man, a far bigger and less diluted example of it than myself, made it all clear and right and natural. We belonged to the same forgotten place and time. Under his lead and guidance, I could find my own—return...."

I whistled a long soft whistle, looking up into the sky. Then, sitting upright like himself, we stared hard at one another, straight in the eye. He was too grave, too serious to trifle with. It would have been unfair too. Besides, I loved to hear him. The way he reared such fabulous superstructures upon slight incidents, interpreting thus his complex being to himself, was uncommonly interesting. It was observing the creative imagination actually at work, and the process in a sense seemed sacred. Only the truth and actuality with which he clothed it all made me a little uncomfortable sometimes.

"I'll put it to you quite simply," he cried suddenly.

"Yes, and 'quite simply' it was—?"

"That he knew the awful spiritual loneliness of living in a world whose tastes and interests were not his own, a world to which he was essentially foreign, and at whose hands he suffered continual rebuff and rejection. Advances from either side were mutually and necessarily repelled because oil and water cannot mix. Rejected, moreover, not merely by a family, tribe, or nation, but by a race and time—by the whole World of Today; an outcast and an alien, a desolate survival."

"An appalling picture!"

"I understood it," he went on, holding up both hands by way of emphasis, "because in miniature I had suffered the same: he was a supreme case of what lay so deeply in myself. He was a survival of other life the modern mind has long since agreed to exile and deny. Humanity stared at him over a barrier, never dreaming of asking him in. Even had it done so he could not by the law of his being have accepted. Outcast myself in some small way, I understood his terrible loneliness, a soul without a country, visible and external country that is. A passion of tenderness and sympathy for him, and so also for myself, awoke. I saw him as chieftain of all the lonely, exiled souls of life."

Breathless a moment, he lay on his back staring at the summer clouds—those thoughts of wind that change and pass before their meanings can be quite seized. Similarly protean was the thought his phrases tried to clothe. The terror, pathos, sadness of this big idea he strove to express touched me deeply, yet never quite with the clarity of his own conviction.

"There are such souls, dépaysées and in exile," he said suddenly again, turning over on the grass. "They do exist. They walk the earth today here and there in the bodies of ordinary men ... and their loneliness is a loneliness that must be whispered."

"You formed any idea what kind of—of survival?" I asked gently, for the notion grew in me that after all these two would prove to be mere revolutionaries in escape, political refugees, or something quite ordinary.

O'Malley buried his face in his hands for a moment without replying. Presently he looked up. I remember that a streak of London black ran from the corner of his mouth across the cheek. He pushed the hair back from his forehead, answering in a manner grown abruptly calm and dispassionate.

"Don't ye see what a foolish question that is," he said quietly, "and how impossible to satisfy, inviting that leap of invention which can be only an imaginative lie...? I can only tell you," and the breeze brought to us the voices of children from the Round Pond where they sailed their ships of equally wonderful adventure, "that my own longing became this: to go with him, to know what he knew, to live where he lived—forever."

"And the alarm you said you felt?"

He hesitated.

"That," he added, "was a kind of mistake. To go involved, I felt, an inner catastrophe that might be Death—that it would be out of the body, I mean, or a going backwards. In reality, it was a going forwards and a way to Life."

VII

And it was just before the steamer made Naples that the jolly Captain unwittingly helped matters forward a good deal. For it was his ambition to include in the safe-conduct of his vessel the happy-conduct also of his passengers. He liked to see them contented and of one accord, a big family, and he noted—or had word brought to him perhaps—that there were one or two whom the attitude of the majority left out in the cold.

It may have been—O'Malley wondered without actually asking—that the man who shared the cabin with the strangers made some appeal for re-arrangement, but in any case Captain Burgenfelder approached the Irishman that afternoon on the bridge and asked if he would object to having them in his stateroom for the balance of the voyage.

"Your present gompanion geds off at Naples," he said. "Berhaps you would not object. I think—they seem lonely. You are friendly with them. They go alzo to Batoum?"

This proposal for close quarters gave him pause. He knew a moment or two of grave hesitation, yet without time to analyze it. Then, driven by a sudden decision of the heart that knew no revision of reason, he agreed.

"I had better, perhaps, suggest it to see if they are willing," he said the next minute, hedging.

"I already ask him dat."

"Oh, you have! And he would like it—not object, I mean?" he added, aware of a subtle sense of half-frightened pleasure.

"Pleased and flattered on the contrary," was the reply, as he handed him the glasses to look at Ischia rising blue from the sea.

O'Malley felt as though his decision was somehow an act of self-committal, almost grave. It meant that impulsively he accepted a friendship which concealed in its immense attraction—danger. He had taken the plunge.

The rush of it broke over him like a wave, setting free a tumult of very deep emotion. He raised the glasses automatically to his eyes, but looking through them he saw not Ischia nor the opening the Captain explained the ship would make, heading that evening for Sicily. He saw quite another picture that drew itself up out of himself—was thrown up, rather, somewhat with violence, as upon a landscape of dream-scenery. The lens of passionate yearning in himself, ever unsatisfied, focused it against a background far, far away, in some faint distance that was neither of space nor time, and might equally have been past as future. Large figures he saw, shadowy yet splendid, that ran free-moving as clouds over mighty hills, vital with the abundant strong life of a younger world.... Yet never quite saw them, never quite overtook them, for their speed and the manner of their motion bewildered the sight....

Moreover, though they evaded him in terms of physical definition he knew a sense of curious, half-remembered familiarity. Some portion of his hidden self, uncaught, unharnessed by anything in modern life, rose with a passionate rush of joy and made after them—something in him untamed as wind. His mind stood up, as it were, and shouted "I am coming." For he saw himself not far behind, as a man, racing with great leaps to join them ... yet never overtaking, never drawing close enough to see quite clearly. The roar of their tramping shook the very blood in his ears....

His decision to accept the strangers had set free in his being something that thus for the first time in his life—escaped.... Symbolically in his mind this Escape had taken picture form....

The Captain's voice was asking for the glasses; with a wrench that caused almost actual physical pain he tore himself away, letting this herd of Flying Thoughts sink back into the shadows and disappear. With sharp regret he saw them go—a regret for long, long, far-off things....

Turning, he placed the field-glasses carefully in that fat open hand stretched out to receive them, and noted as he did so the thick, pink fingers that closed about the strap, the heavy ring of gold, the band of gilt about the sleeve. That wrought gold, those fleshy fingers, the genial gutteral voice saying "Thanks" were symbols of an existence tamed and artificial that caged him in again....

Then he went below and found that the lazy "drummer" who talked harvest-machines to puzzled peasants had landed, and in his place an assortment of indiscriminate clothing belonging to the big Russian and his son lay scattered over the upper berth and upon the sofa-bed beneath the port-hole.

VIII

"For my own part I find in some of these abnormal or supernormal facts the strongest suggestions in favor of a superior consciousness being possible. I doubt whether we shall ever understand some of them without using the very letter of Fechner's conception of a great reservoir in which the memories of earth's inhabitants are pooled and preserved, and from which, when the threshold lowers or the valve opens, information ordinarily shut out leaks into the mind of exceptional individuals among us."

—WILLIAM JAMES, A Pluralistic Universe

And it was some hours later, while the ship made for the open sea, that he told Dr. Stahl casually of the new arrangement and saw the change come so suddenly across his face. Stahl stood back from the compass-box whereon they leaned, and putting a hand upon his companion's shoulder, looked a moment into his eyes. With surprise O'Malley noted that the pose of cynical disbelief was gone; in its place was sympathy, interest, kindness. The words he spoke came from his heart.

"Is that true?" he asked, as though the news disturbed him.

"Of course. Why not? Is there anything wrong?" He felt uneasy. The doctor's manner confirmed the sense that he had done a rash thing. Instantly the barrier between the two crumbled and he lost the first feeling of resentment that his friends should be analyzed. The men thus came together in unhindered sincerity.

"Only," said the doctor thoughtfully, half gravely, "that—I may have done you a wrong, placed you, that is, in a position of—" he hesitated an instant,—"of difficulty. It was I who suggested the change."

O'Malley stared at him.

"I don't understand you quite."

"It is this," continued the other, still holding him with his eyes. He said it deliberately. "I have known you for some time, formed-er—an opinion of your type of mind and being—a very rare and curious one, interesting me deeply—"

"I wasn't aware you'd had me under the microscope," O'Malley laughed, but restlessly.

"Though you felt it and resented it—justly, I may say—to the point of sometimes avoiding me—"

"As doctor, scientist," put in O'Malley, while the other, ignoring the interruption, continued in German:—

"I always had the secret hope, as 'doctor and scientist,' let us put it then, that I might one day see you in circumstances that should bring out certain latent characteristics I thought I divined in you. I wished to observe you—your psychical being—under the stress of certain temptations, favorable to these characteristics. Our brief voyages together, though they have so kindly ripened our acquaintance into friendship"—he put his hand again on the other's shoulder smiling, while O'Malley replied with a little nod of agreement—"have, of course, never provided the opportunity I refer to—"

"Ah—!"

"Until now!" the doctor added. "Until now."

Puzzled and interested the Irishman waited for him to go on, but the man of science, who was now a ship's doctor, hesitated. He found it difficult, apparently, to say what was in his thoughts.

"You refer, of course, though I hardly follow you quite—to our big friends?" O'Malley helped him.

The adjective slipped out before he was aware of it. His companion's expression admitted the accuracy of the remark. "You also see them—big, then?" he said, quickly taking him up. He was not cross-questioning; out of keen sympathetic interest he asked it.

"Sometimes, yes," the Irishman answered, more astonished. "Sometimes only—"

"Exactly. Bigger than they really are as though at times they gave out—emanated—something that extended their appearance. Is that it?"

O'Malley, his confidence wholly won, more surprised, too, than he quite understood, seized Stahl by the arm and drew him toward the rails. They leaned over, watching the sea. A passenger, pacing the decks before dinner, passed close behind them.

"But, doctor," he said in a hushed tone as soon as the steps had died away, "you are saying things that I thought were half in my imagination only, not true in the ordinary sense quite—your sense, I mean?"

For some moments the doctor made no reply. In his eyes a curious steady gaze replaced the usual twinkle. When at length he spoke, it was evidently following a train of thought of his own, playing round a subject he seemed half ashamed of and yet desired to state with direct language.

"A being akin to yourself," he said in low tones, "only developed, enormously developed; a Master in your own peculiar region, and a man whose influence acting upon you at close quarters could not fail to arouse the latent mind-storms"—he chose the word hesitatingly, as though seeking for a better he could not find on the moment,—"always brewing in you just below the horizon."

He turned and watched his companion's face keenly. O'Malley was too impressed to feel annoyance.

"Well—?" he asked, feeling the adventure closing round him with quite a new sense of reality. "Well?" he repeated louder. "Please go on. I'm not offended, only uncommonly interested. You leave me in a fog, so far. I think you owe me more than hints."

"I do," said the other simply. "About that man is a singular quality too rare for language to have yet coined its precise description: something that is essentially"—they had lapsed into German now, and he used the German word—"unheimlich."

The Irishman started. He recognized this for truth. At the same time the old resentment stirred a little in him, creeping into his reply.

"You have studied him closely then—had him, too, under the microscope?
In this short time?"

This time the answer did not surprise him, however.

"My friend," he heard, while the other turned from him and gazed out over the misty sea, "I have not been a ship's doctor—always. I am one now only because the leisure and quiet give me the opportunity to finish certain work, recording work. For years I was in the H——"—he mentioned the German equivalent for the Salpêtrière—"years of research and investigation into the astonishing vagaries of the human mind and spirit—with certain results, followed later privately, that it is now my work to record. And among many cases that might well seem—er—beyond either credence or explanation,"—he hesitated again slightly—"I came across one, one in a million, let us admit, that an entire section of my work deals with under the generic term of Urmenschen."

"Primitive men," O'Malley snapped him up, translating. Through his growing bewilderment ran also a growing uneasiness shot strangely with delight. Intuitively he divined what was coming.

"Beings," the doctor corrected him, "not men. The prefix Ur-, moreover, I use in a deeper sense than is usually attached to it as in Urwald, Urwelt and the like. An Urmensch in the world today must suggest a survival of an almost incredible kind—a kind, too, utterly inadmissible and inexplicable to the materialist perhaps—"

"Paganistic?" interrupted the other sharply, joy and fright rising over him.

"Older, older by far," was the rejoinder, given with a curious hush and a lowering of the voice.

The suggestion rushed into full possession of O'Malley's mind. There rose in him something that claimed for his companions the sea, the wind, the stars—tumultuous and terrific. But he said nothing. The conception, blown into him thus for the first time at full strength, took all his life into its keeping. No energy was left over for mere words. The doctor, he was aware, was looking at him, the passion of discovery and belief in his eyes. His manner kindled. It was the hidden Stahl emerging.

"... a type, let me put it," he went on in a voice whose very steadiness thrilled his listener afresh, "that in its strongest development would experience in the world today the loneliness of a complete and absolute exile. A return to humanity, you see, of some unexpended power of mythological values...."

"Doctor...!"

The shudder passed through him and away almost as soon as it came. Again, the sea grew splendid, the thunder of the waves held voices calling, and the foam framed shapes and faces, wildly seductive, though fugitive as dreams. The words he had heard moved him profoundly. He remembered how the presence of the stranger had turned the world alive.

He knew what was coming, too, and gave the lead direct, while yet half afraid to ask the question.

"So, my friend—this big 'Russian'—?"

"I have known before, yes, and carefully studied."

IX

"Is it not just possible that there is a mode of being as transcending Intelligence and Will as these transcend mechanical motion?"

—HERBERT SPENCER, First Principles

The two men left the rail and walked arm in arm along the deserted deck, speaking in lowered voices.

"He came first to us, brought by the keeper of an obscure hotel where he was staying, as a case of lapse of memory—loss of memory, I should say, for it was complete. He was unable to say who he was, whence he came, or to whom he belonged. Of his land or people, we could learn nothing. His antecedents were an utter blank. Speech he had practically none of his own—nothing but the merest smattering of many tongues, a word here, a word there. Utterance, indeed, of any kind was exceedingly difficult to him. For years, evidently, he had wandered over the world, companionless among men, seeking his own, finding no place where to lay his head. People, it seemed, both men and women, kept him at arm's-length, feeling afraid; the keeper of the little hotel was clearly terrified. This quality he had that I mentioned just now, repelled human beings—even in the Hospital it was noticeable—and placed him in the midst of humanity thus absolutely alone. It is a quality rarer than"—hesitating, searching for a word—"purity, one almost extinct today, one that I have never before or since come across in any other being—hardly ever, that is to say," he qualified the sentence, glancing significantly at his companion.

"And the boy?" O'Malley asked quickly, anxious to avoid any discussion of himself.

"There was no boy then. He has found him since. He may find others too—possibly!" The Irishman drew his arm out, edging away imperceptibly. That shiver of joy reached him from the air and sea, perhaps.

"And two years ago," continued Dr. Stahl, as if nothing had happened, "he was discharged, harmless"—he lingered a moment on the word, "if not cured. He was to report to us every six months. He has never done so."

"You think he remembers you?"

"No. It is quite clear that he has lapsed back completely again into the—er—state whence he came to us, that unknown world where he passed his youth with others of his kind, but of which he has been able to reveal no single detail to us, nor we to trace the slightest clue."

They stopped beneath the covered portion of the deck, for the mist had now turned to rain. They leaned against the smoking-room outer wall. In O'Malley's mind the thoughts and feelings plunged and reared. Only with difficulty did he control himself.

"And this man, you think," he asked with outward calmness, "is of—of my kind?"

"'Akin,' I said. I suggest—" But O'Malley cut him short.

"So that you engineered our sharing a cabin with a view to putting him again—putting us both—under the microscope?"

"My scientific interest was very strong," Dr. Stahl replied carefully. "But it is not too late to change. I offer you a bed in my own roomy cabin on the promenade deck. Also, I ask your forgiveness."

The Irishman, large though his imaginative creed was, felt oddly checked, baffled, stupefied by what he had heard. He knew perfectly well what Stahl was driving at, and that revelations of another kind were yet to follow. What bereft him of very definite speech was this new fact slowly awakening in his consciousness which hypnotized him, as it were, with its grandeur. It seemed to portend that his own primitive yearnings, so-called, grew out of far deeper foundations than he had yet dreamed of even. Stahl, should he choose to listen, meant to give him explanation, quasi-scientific explanation. This talk about a survival of "unexpended mythological values" carried him off his feet. He knew it was true. Veiled behind that carefully chosen phrase was something more—a truth brilliantly discovered. He knew, too, that it bit at the platform-boards upon which his personality, his sanity, his very life, perhaps, rested—his modern life.

"I forgive you, Dr. Stahl," he heard himself saying with a deceptive calmness of voice as they stood shoulder to shoulder in that dark corner, "for there is really nothing to forgive. The characteristics of these Urmenschen you describe attract me very greatly. Your words merely give my imagination a letter of introduction to my reason. They burrow among the foundations of my life and being. At least—you have done me no wrong...." He knew the words were wild, impulsive, yet he could find no better. Above all things he wished to conceal his rising, grand delight.

"I thank you," Stahl said simply, yet with a certain confusion. "I—felt I owed you this explanation—er—this confession."

"You wished to warn me?"

"I wished to say 'Be careful' rather. I say it now—Be careful! I give you this invitation to share my cabin for the remainder of the voyage, and I urge you to accept it." The offer was from the heart, while the scientific interest in the man obviously half hoped for a refusal.

"You think harm might come to me?"

"Not physically. The man is gentle and safe in every way."

"But there is danger—in your opinion?" insisted the other.

"There is danger—"

"That his influence may make me as himself—an Urmensch?"

"That he may—get you," was the curious answer, given steadily after a moment's pause.

Again, the words thrilled O'Malley to the core of his delighted, half-frightened soul. "You really mean that?" he asked again; "as 'doctor and scientist,' you mean it?"

Stahl replied with a solemn anxiety in eyes and voice. "I mean that you have in yourself that 'quality' which makes the proximity of this 'being' dangerous: in a word that he may take you—er—with him."

"Conversion?"

"Appropriation."

They moved further up the deck together for some minutes in silence, but the Irishman's feelings, irritated by the man's prolonged evasion, reached a degree of impatience that was almost anger. "Let us be more definite," he exclaimed at length a trifle hotly. "You mean that I might go insane?"

"Not in the ordinary sense," came the answer without a sign of annoyance or hesitation; "but that something might happen to you—something that science could not recognize, and medical science could not treat—"

Then O'Malley interrupted him with the vital question that rushed out before he could consider its wisdom or legitimacy.

"Then what really is he—this man, this 'being' whom you call a 'survival,' and who makes you fear for my safety. Tell me exactly what he is?"

They found themselves just then by the doctor's cabin, and Stahl, pushing the door open, led him in. Taking the sofa for himself, he pointed to an armchair opposite.

X

"Superstition is outside reason; so is revelation."

—OLD SAYING

And O'Malley understood that he had pressed the doctor to the verge of confessing some belief that he was ashamed to utter or to hold, something forced upon him by his out-of-the-way experience of life to which his scientific training said peremptorily "No." Further, that he watched him keenly all the time, noting the effect his words produced.

"He is not a human being at all," he continued with a queer thin whisper that conveyed a gravity of conviction singularly impressive, "in the sense in which you and I are accustomed to use the term. His inner being is not shaped, as his outer body, upon quite—human lines. He is a Cosmic Being—a direct expression of cosmic life. A little bit, a fragment, of the Soul of the World, and in that sense a survival—a survival of her youth."

The Irishman, as he listened to these utterly unexpected words, felt something rise within him that threatened to tear him asunder. Whether it was joy or terror, or compounded strangely of the two, he could not tell. It seemed as if he stood upon the edge of hearing something—spoken by a man who was no mere dreamer like himself—that would explain the world, himself, and all his wildest cravings. He both longed and feared to hear it. In his hidden and most secret thoughts, those thoughts he never uttered to another, this deep belief in the Earth as a conscious, sentient, living Being had persisted in spite of all the forces education and modern life had turned against it. It seemed in him an undying instinct, an unmovable conviction, though he hardly dared acknowledge it even to himself.

He had always "dreamed" the Earth alive, a mothering organism to humanity; and himself, via his love of Nature, in some sweet close relation to her that other men had forgotten or ignored. Now, therefore, to hear Stahl talk of Cosmic Beings, fragments of the Soul of the World, and "survivals of her early life" was like hearing a great shout of command to his soul to come forth and share it in complete acknowledgment.

He bit his lips, pinched himself, stared. Then he took the black cigar he was aware was being handed to him, lit it with fingers that trembled absurdly, and smoked as hard as though his sanity depended on his finishing it in a prescribed time. Great clouds rose before his face. But his soul within him came up with a flaming rush of speed, shouting, singing....

There was enough ash to knock off into the bronze tray beside him before either said a word. He watched the little operation as closely as though he were aiming a rifle. The ash, he saw, broke firmly. "This must be a really good cigar," he thought to himself, for as yet he had not been conscious of tasting it. The ash-tray, he also saw, was a kind of nymph, her spread drapery forming the receptacle. "I must get one of those," he thought. "I wonder what they cost." Then he puffed violently again. The doctor had risen and was pacing the cabin floor slowly over by the red curtain that concealed the bunk. O'Malley absent-mindedly watched him, and as he did so the words he had heard kept on roaring at the back of his mind.

And then, while silence still held the room,—swift, too, as a second although it takes time to write—flashed through him a memory of Fechner, the German philosopher who held that the Universe was everywhere consciously alive, and that the Earth was the body of a living Entity, and that the World-Soul or Cosmic Consciousness is something more than a picturesque dream of the ancients....

The doctor came to anchor again on the sofa opposite. To his great relief he was the first to break the silence, for O'Malley simply did not know how or where to begin.

"We know today—you certainly know for I've read it accurately described in your books—that the human personality can extend itself under certain conditions called abnormal. It can project portions of itself, show itself even at a distance, operate away from the central covering body. In exactly similar fashion may the Being of the Earth have projected portions of herself in the past. Of such great powers or beings there may be conceivably a survival ... a survival of a hugely remote period when her Consciousness was manifested, perhaps, in shapes and forms long since withdrawn before the tide of advancing humanity ... forms of which poetry and legend alone have caught a flying memory and called them gods, monsters, mythical beings of all sorts and kinds...."

And then, suddenly, as though he had been deliberately giving his imagination rein yet now regretted it, his voice altered, his manner assumed a shade of something colder. He shifted the key, as though to another aspect of his belief. The man was talking swiftly of his experiences in the big and private hospitals. He was describing the very belief to which he had first found himself driven—the belief that had opened the door to so much more. So far as O'Malley could follow it in his curiously excited condition of mind, it was little more or less than a belief he himself had often played lovingly with—the theory that a man has a fluid or etheric counterpart of himself which is obedient to strong desire and can, under certain conditions, be detached—projected in a shape dictated by that desire.

He only realized this fully later perhaps, for the doctor used a phraseology of his own. Stahl was telling calmly how he had been driven to some such belief by the facts that had come under his notice both in the asylums and in his private practice.

"...That in the amazingly complex personality of a human being," he went on, "there does exist some vital constituent, a part of consciousness, that can leave the body for a short time without involving death; that it is something occasionally visible to others; something malleable by thought and desire—especially by intense and prolonged yearning; and that it can even bring relief to its owner by satisfying in some subjective fashion the very yearnings that drew it forth."

"Doctor! You mean the 'astral'?"

"There is no name I know of. I can give it none. I mean in other words that it can create the conditions for such satisfaction—dream-like, perhaps, yet intense and seemingly very real at the time. Great emotion, for instance, drives it forth, explaining thus appearances at a distance, and a hundred other phenomena that my investigations of abnormal personality have forced me to recognize as true. And nostalgia often is the means of egress, the channel along which all the inner forces and desires of the heart stream elsewhere toward their fulfillment in some person, place, or dream."

Stahl was giving himself his head, talking freely of beliefs that rarely found utterance. Clearly it was a relief to him to do so—to let himself be carried away. There was, after all, the poet in him side by side with the observer and analyst, and the fundamental contradiction in his character stood most interestingly revealed. O'Malley listened, half in a dream, wondering what this had to do with the Cosmic Life just mentioned.

"Moreover, the appearance, the aspect of this etheric Double, molded thus by thought, longing, and desire, corresponds to such thought, longing, and desire. Its shape, when visible shape is assumed, may be various—very various. The form might conceivably be felt, discerned clairvoyantly as an emanation rather than actually seen," he continued.

Then he added, looking closely at his companion, "and in your own case this Double—it has always seemed to me—may be peculiarly easy of detachment from the rest of you."

"I certainly create my own world and slip into it—to some extent," murmured the Irishman, absorbingly interested; "—reverie and so forth; partially, at any rate."

"'Partially,' yes, in your reveries of waking consciousness," Stahl took him up, "but in sleep—in the trance consciousness—completely! And therein lies your danger," he added gravely; "for to pass out completely in waking consciousness, is the next step—an easy one;

and it constitutes, not so much a disorder of your being, as a readjustment, but a readjustment difficult of sane control." He paused again. "You pass out while fully awake—a waking delusion. It is usually labeled—though in my opinion wrongly so—insanity."

"I'm not afraid of that," O'Malley laughed, almost nettled. "I can manage myself all right—have done so far, at any rate."

It was curious how the roles had shifted. O'Malley it was now who checked and criticized.

"I suggest caution," was the reply, made earnestly. "I suggest caution."

"I should keep your warnings for mediums, clairvoyants, and the like," said the other tartly. He was half amazed, half alarmed even while he said it. It was the personal application that annoyed him. "They are rather apt to go off their heads, I believe."

Dr. Stahl rose and stood before him as though the words had given him a cue he wanted. "From that very medium-class," he said, "my most suggestive 'cases' have come, though not for one moment do I think of including you with them. Yet these very 'cases' have been due one and all to the same cause—the singular disorder I have just mentioned."

They stared at one another a moment in silence. Stahl, whether O'Malley liked it or no, was impressive. He gazed at the little figure in front of him, the ragged, untidy beard, the light shining on the bald skull, wondering what was coming next and what this bewildering confession of unorthodox belief was leading up to. He longed to hear more about that hinted Cosmic Life ... and how yearning might lead to its realization.

"For any phenomena of the séance-room that may be genuine," he heard him saying, "are produced by this fluid, detachable portion of the personality, the very thing we have been speaking about. They are projections of the personality—automatic projections of the consciousness."

And then, like a clap of thunder upon his bewildered mind, came this man's amazing ultimatum, linking together all the points touched upon and bringing them to a head. He repeated it emphatically.

"And in similar fashion," concluded the calm, dispassionate voice beside him, "there have been projections of the Earth's great consciousness—direct expressions of her cosmic life—Cosmic Beings. And of these distant and primitive manifestations, it is conceivable that one or two may still—here and there in places humanity has never stained—actually survive. This man is one of them."

He turned on the two electric lights behind him with an admirable air of finality. The extraordinary talk was at an end. He moved about the cabin, putting chairs straight and toying with the papers on his desk. Occasionally he threw a swift and searching glance at his companion, like a man who wished to note the effect of an attack.

For, indeed, this was the impression that his listener retained above all else. This flood of wild, unorthodox, speculative ideas had been poured upon him helter-skelter with a purpose. And the abruptness of the climax was cleverly planned to induce impulsive, hot confession.

But O'Malley found no words. He sat there in his armchair, passing his fingers through his tumbled hair. His inner turmoil was too much for speech or questions ... and presently, when the gong for dinner rang noisily outside the cabin door, he rose abruptly and went out without a single word. Stahl turned to see him go. He merely nodded with a little smile.

But he did not go to his stateroom. He walked the deck alone for a time, and when he reached the dining room, Stahl, he saw, had already come and gone. Halfway down the table, diagonally across, the face of the big Russian looked up occasionally at him and smiled, and every time he did so the Irishman felt a sense of mingled alarm and wonder greater than anything he had ever known in his life before. One of the great doors of life again had opened. The barriers of his heart broke away. He was no longer caged and manacled within the prison of a puny individuality. The world that so distressed him faded. The people in it were dolls. The fur-merchant, the Armenian priest, the tourists and the rest were mere automatic puppets, all made to scale—petty scale, amazingly dull, all exactly alike—tiny, unreal, half alive.

The ship, meanwhile, he reflected with a joy that was passion, was being borne over the blue sea, and this sea lay spread upon the curved breast of the round and spinning earth. He, too, and the big Russian lay upon her breast, held close by gravity so-called, caught closer still, though, by something else besides. And his longings increased with his understanding. Stahl, wittingly or unwittingly, had given them an immense push forwards.

XI

"In scientific terms one can say: Consciousness is everywhere; it is awake when and wherever the bodily energy underlying the spiritual exceeds that degree of strength which we call the threshold. According to this, consciousness can be localized in time and space."

—FECHNER, Buchlein vom Leben nach dem Tode

The offer of the cabin, meanwhile, remained open. In the solitude that O'Malley found necessary that evening he toyed with it, though knowing that he would never really accept.

Like a true Celt his imagination took the main body of Stahl's words and ensouled them with his own vivid temperament. There stirred in him this nameless and disquieting joy that wrought for itself a Body from material just beyond his thoughts—that region of enormous experience that ever fringes the consciousness of imaginative men. He took the picture at its face value, took it inside with his own thoughts, delighted in it, raised it, of course, very soon to a still higher scale. If he criticized at all it was with phrases like "The man's a poet after all! Why, he's got creative imagination!" To find his own intuitions endorsed, even half explained, by a mind of opposite type was a new experience. It emphasized amazingly the reality of that inner world he lived in.

This explanation of the big Russian's effect upon himself was terrific, and that a "doctor" should have conceived it, glorious. That some portion of a man's spirit might assume the shape of his thoughts and project itself visibly seemed likely enough. Indeed, to him, it seemed already a "fact," and his temperament did not linger over it. But that other suggestion fairly savaged him with its strange grandeur. He played lovingly with it.

That the Earth was a living being was a conception divine in size as in simplicity, and that the Gods and mythological figures had been projections of her consciousness—this thought ran with a magnificent new thunder about his mind. It was overwhelming, beautiful as Heaven and as gracious. He saw the ancient shapes of myth and legend still alive in some gorgeous garden of the primal world, a corner too remote for humanity to have yet stained it with their trail of uglier life. He understood in quite a new way, at last, those deep primitive longings that hitherto had vainly craved their full acknowledgment. It meant that he lay so close to the Earth that he felt her pulses as his own. The idea stormed his belief.

It was the Soul of the Earth herself that all these years had been calling to him.

And while he let his imagination play with the soaring beauty of the idea, he remembered certain odd little facts. He marshaled them before him in a row and questioned them: The picture he had seen with the Captain's glasses—those speeding shapes of beauty; the new aspect of a living Nature that the Russian's presence stirred in him; the man's broken words as they had leaned above the sea in the dusk; the curious passion that leaped to his eyes when certain chance words had touched him at the dinner-table. And, lastly, the singular impression of giant bulk he produced sometimes upon the mind, almost as though a portion of him—this detachable portion molded by the quality of his spirit as he felt himself to be—emerged visibly to cause it.

Vaguely, in this way, O'Malley divined how inevitable was the apparent isolation of these two, and why others instinctively avoided them. They seemed by themselves in an enclosure where the parent lumberingly, and the boy defiantly, disported themselves with a kind of lonely majesty that forbade approach.

And it was later that same night, as the steamer approached the Lipari Islands, that the drive forward he had received from the doctor's words was increased by a succession of singular occurrences. At the same time, Stahl's deliberate and as he deemed it unjustifiable interference, helped him to make up his mind decisively on certain other points.

The first "occurrence" was of the same order as the "bigness"—extraordinarily difficult, that is, to confirm by actual measurement.

It was ten o'clock, Stahl still apparently in his cabin by himself, and most of the passengers below at an impromptu concert, when the Irishman, coming down from his long solitude, caught sight of the Russian and his boy moving about the dark after-deck with a speed and vigor that instantly arrested his attention. The suggestion of size, and of rapidity of movement, had never been more marked. It was as though a cloud of the summer darkness moved beside them.

Then, going cautiously nearer, he saw that they were neither walking quickly, nor running, as he had first supposed, but—to his amazement—were standing side by side upon the deck—stock still. The appearance of motion, however, was not entirely a delusion, for he next saw that, while standing there steady as the mast and life-boats behind them, something emanated shadow-like from both their persons and seemed to hover and play about them—something that was only approximately of their own outer shapes, and very considerably larger. Now it veiled them, now left them clear. He thought of smoke-clouds moving to and fro about dark statues.

So far as he could focus his sight upon them, these "shadows," without any light to cast them, moved in distorted guise there on the deck with a motion that was somehow rhythmical—a great movement as of dance or gambol.

As with the appearance of "bigness," he perceived it first out of the corner of his eye. When he looked again he saw only two dark figures, motionless.

He experienced the sensation a man sometimes knows on entering a deserted chamber in the nighttime and is aware that the things in it have just that instant—stopped. His arrival puts abrupt end to some busy activity they were engaged in, which begins again the moment he goes. Chairs, tables, cupboards, the very spots and patterns of the wall have just flown back to their usual places whence they watch impatiently for his departure—with the candle.

This time, on a deck instead of in a room, O'Malley with his candle had surprised them in the act: people, moreover, not furniture. And this shadowy gambol, this silent Dance of the Emanations, immense yet graceful, made him think of Winds flying, visible and uncloaked, somewhere across long hills, or of Clouds passing to a stately, elemental measure over the blue dancing-halls of an open sky. His imagery was confused and gigantic, yet very splendid. Again, he recalled the pictured shapes seen with his mind's eye through the Captain's glasses. And as he watched, he felt in himself what he called "the wild, tearing instinct to run and join them," more even—that by rights he ought to have been there from the beginning—dancing with them—indulging a natural and instinctive and rhythmical movement that he had somehow forgotten.

The passion in him was very strong, very urgent, it seems, for he took a step forward, a call of some kind rose in his throat, and in another second he would have been similarly cavorting upon the deck, when he felt his arm clutched suddenly with vigor from behind. Someone seized him and held him back. A German voice spoke with a guttural whisper in his ear.

Dr. Stahl, crouching and visibly excited, drew him forward a little. "Hold up!" he heard whispered—for their India rubber soles slithered on the wet decks. "We shall see from here, eh? See something at last?" He still whispered. O'Malley's sudden anger died down. He could not give vent to it without making noise, for one thing, and above all else he wished to—see. He merely felt a vague wonder how long Stahl had been watching.

They crouched behind the lee of a boat. The outline of the ship rose, distinctly visible against the starry sky, masts, spars, and cordage. A faint gleam came through the glass below the compass-box. The wheel and the heaps of coiled rope beyond rose and fell with the motion of the vessel, now against the stars, now black against the phosphorescent foam that trailed along the sea like shining lace. But the human figures, he next saw, were now doing nothing, not even pacing the deck; they were no longer of unusual size either. Quietly leaning over the rail, father and son side by side, they were guiltless of anything more uncommon than gazing into the sea. Like the furniture, they had just—stopped!

Dr. Stahl and his companion waited motionless for several minutes in silence. There was no sound but the dull thunder of the screws, and a faint windy whistle the ship's speed made in the rigging. The passengers were all below. Then, suddenly, a burst of music came up as someone opened a saloon port-hole and quickly closed it again—a tenor voice singing to the piano some trivial modern song with a trashy sentimental lilt. It was—in this setting of sea and sky—painful; O'Malley caught himself thinking of a barrel-organ in a Greek temple.

The same instant father and son, as though startled, moved slowly away down the deck into the further darkness, and Dr. Stahl tightened his grip of the Irishman's arm with a force that almost made him cry out. A gleam of light from the opened port-hole had fallen about them before they moved. Quite clearly it revealed them bending busily over, heads close together, necks and shoulders thrust forward and down a little.

"Look, by God!" whispered Stahl hoarsely as they moved off. "There's a third!"

He pointed. Where the two had been standing something, indeed, still remained. Concealed hitherto by their bulk, this other figure had been left. They saw its large, dim outline. It moved. Apparently it began to climb over the rails, or to move in some way just outside them, hanging half above the sea. There was a free, swaying movement about it, not ungainly so much as big—very big.

"Now, quick!" whispered the doctor excited, in English; "this time I find out, sure!"

He made a violent movement forward, a pocket electric lamp in his hand, then turned angrily, furiously, to find that O'Malley held him fast. There was a most unseemly struggle—for a minute, and it was caused by the younger man's sudden passionate instinct to protect his own from discovery, if not from actual capture and destruction.

Stahl fought in vain, being easily overmatched; he swore vehement German oaths under his breath; and the pocket-lamp, of course unlighted, fell and rattled over the deck, sliding with the gentle roll of the steamer to leeward. But O'Malley's eyes, even while he struggled, never for one instant left the spot where the figure and the "movement" had been; and it seemed to him that when the bulwarks dipped against the dark of the sea, the moving thing completed its efforts and passed into the waves with a swift leap. When the vessel righted herself again the outline of the rail was clear.

Dr. Stahl, he then saw, had picked up the lamp and was bending over some mark upon the deck, examining a wide splash of wet upon which he directed the electric flash. The sense of revived antagonism between the men for the moment was strong, too strong for speech. O'Malley feeling half ashamed, yet realized that his action had been instinctive, and that another time he would do just the same. He would fight to the death any too close inspection, since such inspection included also now—himself.

The doctor presently looked up. His eyes shone keenly in the gleam of the lamp, but he was no longer agitated.

"There is too much water," he said calmly, as though diagnosing a case; "too much to permit of definite traces." He glanced round, flashing the beam about the decks. The other two had disappeared. They were alone. "It was outside the rail all the time, you see," he added, "and never quite reached the decks." He stooped down and examined the splash once more. It looked as though a wave had topped the scuppers and left a running line of foam and water. "Nothing to indicate its exact nature," he said in a whisper that conveyed something between uneasiness and awe, again turning the light sharply in every direction and peering about him. "It came to them—er—from the sea, though; it came from the sea right enough. That, at least, is positive." And in his manner was perhaps just a touch to indicate relief.

"And it returned into the sea," exclaimed O'Malley triumphantly. It was as though he related his own escape.

The two men were now standing upright, facing one another. Dr. Stahl, betraying no sign of resentment, looked him steadily in the eye. He put the lamp back into his pocket. When he spoke at length in the darkness, the words were not precisely what the Irishman had expected. Under them his own vexation and excitement faded instantly. He felt almost sheepish when he remembered his violence.

"I forgive your behavior, of course," Stahl said, "for it is consistent—splendidly consistent—with my theory of you; and of value, therefore. I only now urge you again"—he moved closer, speaking almost solemnly—"to accept the offer of a berth in my cabin. Take it, my friend, take it—tonight."

"Because you wish to watch me at close quarters."

"No," was the reply, and there was sympathy in the voice, "but because you are in danger—especially in sleep."

There was a moment's pause before O'Malley said anything.

"It is kind of you, Dr. Stahl, very kind," he answered slowly, and this time with grave politeness; "but I am not afraid, and I see no reason to make the change. And as it's now late," he added somewhat abruptly, almost as though he feared he might be persuaded to alter his mind, "I will say good-night and turn in—if you will forgive me—at once."

Dr. Stahl said no further word. He watched him, the other was aware, as he moved down the deck toward the saloon staircase, and then turned once more with his lamp to stoop over the splashed portion of the boards. He examined the place apparently for a long time.

But O'Malley, as he went slowly down the hot and stuffy stairs, realized with a wild and rushing tumult of joy that the "third" he had seen was of a splendor surpassing the little figures of men, and that something deep within his own soul was most gloriously akin with it. A link with the Universe had been subconsciously established, tightened up, adjusted. From all this living Nature breathing about him in the night, a message had reached the strangers and himself—a message shaped in beauty and in power. Nature had become at last aware of his presence close against her ancient face. Henceforth would every sight of Beauty take him direct to the place where Beauty comes from. No middleman, no Art was necessary. The gates were opening. Already he had caught a glimpse.

XII

In the stateroom he found, without surprise somehow, that his new companions had already retired for the night. The curtain of the upper berth was drawn, and on the sofa-bed below the opened port-hole the boy already slept. Standing a moment in the little room with these two close, he felt that he had come into a new existence almost. Deep within him this sense of new life thrilled and glowed. He was shaking a little all over, not with the mere tremor of excitement, however, but with the tide of a vast and rising exultation he could scarce contain. For his normal self was too small to hold it. It demanded expansion, and the expansion it claimed had already begun. The boundaries of his personality were enormously extending.

In words this change escaped him wholly. He only knew that something in him of an old unrest lay down at length and slept. Less acute grew those pangs of starvation his life had ever felt—the ache of that inappeasable hunger for the beauty and innocence of some primal state before thick human crowds had stained the world with all their strife and clamor. The glory of it burned white within him.

And the way he described it to himself was significant of its true nature. For it vans the analogy of childhood. The passion of a boy's longing swept over him. He knew again the feelings of those early days when—

A boy's will is the wind's will,
And the thoughts of youth are long, long thoughts,

—when all the world smells sweet and golden as a summer's day, and a village street is endless as the sky....

This it was, raised to its highest power, that dropped a hint of explanation into that queer heart of his wherein had ever burned the strange desire for primitive existence. It was the Call, though, not of his own youth alone, but of the youth of the world. A mood of the Earth's consciousness—some giant expression of her cosmic emotion—caught him. And it was the big Russian who acted as channel and interpreter.

Before getting into bed, he drew aside the little red curtain that screened his companion and peered cautiously through the narrow slit. The big occupant of the bunk also slept, his mane-like hair spread about him over the pillow, and on his great, placid face a look of peace that seemed to deepen with every day the steamer neared her destination. O'Malley gazed for a full minute and more. Then the sleeper felt the gaze, for suddenly the eyelids quivered, moved, and lifted. The large brown eyes peered straight into his own. The Irishman, unable to turn away in time, stood fixed and staring in return. The gentleness and power of the look passed straight down into his heart, filled him to the brim with things their owner knew, and confirmed that appeasement of his own hunger, already begun.

"I tried—to prevent the—interference," he stammered in a low voice.

"I held him back. You saw me?"

A huge hand stretched forth from the bunk to stop him. Impulsively he seized it with both his own. At the first contact he started—a little frightened. It felt so wonderful, so mighty. Thus, might a gust of wind or a billow of the sea have thrust against him.

"A messenger—came," said the man with that laborious slow utterance, and deep as thunder, "from—the—sea."

"From—the—sea, yes," repeated O'Malley beneath his breath, yet conscious rather that he wanted to shout and sing it. He saw the big man smile. His own small hands were crushed in the grasp of power. "I—understand," he added in a whisper. He found himself speaking with a similar clogged utterance. Somehow, it seemed, the language they ought to have used was either forgotten or unborn. Yet whereas his friend was inarticulate perhaps, he himself was—dumb. These little modern words were all wrong and inadequate. Modern speech could only deal with modern smaller things.

The giant half rose in his bed, as though at first to leap forward and away from it. He tightened an instant the grasp upon his companion's hands, then suddenly released them and pointed across the cabin. That smile of happiness spread upon his face. O'Malley turned. There the boy lay, deeply slumbering, the clothes flung back so that the air from the port-hole played over the bare neck and chest; upon his face, too, shone the look of peace and rest his father wore, the hunted expression all gone, as though the spirit had escaped in sleep. The parent pointed, first to the boy, then to himself, then to this new friend standing beside his bed. The gesture including the three of them was of singular authority—invitation, welcome, and command lay in it. More—in some incomprehensible way it was majestic. O'Malley's thought flashed upon him the limb of some great oak tree, swaying in the wind.

Next, placing a finger on his lips, his eyes once more swept O'Malley and the boy, and he turned again into the little bunk that so difficultly held him, and lay back. The hair flowed down and mingled with the beard, over pillow and neck, almost to the shoulders. And something that was enormous and magnificent lay back with him, carrying with it again that sudden atmosphere of greater bulk. With a deep sound in his throat that was certainly no actual word and yet more expressive than any speech, he turned hugely over among the little, scanty sheets, drew the curtain again before his face, and returned into the world of—sleep.

XIII

"It may happen that the earthly body falls asleep in one direction deeply enough to allow it in others to awaken far beyond its usual limits, and yet not so deeply and completely as to awaken no more. Or, to the subjective vision there comes a flash so unusually vivid as to bring to the earthly sense an impression rising above the threshold from an otherwise inaccessible distance. Here begin the wonders of clairvoyance, of presentiments, and premonitions in dreams;—pure fables, if the future body and the future life are fables; otherwise, signs of the one and predictions of the other; but what has signs exists, and what has prophecies will come."

—FECHNER, Buchlein vom Leben nach dem Tode

But O'Malley rolled into his own berth below without undressing, sleep far from his eyes. He had heard the Gates of ivory and horn swing softly upon their opening hinges, and the glimpse he caught of the garden beyond made any question of slumber impossible. Again, he saw those shapes of cloud and wind flying over the long hills, while the name that should describe them ran, hauntingly splendid, along the mysterious passages of his being, though never coming quite to the surface for capture.

Perhaps, too, he was glad that the revelation was only partial. The size of the vision thus invoked awed him a little, so that he lay there half wondering at the complete surrender he had made to this guidance of another soul.

Stahl's warnings ran far away and laughed. The idea even came to him that Stahl was playing with him: that his portentous words had been carefully chosen for their heightening effect upon his own imagination so that the doctor might study an uncommon and extreme "case." The notion passed through him merely, without lingering.

In any event it was idle to put the brakes on now. He was internally committed and must go wherever it might lead. And the thought rejoiced him. He had climbed upon a pendulum that swung into an immense past; but its return swing would bring him safely back. It was rushing now into that nameless place of freedom that the primitive portion of his being had hitherto sought in vain, and a fundamental, starved craving of his life would know satisfaction at last. Already life had grown all glorious without. It was not steel engines but a speeding sense of beauty that drove the ship over the sea with feet of winged blue darkness. The stars fled with them across the sky, dropping golden leashes to draw him faster and faster forwards—yet within—to the dim days when this old world yet was young. He took his fire of youth and spread it, as it were, all over life till it covered the entire world, far, far away. Then he stepped back into it, and the world herself, he found, stepped with him.

He lay listening to the noises of the ship, the thump and bumble of the engines, the distant droning of the screws under water. From time-to-time stewards moved down the corridor outside, and the footsteps of some late passenger still paced the decks overhead. He heard voices, too, and occasionally the clattering of doors. Once or twice, he fancied someone moved stealthily to the cabin door and lingered there, but the matter never drew him to investigate, for the sound each time resolved itself naturally into the music of the ship's noises.

And everything, meanwhile, heard or thought, fed the central concern upon which his mind was busy. These superficial sounds, for instance, had nothing to do with the real business of the ship; that lay below with the buried engines and the invisible screws that worked like demons to bring her into port. And with himself and his slumbering companions the case was similar. Their respective power-stations, working in the subconscious, had urged them toward one another inevitably. How long, he wondered, had the spirit of that lonely, alien "being" flashed messages into the void that reached no receiving-station tuned to their acceptance? Their accumulated power was great, the currents they generated immense. He knew. For had they not charged full into himself the instant he came on board, bringing an intimacy that was immediate and full-fledged?

The untamed longings that always tore him when he felt the great winds, moved through forests, or found himself in desolate places, were at last on the high road to satisfaction—to some "state" where all that they represented would be explained and fulfilled. And whether such "state" should prove to be upon the solid surface of the earth, objective; or in the fluid regions of his inner being, subjective—was of no account whatever. It would be true. The great figure that filled the berth above him, now deeply slumbering, had in him subterraneans that gave access not only to Greece, but far beyond that haunted land, to a state of existence symbolized in the legends of the early world by Eden and the Golden Age....

"You are in danger," that wise old speculative doctor had whispered, "and especially in sleep!" But he did not sleep. He lay there thinking, thinking, thinking, a rising exaltation of desire paving busily the path along which eventually he might escape.

As the night advanced and the lesser noises retired, leaving only the deep sound of the steamer talking to the sea, he became aware, too, that a change, at first imperceptibly, then swiftly, was stealing over the cabin. It came with a riot of silent Beauty. At a loss to describe it with precision, he nevertheless divined that it proceeded from the sleeping figure overhead and in a lesser pleasure, too, from the boy upon the sofa opposite. It emanated from these two, he felt, in proportion as their bodies passed into deeper and deeper slumber, as though what occurred sometimes upon the decks by an act of direct volition, took place now automatically and with a fuller measure of release. Their spirits, free of that other world in sleep, were alert and potently discharging. Unconsciously, their vital, underlying essence escaped into activity.

Growing about his own person, next, it softly folded him in, casing his inner being with glory and this crowding sense of beauty. This increased manifestation of psychic activity reached down into the very core of himself, like invisible fingers playing upon an instrument. Notes—powers—in his soul, hitherto silent because none had known how to sound them, rose singing to the surface. For it seemed at length that forms of some intense life, busily operating, moved to and fro within the painted white walls of that little cabin, working subtly to bring about a transformation of himself. A singular change was fast and cleverly at work in his own being. It was, he puts it, a silent and irresistible Evocation.

No one of his senses was directly affected; certainly, he neither saw, felt, nor heard anything in the usual acceptance of the terms; but any instant surely, it seemed that all his senses must awake and report to the mind things that were splendid beyond the common order. In the crudest aspect of it, he felt as though he extended and grew large—that he dreaded to see himself in the mirror lest he might witness an external appearance of bigness which corresponded to this interior expansion.

For a long time, he lay unresisting, letting the currents of this subjective tempest play through and round him. Entrancing sensations of beauty and rapture came with it. The outer world seemed remote and trivial, the passengers unreal—the priest, the voluble merchant, the jovial Captain, all spun like dead things at the periphery of life, whereas he was moving toward the Center. Stahl—! the thought of Dr. Stahl, alone intruded with a certain unwelcome air of hindrance, almost as though he sought to end it, or call a halt. But Stahl, too, himself presently spun off like a leaf before the rising wind…

And then it was that an external sense was tapped, and he did hear something. From the berth overhead came a faint sound that made his heart stand still, though not with common fear. He listened intently. The blood tearing through his ears at first concealed its actual nature. It was far, far away; then came closer, as a waft of wind brings near and carries off again a sound of bells in mountains. It fled over vales and hills, to return a moment after with suddenness—a little louder, a little nearer. And with it came an increase of this sense of beauty that stretched his heart, as it were, to some deep ancient scale of joy once known, but long forgotten…

Across the cabin, the boy moved uneasily in his sleep.

"Oh, that I could be with him where he now is!" he cried, "in that place of eternal youth and eternal companionship!" The cry was instinctive utterly; his whole being, condensed in the single yearning, pressed through it—drove behind it. The place, the companionship, the youth—all, he knew, would prove in some strange way enormous, vast, ultimately satisfying forever and ever, far out of this little modern world that imprisoned him…

Again, most unwelcome and unexplained, the face of Stahl flashed suddenly before him to hinder and interrupt. He banished it with an effort, for it brought a smaller comprehension that somehow involved—fear.

"Curse the man!" flamed in anger across his world of beauty, and the violence of the contrast broke something in his mind like a globe of colored glass that had focused the exquisiteness of the vision…. The sound continued as before, but its power of evocation lessened. The thought of Stahl—Stahl in his denying aspect—dimmed it.

Glancing up at the frosted electric light, O'Malley felt vaguely that if he turned it out he would somehow yet see better, hear better, understand more; and it was this practical consideration, introduced indirectly by the thought of Stahl, that made him realize now for the first time that he actually and definitely was—afraid. For, to leave his bunk with its comparative, protective dark, and step into the middle of a cabin he knew to be alive with a seethe of invisible charging forces, made him realize that distinct effort was necessary—effort of will. If he yielded he would be caught up and away, swept from his known moorings, borne through high space out of himself. And Stahl with his cowardly warnings and belittlements set fear, thus, in the place of free acceptance. Otherwise, he might even have come to these long blue hills where danced and raced the giant shapes of cloud, singing while....

"Singing!" Ah! There was the clue! The sound he heard was singing—faint, low singing; close beside him too. It was the big man, singing softly in his sleep.

This ordinary explanation of the "wonder-sound" brought him down to earth, and so to a more normal feeling of security again. He stepped cautiously from the bed, careful not to let the rings rattle on the rod of brass, and slowly raised himself upright. And then, through a slit of the curtain, he—saw. The lips of the big sleeper moved gently, the beard rising and falling very slightly with them, and this murmur that he had thought so far away, came out and sang deliriously and faint before his very face. It most curiously—flowed. Easily, naturally, almost automatically, it poured softly forth, and the Irishman at once understood why he had first mistaken it for an echo of wind from distant hills. The imagery was entirely accurate. For it was precisely the singing cry that wind makes in a keyhole, in a chimney, or passing idly over the sweep of grassy hills. Exactly thus had he often listened to it swishing through the crannies of high rocks, tuneless yet searching. In it, too, there lay some accent of a secret, dim sublimity, deeper far than any other human sound could touch. The terror of a great freedom caught him, a freedom most awfully remote from the smaller personal existence he knew Today ... for it suggested, with awe and wonder, the kind of primitive utterance that was before speech or the development of language; when emotions were still too vague and mighty to be caught by little words, but when beings, close to the heart of their great Mother, expressed the feelings, enormous and uncomplex, of the greater life they shared as portions of her—projections of the Earth herself.

With a crash in his brain, O'Malley stopped. These thoughts, he suddenly realized, were not his own. An attack of unwonted sensations stung and scattered his mind with a rush of giant splendor that threatened to overwhelm him. He was in the very act of being carried away; his sense of personal identity menaced; surrender well-nigh already complete.

Another moment, especially if those eyes opened and caught him, and he would be beyond recall in the region of these other two. The narrow space of that little cabin was charged already to the brim, filled with some overpowering loveliness of wild and simple things, the beauty of stars and winds and flowers, the terror of seas and mountains; strange radiant forms of gods and heroes, nymphs, fauns and satyrs; the fierce sunshine of some Golden Age unspoiled, of a stainless region now long forgotten and denied—that world of splendor his heart had ever craved in vain, and beside which the life of Today faded to a wretched dream.

It was the Urwelt calling....

With a violent internal effort, he tore his gaze from those eyelids that fortunately opened not. At the same moment, though he did not hear them, steps came close in the corridor, and there was a rattling of the knob. Behind him, a movement from the berth below the port-hole warned him that he was but just in time. The Vision he was afraid as yet to acknowledge drew with such awful speed toward the climax.

Quickly he turned away, lifted the hook of the cabin door, and passed into the passage, strangely faint. A great commotion followed him out: father and son both, it seemed, suddenly upon their feet. And at the same time the sound of "singing" rolled into the body of a great hushed chorus, as it were of galloping winds that filled big valleys far away with a gust of splendor, faintly roaring in some incredible distance where no cities were, nor habitations of men; with a freedom, too, that was majestic and sublime. Oh! the terrific gait of that life in an open world!—Golden to the winds!—uncrowded!—The cosmic life—!

O'Malley shivered as he heard. For an instant, the true grain of his inner life, picked out in flame and silver, flashed clear. Almost—he knew himself caught back.

And there, in the dimly-lighted corridor, against the paneling of the cabin wall, crouched Dr. Stahl—listening. The pain of the contrast was vivid beyond words. It seemed as if he had passed from the thunder of organs to hear the rattling of tin cans. Instantly he understood the force that all along had held him back: the positive, denying aspect of this man's mind—afraid.

"You!" he exclaimed in a high whisper. "What are you doing here?" He hardly remembers what he said. The doctor straightened up and came on tiptoe to his side. He moved hurriedly.

"Come away," he said vehemently under his breath. "Come with me to my cabin—to the decks—anywhere away from this—before it's too late."

And the Irishman then realized that his face was white and that his voice shook. The hand that gripped him by the arm shook too.

They went quickly along the deserted corridor and up the stairs, O'Malley making no resistance, moving in a kind of dream. He has a fleeting recollection of an odor, sweet and slightly pungent as of horses, in his nostrils. The wind of the open decks revived him, and he saw to his amazement that the East was brightening. In that cabin, then, hours had been compressed into minutes.

The steamer had already slipped by the Straits of Messina. To the right he saw the cones of Etna, shadowy in the sky, calling across the dawn to Stromboli their smoking brother of the Lipari. To the left over the blue Ionian Sea the lights of a cloudless sunrise rose softly above the world.

And the hour of enchantment seized and shook him anew. Somewhere, across those faint blue waves, lay the things that he so passionately sought. It was the very essence of their loveliness and wonder that had charged down between the walls of that stuffy cabin below. For every morning still, at dawn, the tired world knows again the splendors of her youth; and the Irishman, shuddering a little in his sacred joy, felt that he must burst his bonds and fly to join the sunrise and the sea. The yearning, he was aware, had now increased a thousandfold: its fulfillment was merely delayed.

He passed along the decks all slippery with dew into Dr. Stahl's cabin and flung himself on the broad sofa to sleep. Sleep, too, came at once;

he was profoundly exhausted; and, while he slept, Stahl watched over him, covering his body with a thick blanket.

XIV

"It is a lovely imagination responding to the deepest desires, instincts, cravings of spiritual man, that spiritual rapture should find an echo in the material world; that in mental communion with God we should find sensible communion with nature; and that, when the faithful rejoice together, bird and beast, hill and forest should be not felt only but seen to rejoice along with them. It is not the truth; between us and our environment, whatever links there are, this link is wanting. But the yearning for it, the passion which made Wordsworth cry out for something, even were it the imagination of a pagan which would make him 'less forlorn,' is natural to man and simplicity leaps at the lovely fiction of a response. Just here is the opportunity for such alliances between spiritualism and superstition as are the daily despair of seekers after truth."

—Dr. VERRALL

And though he slept for hours the doctor never once left his side, but sat there with pencil and notebook, striving to catch, yet in vain, some accurate record of the strange fragmentary words that fell from his lips at intervals. His own face was aflame with an interest that amounted to excitement. The very hand that held the pencil trembled. One would have said that thus somewhat a man might behave who found himself faced with confirmation of some vast, speculative theory his mind had played with hitherto from a distance only.

Toward noon the Irishman awoke. The steamer, still loading oranges and sacks of sulfur in the Catania harbor, was dusty and noisy. Most of the passengers were ashore, hurrying with guidebooks and field-glasses to see the statue of the dead Bellini or watch the lava flow. A blazing, suffocating heat lay over the oily sea, and the summit of the volcano, with its tiny, ever-changing puff of smoke, soared through blue haze.

To Stahl's remark, "You've slept eight hours," he replied, "But I feel as though I'd slept eight centuries away." He took the coffee and rolls provided, and then smoked. The doctor lit a cigar. The red curtains over the port-holes shut out the fierce sun, leaving the cabin cool and dim. The shouting of the lightermen and officers mingled with the roar and scuttle of the donkey-engine. And O'Malley knew perfectly well that while the other moved about carelessly, playing with books and papers on his desk, he was all the time keeping him under close observation.

"Yes," he continued, half to himself, "I feel as if I'd fallen asleep in one world and awakened into another where life is trivial and insignificant, where men work like devils for things of no value in order to accumulate them in great ugly houses; always collecting and collecting, like mad children, possessions that they never really possess—things external to themselves, valueless and unreal—"

Dr. Stahl came up quietly and sat down beside him. He spoke gently, his manner kind and grave rather. He put a hand upon his shoulder.

"But, my dear boy," he said, the critical mood all melted away, "do not let yourself go too completely. That is vicious thinking, believe me. All details are important—here and now—spiritually important, if you prefer the term. The symbols change with the ages, that is all." Then, as the other did not reply, he added: "Keep yourself well in hand. Your experience is of extraordinary interest—may even be of value, to yourself as well as to—er—others. And what happened to you last night is worthy of record—if you can use it without surrendering your soul to it altogether. Perhaps, later, you will feel able to speak of it—to tell me in detail a little—?"

His keen desire to know more evidently fought with his desire to protect, to heal, possibly even to prevent.

"If I felt sure that your control were sufficient, I could tell you in return some results of my own study of—certain cases in the hospitals, you see, that might throw light upon—upon your own curious experience."

O'Malley turned with such abruptness that the cigar ash fell down over his clothes. The bait was strong, but the man's sympathy was not sufficiently of a piece, he felt, to win his entire confidence.

"I cannot discuss beliefs," he said shortly, "in the speculative way you do. They are too real. A man doesn't argue about his love, does he?" He spoke passionately. "Today everybody argues, discusses, speculates no one believes. If you had your way, you'd take away my beliefs and put in their place some wretched little formula of science that the next generation will prove all wrong again. It's like the N rays one of you discovered: they never really existed at all." He laughed. Then his flushed face turned grave again. "Beliefs are deeper than discoveries. They are eternal."

Stahl looked at him a moment with admiration. He moved across the cabin toward his desk.

"I am more with you than perhaps you understand," he said quietly, yet without too obviously humoring him. "I am more—divided, that's all."

"Modern!" exclaimed the other, noticing the ashes on his coat for the first time and brushing them off impatiently. "Everything in you expresses itself in terms of matter, forgetting that matter being in continual state of flux is the least real of all things—"

"Our training has been different," observed Stahl simply, interrupting him. "I use another phraseology. Fundamentally, we are not so far apart as you think. Our conversation of yesterday proves it, if you have not forgotten. It is people like yourself who supply the material that teaches people like me—helps me to advance—to speculate, though you dislike the term."

The Irishman was mollified, though for some time he continued in the same strain. And the doctor let him talk, realizing that his emotion needed the relief of this safety-valve. He used words loosely, but Stahl did not check him; it was merely that the effort to express himself—this self that could believe so much—found difficulty in doing so coherently in modern language. He went very far. For the fact that while Stahl criticized and denied, he yet understood, was a strong incentive to talk. O'Malley plunged repeatedly over his depth, and each time the doctor helped him in to shore.

"Perhaps," said Stahl at length in a pause, "the greatest difference between us is merely that whereas you jump headlong, ignoring details by the way, I climb slowly, counting the steps and making them secure. I deny at first because if the steps survive such denial, I know that they are permanent. I build scaffolding. You fly."

"Flight is quicker," put in the Irishman.

"It is for the few," was the reply; "scaffolding is for all."

"You spoke a few days ago of strange things," O'Malley said presently with abruptness, "and spoke seriously too. Tell me more about that, if you will." He sought to lead the talk away from himself, since he did not intend to be fully drawn. "You said something about the theory that the Earth is alive, a living being, and that the early legendary forms of life may have been emanations—projections of herself—detached portions of her consciousness—or something of the sort. Tell me about that theory. Can there be really men who are thus children of the earth, fruit of pure passion—Cosmic Beings as you hinted? It interests me deeply."

Dr. Stahl appeared to hesitate.

"It is not new to me, of course," pursued the other, "but I should like to know more."

Stahl still seemed irresolute. "It is true," he replied at length slowly, "that in an unguarded moment I let drop certain observations. It is better you should consider them unsaid perhaps: forget them."

"And why, pray?"

The answer was well calculated to whet his appetite.

"Because" answered the doctor, bending over to him as he crossed over to his side, "they are dangerous thoughts to play with, dangerous to the interests of humanity in its present state today, unsettling to the soul, shaking the foundations of sane consciousness." He looked hard at him. "Your own mind," he added softly, "appears to me to be already on their track. Whether you are aware of it or not, you have in you that kind of very passionate desire—of yearning—which might reconstruct them and make them come true—for yourself—if you get out."

O'Malley, his eyes shining, looked up into his face.

"'Reconstruct—make them come true—if I get out'!" he repeated stammeringly, fearful that if he appeared too eager the other would stop. "You mean, of course, that this Double in me would escape and build its own heaven?"

Stahl nodded darkly. "Driven forth by your intense desire." After a pause he added, "The process already begun in you would complete itself."

Ah! So obviously what the doctor wanted was a description of his sensations in that haunted cabin.

"Temporarily?" asked the Irishman under his breath.

The other did not answer for a moment. O'Malley repeated the question.

"Temporarily," said Stahl, turning away again toward his desk, "unless—the yearning were too strong."

"In which case—?"

"Permanently. For it would draw the entire personality with it...."

"The soul?"

Stahl was bending over his books and papers. The answer was barely audible.

"Death," was the whispered word that floated across the heavy air of that little sunbaked cabin.

The word if spoken at all was so softly spoken that the Irishman scarcely knew whether he actually heard it, or whether it was uttered by his own thought. He only realized—catching some vivid current from the other man's mind—that this separation of a vital portion of himself that Stahl hinted at might involve a kind of nameless inner catastrophe which should mean the loss of his personality as it existed today—an idea, however, that held no terror for him if it meant at the same time the recovery of what he so passionately sought.

And another intuition flashed upon its heels—namely, that this extraordinary doctor spoke of something he knew as a certainty; that his amazing belief, though paraded as theory, was to him more than theory. Had he himself undergone some experience that he dared not speak of, and were his words based upon a personal experience instead of, as he pretended, merely upon the observation of others? Was this a result of his study of the big man two years ago? Was this the true explanation of his being no longer an assistant at the H—hospital, but only a ship's doctor? Had this "modern" man, after all, a flaming volcano of ancient and splendid belief in him, akin to what was in himself, yet ever fighting it?

Thoughts raced and thundered through his mind as he watched him across the cigar smoke. The rattling of that donkey-engine, the shouts of the lightermen, the thuds of the sulfur-sacks—how ridiculous they all sounded, the clatter of a futile, meaningless existence where men gathered—rubbish, for mere bodies that lived amid dust a few years, then returned to dust forever.

He sprang from his sofa and crossed over to the doctor's side. Stahl was still bending over a littered desk.

"You, too," he cried, and though trying to say it loud, his voice could only whisper, "you, too, must have the Urmensch in your heart and blood, for how else, by my soul, could you know it all? Tell me, doctor, tell me!" And he was on the very verge of adding, "Join us! Come and join us!" when the little German turned his bald head slowly round and fixed upon the excited Irishman such a cool and quenching stare that instantly he felt himself convicted of foolishness, almost of impertinence.

He dropped backwards into an armchair, and the doctor at the same moment let himself down upon the revolving stool that was nailed to the floor in front of the desk. His hands smoothed out papers. Then he leaned forward, still holding his companion's eyes with that steady stare which forbade familiarity.

"My friend," he said quietly in German, "you asked me just now to tell you of the theory—Fechner's theory—that the Earth is a living, conscious Being. If you care to listen, I will do so. We have time." He glanced round at the shady cabin, took down a book from the shelf before him, puffed his black cigar and began to read.

"It is from one of your own people—William James; what you call a 'Hibbert Lecture' at Manchester College. It gives you an idea, at least, of what Fechner saw. It is better than my own words."

So Stahl, in his turn, refused to be "drawn." O'Malley, as soon as he recovered from the abruptness of the change from that other conversation, gave all his attention. The uneasy feeling that he was being played with, coaxed as a specimen to the best possible point for the microscope, passed away as the splendor of the vast and beautiful conception dawned upon him, and shaped those nameless yearnings of his life in glowing language.

XV

The shadows of the September afternoon were lengthening toward us from the Round Pond by the time O'Malley reached this stage of his curious and fascinating story. It was chilly under the trees, and the "wupsey-up, wupsey-down" babies, as he termed them, had long since gone into their teas, or whatever it is that London babies take at six o'clock.

We strolled home together, and he welcomed the idea of sharing a dinner we should cook ourselves in the tiny Knightsbridge flat. "Stewpot evenings," he called these occasions. They reminded us of camping trips together, although it must be confessed that in the cage-like room the "stew" never tasted quite as it did beside running water on the skirts of the forest when the dews were gathering on the little gleaming tent, and the wood-smoke mingled with the scents of earth and leaves.

Passing that grotesque erection opposite the Albert Hall, gaudy in the last touch of sunset, I saw him shudder. The spell of the ship and sea and the blazing Sicilian sunshine lay still upon us, Etna's cones towering beyond those gilded spikes of the tawdry Memorial. I stole a glance at my companion. His light blue eyes shone, but with the reflection of another sunset—the sunset of forgotten, ancient, far-off scenes when the world was young.

His personality held something of magic in that silent stroll homewards, for no word fell from either one of us to break its charm.

The untidy hair escaped from beneath the broad-brimmed old hat, and his faded coat of grey flannel seemed touched with the shadows that the dusk brings beneath wild-olive trees. I noticed the set of his ears, and how the upper points of them ran so sharply into the hair. His walk was springy, light, very quiet, suggesting that he moved on open turf where a sudden running jump would land him, not into a motor-bus, but into a mossy covert where ferns grew. There was a certain fling of the shoulders that had an air of rejecting streets and houses. Some fancy, wild and sweet, caught me of a faun passing down through underbrush of woodland glades to drink at a forest pool; and, chance giving back to me a little verse of Alice Corbin's, I turned and murmured it while watching him:

What dim Arcadian pastures
Have I known,
That suddenly, out of nothing,
A wind is blown,
Lifting a veil and a darkness,
Showing a purple sea—
And under your hair, the faun's eyes
Look out on me?

It was, of course, that whereas his body marched along Hill Street and through Montpelier Square, his thoughts and spirit flitted through the haunted, old-time garden he forever craved. I thought of the morrow—of my desk in the Life Insurance Office, of the clerks with oiled hair brushed back from the forehead, all exactly alike, trousers neatly turned up to show fancy-colored socks from bargain sales, their pockets full of cheap cigarettes, their minds busy with painted actresses and the names of horses! A Life Insurance Office! All London paying yearly sums to protect themselves against—against the most interesting moment of life. Premiums upon escape and freedom!

Again, it was the spell of my companion's personality that turned all this paraphernalia of the busy, modern existence into the counters in some grotesque and rather sordid game. Tomorrow, of course, it would all turn real and earnest again, O'Malley's story a mere poetic fancy. But for the moment I lived it with him and found it magnificent.

And the talk we had that evening when the stew-pot was empty and we were smoking on the narrow-ledged roof of the prison-house—for he always begged for open air, and with cushions we often sat beneath the stars and against the grimy chimney-pots—that talk I shall never forget. Life became constructed all anew. The power of the greatest fairy tale this world can ever know lay about me, raised to its highest expression. I caught at least some touch of reality—of awful reality—in the idea that this splendid globe whereon we perched like insects peeping timidly from tiny cells, might be the body of a glorious Being—the mighty frame to which some immense Collective Consciousness, vaster than that of men, and wholly different in kind, might be attached.

In the story, as I found it later in the dusty little Paddington room, O'Malley reported, somewhat heavily, it seemed to me, the excerpts chosen by Dr. Stahl. As an imaginative essay, they were interesting, of course, and vitally suggestive, but in a tale of adventure such as this they overweight the barque of fancy. Yet, in order to appreciate what followed, it seems necessary for the mind to steep itself in something of his ideas. The reader who dreads to think, and likes his imagination to soar unsupported, may perhaps dispense with the balance of this section; but to be faithful to the scaffolding whereon this Irishman built his amazing dream, I must attempt as best I can some précis of that conversation.

XVI

"Every fragment of visible Nature might, as far as is known, serve as part in some organism unlike our bodies.... As to that which can, and that which cannot, play the part of an organism, we know very little. A sameness greater or less with our own bodies is the basis from which we conclude to other bodies and souls.... A certain likeness of outward form, and again some amount of similarity in action, are what we stand on when we argue to psychical life. But our failure, on the other side, to discover these symptoms is no sufficient warrant for positive denial. It is natural in this connection to refer to Fechner's vigorous advocacy."

—F.H. BRADLEY, Appearance and Reality

It was with an innate resistance—at least a stubborn prejudice—that I heard him begin. The earth, of course, was but a bubble of dried fire, a huge round clod, dead as mutton. How could it be, in any permissible sense of the word—alive?

Then, gradually, as he talked there among the chimney-pots of old smoky London, there stole over me this new and disquieting sense of reality—a strange, vast splendor, too mighty to lie in the mind with comfort. Laughter fled away, ashamed. A new beauty, as of some amazing dawn, flashed and broke upon the world. The autumn sky overhead, thick-sown with its myriad stars, came down close, sifting gold and fire about my life's dull ways. That desk in the Insurance Office of Cornhill gleamed beyond as an altar or a possible throne.

The glory of Fechner's immense speculation flamed about us both, majestic yet divinely simple. Only a dim suggestion of it, of course, lay caught in the words the Irishman used—words, as I found later, that were a mixture of Professor James and Dr. Stahl, flavored strongly with Terence O'Malley—but a suggestion potent enough to have haunted me ever since and to have instilled meanings of stupendous divinity into all the commonest things of daily existence. Mountains, seas, wide landscapes, forests,—all I see now with emotions of wonder, delight, and awe unknown to me before. Flowers, rain, wind, even a London fog, have come to hold new meanings.

I never realized before that the mere size of our old planet could have hindered the perception of so fair a vision, or her mere quantitative bulk have killed automatically in the mind the possible idea of her being in some sense living. A microbe, endowed with our powers of consciousness, might similarly deny life to the body of the elephant on which it rode; or some were arguing atom, endowed with mind and senses, persuade itself that the monster upon whose flesh it dwelt were similarly a "heavenly body" of dead, inert matter; the bulk of the "world" that carried them obstructing their perception of its Life.

And Fechner, as it seems, was no mere dreamer, playing with a huge poetical conception. Professor of Physics in Leipsic University, he found time amid voluminous labors in chemistry to study electrical science with the result that his measurements in galvanism are classic to this day. His philosophical work was more than considerable. "A book on the atomic theory, classic also; four elaborate mathematical and experimental volumes on what he called psychophysics (many persons consider Fechner to have practically founded scientific psychology in the first of these books); a volume on organic evolution, and two works on experimental æsthetics, in which again Fechner is thought by some judges to have laid the foundations of a new science," are among his other performances.... "All Leipsic mourned him when he died, for he was the pattern of the ideal German scholar, as daringly original in his thought as he was homely in his life, a modest, genial, laborious slave to truth and learning.... His mind was indeed one of those multitudinously organized crossroads of truth which are occupied only at rare intervals by children of men, and from which nothing is either too far or too near to be seen in due perspective. Patientest observation, exactest mathematics, shrewdest discrimination, humanest feeling, flourished in him on the largest scale, with no apparent detriment to one another. He was in fact a philosopher in the 'great' sense."

"Yes," said O'Malley softly in my ear as we leaned against the chimneys and watched the tobacco curl up to the stars, "and it was this man's imagination that had evidently caught old Stahl and bowled him over. I never fathomed the doctor quite. His critical and imaginative apparatus got a bit mixed up, I suspect, for one moment he cursed me for asking 'suspicious questions,' and the next sneered sarcastically at me for boiling over with a sudden inspirational fancy of my own. He never gave himself away completely and left me to guess that he made that Hospital place too hot to hold him. He was a wonderful bird. But every time I aimed at him I shot wide and hit a cloud. Meantime he peppered me all over—one minute urging me into closer intimacy with my Russian—his cosmic being, his Urmensch type—so that he might study my destruction, and half an hour later doing his utmost apparently to protect me from him and keep me sane and balanced." His laugh rang out over the roofs.

"The net result," he added, his face tilted toward the stars as though he said it to the open sky rather than to me, "was that he pushed me forwards into the greatest adventure life has ever brought to me. I believe, I verily believe that sometimes, there were moments of unconsciousness—semi-consciousness perhaps—when I really did leave my body—caught away as Moses or was it Job or Paul?—into a Third Heaven, where I touched a bit of Reality that fairly made me reel with happiness and wonder."

"Well, but Fechner—and his great idea?" I brought him back.

He tossed his cigarette down into the back-garden that fringed the Park, leaning over to watch its zigzag flight of flame.

"Is simply this," he replied, "—'that not alone the earth but the whole Universe in its different spans and wave-lengths, is everywhere alive and conscious.' He regards the spiritual as the rule in Nature, not the exception. The professorial philosophers have no vision. Fechner towers above them as a man of vision. He dared to imagine. He made discoveries—whew!!" he whistled, "and such discoveries!"

"To which the scholars and professors of today," I suggested, "would think reply not even called for?"

"Ah," he laughed, "the solemn-faced Intellectuals with their narrow outlook, their atrophied vision, and their long words! Perhaps! But in Fechner's universe there is room for every grade of spiritual being between man and God. The vaster orders of mind go with the vaster orders of body. He believes passionately in the Earth Soul; he treats her as our special guardian angel; we can pray to the Earth as men pray to their saints. The Earth has a Collective Consciousness. We rise upon the Earth as wavelets rise upon the ocean. We grow out of her soil as leaves grow from a tree. Sometimes we find our bigger life and realize that we are parts of her bigger collective consciousness, but as a rule we are aware only of our separateness, as individuals. These moments of cosmic consciousness are rare. They come with love, sometimes with pain, music may bring them too, but above all—landscape and the beauty of Nature! Men are too petty, conceited, egoistic to welcome them, clinging for dear life to their precious individualities."

He drew breath and then went on: "'Fechner likens our individual persons on the earth to so many sense-organs of her soul, adding to her perceptive life so long as our own life lasts. She absorbs our perceptions, just as they occur, into her larger sphere of knowledge. When one of us dies, it is as if an eye of the world were closed, for all perceptive contributions from that particular quarter cease.'"

"Go on," I exclaimed, realizing that he was obviously quoting verbatim fragments from James that he had since pondered over till they had become his own, "Tell me more. It is delightful and very splendid."

"Yes," he said, "I'll go on quick enough, provided you promise me one thing: and that is—to understand that Fechner does not regard the Earth as a sort of big human being. If a being at all, she is a being utterly different from us in kind, as of course we know she is in structure. Planetary beings, as a class, would be totally different from any other beings that we know. He merely protests at the presumption of our insignificant human knowledge in denying some kind of life and consciousness to a form so beautifully and marvelously organized as that of the earth! The heavenly bodies, he holds, are beings superior to men in the scale of life—a vaster order of intelligence altogether. A little two-legged man with his cocksure reason strutting on its tiny brain as the apex of attainment he ridicules. D'ye see, now?"

I gasped, I lit a big pipe—and listened. He went on. This time it was clearly a page from that Hibbert Lecture Stahl had mentioned—the one in which Professor James tries to give some idea of Fechner's aim and scope, while admitting that he "inevitably does him miserable injustice by summarizing and abridging him."

"Ages ago the earth was called an animal," I ventured. "We all know that."

"But Fechner," he replied, "insists that a planet is a higher class of being than either man or animal—'a being whose enormous size requires an altogether different plan of life.'"

"An inhabitant of the ether—?"

"You've hit it," he replied eagerly. "Every element has its own living denizens. Ether, then, also has hers—the globes. 'The ocean of ether, whose waves are light, has also her denizens—higher by as much as their element is higher, swimming without fins, flying without wings, moving, immense and tranquil, as by a half-spiritual force through the half-spiritual sea which they inhabit,' sensitive to the slightest pull of one another's attraction: beings in every way superior to us. Any imagination, you know," he added, "can play with the idea. It is old as the hills. But this chap showed how and why it could be actually true."

"This superiority, though?" I queried. "I should have guessed their stage of development lower than ours, rather than higher."

"Different," he answered, "different. That's the point."

"Ah!" I watched a shooting star dive across our thick, wet atmosphere, and caught myself wondering whether the flash and heat of that hurrying little visitor produced any reaction in this Collective Consciousness of the huge Body whereon we perched and chattered, and upon which later it would fall in finest dust.

"It is by insisting on the differences as well as on the resemblances," rushed on the excited O'Malley, "that he makes the picture of the earth's life so concrete. Think a moment. For instance, our animal organization comes from our inferiority. Our need of moving to and fro, of stretching our limbs and bending our bodies, shows only our defect."

"Defect!" I cried. "But we're so proud of it!"

'"What are our legs,'" he laughed, "'but crutches, by means of which, with restless efforts, we go hunting after the things we have not inside ourselves? The Earth is no such cripple; why should she who already possesses within herself the things we so painfully pursue, have limbs analogous to ours? What need has she of arms, with nothing to reach for? Of a neck with no head to carry? Of eyes or nose, when she finds her way through space without either, and has the millions of eyes of all her animals to guide their movements on her surface, and all their noses to smell the flowers she grows?'"

"We are literally a part of her, then—projections of her immense life, as it were—one of the projections, at least?"

"Exactly. And just as we are ourselves a part of the earth," he continued, taking up my thought at once, "so are our organs her organs. 'She is, as it were, eye and ear over her whole extent—all that we see and hear in separation she sees and hears at once.'" He stood up beside me and spread his hands out to the stars and over the trees and paths of the Park at our feet, where the throngs of men and women walked and talked together in the cool of the evening. His enthusiasm grew as the idea of this German's towering imagination possessed him.

"'She brings forth living beings of countless kinds upon her surface, and their multitudinous conscious relations with each other she takes up into her higher and more general conscious life.'"

He leaned over the parapet and drew me to his side. I stared with him at the reflection of London town in the sky, thinking of the glow and heat and restless stir of the great city and of the frantic strivings of its millions for success—money, power, fame, a few, here and there, for spiritual success. The roar of its huge trafficking beat across the night in ugly thunder to our ears. I thought of the other cities of the world; of its villages; of shepherds among the lonely hills; of its myriad wild creatures in forest, plain, and mountain...

"All this she takes up into her great heart as part of herself!" I murmured.

"All this," he replied softly, as the sound of the Band beyond the Serpentine floated over to us on our roof; "—the separate little consciousnesses of all the cities, all the tribes, all the nations of men, animals, flowers, insects—everything." He again opened his arms to the sky. He drew in deep breaths of the night air. The dew glistened on the slates behind us. Far across the towers of Westminster a yellow moon rose slowly, dimming the stars. Big Ben, deeply booming, trembled on the air nine of her stupendous vibrations. Automatically, I counted them—subconsciously.

"And all our subconscious sensations are also hers," he added, catching my thought again; "our dreams but half divined, our aspirations half confessed, our tears, our yearnings, and our—prayers."

At the moment it almost seemed to me as if our two minds joined, each knowing the currents of the other's thought, and both caught up, gathered ill, folded comfortably away into the stream of a

Consciousness far bigger than either. It was like a momentary, specific proof of what he urged—a faint pulse-beat we heard of the soul of the earth; and it was amazingly uplifting.

"Every form of life, then, is of importance," I heard myself thinking, or saying, for I hardly knew which. "The tiniest efforts of value—even the unrecognized ones, and those that seem futile."

"Even the failures," he whispered, "—the moments when we do not trust her."

We stood for some moments in silence. Presently, with a hand upon my shoulder, he drew me down again among our rugs against the chimney-stack.

"And there are some of us," he said gently, yet with a voice that held the trembling of an immense joy, "who know a more intimate relationship with their great Mother than the rest, perhaps. By the so-called Love of Nature, or by some artless simplicity of soul, wholly unmodern of course, perhaps felt by children or poets mostly, they lie caught close to her own deep life, knowing the immense sweet guidance of her mighty soul, divinely mothered, strangers to all the strife for material gain—to that 'unrest which men miscall delight,'—primitive children of her potent youth … offspring of pure passion … each individual conscious of her weight and drive behind him—" His words faded away into a whisper that became unintelligible, then inaudible; but his thought somehow continued itself in my own mind.

"The simple life," I said in a low tone; "the Call of the Wild, raised to its highest power?"

But he changed my sentence a little.

"The call," he answered, without turning to look at me, speaking it into the night about us, "the call to childhood, the true, pure, vital childhood of the Earth—the Golden Age—before men tasted of the Tree and knew themselves separate; when the lion and the lamb lay down together and a little child could lead them. A time and state, that is, of which such phrases can be symbolical."

"And of which there may be here and there some fearful exquisite survival?" I suggested, remembering Stahl's words.

His eyes shone with the fire of his passion. "Of which on that little tourist steamer I found one!"

The wind that fanned our faces came perhaps across the arid wastes of Bayswater and the North-West. It also came from the mountains and gardens of this lost Arcadia, vanished for most beyond recovery....

"The Hebrew poets called it Before the Fall," he went on, "and later poets the Golden Age; today it shines through phrases like the Land of Heart's Desire, the Promised Land, Paradise, and what not; while the minds of saint and mystic have ever dreamed of it as union with their deity. For it is possible and open to all, to every heart, that is, not blinded by the cloaking horror of materialism which blocks the doorways of escape and prisons self behind the drab illusion that the outer form is the reality and riot the inner thought...."

The hoarse shouting of a couple of drunken men floated to us from the pavements, and crossing over, we peered down toward the opening of Sloane Street, watching a moment the stream of broughams, motors, and pedestrians. The two men with the rage of an artificial stimulant in their brains reeled out of sight. A big policeman followed slowly. The night-life of the great glaring city poured on unceasingly—the stream of souls all hurrying by divers routes and means toward a state where they sought to lose themselves—to forget the pressure of the bars that held them—to escape the fret and worry of their harassing personalities and touch some fringe of happiness! All so sure they knew the way—yet hurrying really in the wrong direction—outwards instead of inwards; afraid to be—simple....

We moved back to our rugs. For a long time neither of us found anything to say. Soon I led the way down the creaking ladder indoors again, and we entered the stuffy little sitting-room of the tiny flat he temporarily occupied. I turned up an electric light, but O'Malley begged me to lower it. I only had time to see that his eyes were still aglow. We sat by the open window. He drew a worn notebook from his still more worn coat; but it was too dark for him to read. He knew it all by heart.

XVII

Some of Fechner's reasons for thinking the Earth a being superior in the scale to us, he gave, but it was another passage that lingered chiefly in my heart, the description of the daring German's joy in dwelling upon her perfections—later, too, of his first simple vision. Though myself wholly of the earth, earthy in the ordinary sense, the beauty of the thoughts live in my spirit to this day, transfiguring even that dingy Insurance Office, streaming through all my dullest, hardest daily tasks with the inspiration of a simple delight that helps me over many a difficult weary time of work and duty.

"'To carry her precious freight through the hours and seasons what form could be more excellent than hers—being as it is horse, wheels, and wagon all in one. Think of her beauty—a shining ball, sky-blue and sunlit over one half, the other bathed in starry night, reflecting the heavens from all her waters, myriads of lights and shadows in the folds of her mountains and windings of her valleys she would be a spectacle of rainbow glory, could one only see her from afar as we see parts of her from her own mountain tops. Every quality of landscape that has a name would then be visible in her all at once—all that is delicate or graceful, all that is quiet, or wild, or romantic, or desolate, or cheerful, or luxuriant, or fresh. That landscape is her face—a peopled landscape, too, for men's eyes would appear in it like diamonds among the dew-drops. Green would be the dominant color, but the blue atmosphere and the clouds would enfold her as a bride is shrouded in her veil—a veil the vapory, transparent folds of which the earth, through her ministers the winds, never tires of laying and folding about herself anew.'

"She needs, as a sentient organism," he continued, pointing into the curtain of blue night beyond the window, "no heart or brain or lungs as we do, for she is—different. 'Their functions she performs through us! She has no proper muscles or limbs of her own, and the only objects external to her are the other stars. To these her whole mass reacts by the most exquisite alterations in its total gait and by the still more exquisite vibratory responses in its substance. Her ocean reflects the lights of heaven as in a mighty mirror, her atmosphere refracts them like a monstrous lens, the clouds and snowfields combine them into white, the woods and flowers disperse them into colors.... Men have always made fables about angels, dwelling in the light, needing no earthly food or drink, messengers between us and God. Here are actually existent beings, dwelling in the light and moving through the sky, needing neither food nor drink, intermediaries between God and us, obeying His commands. So, if the heavens really are the home of angels, the heavenly bodies must be those very angels, for other creatures there are none. Yes! the Earth is our great common guardian angel, who watches over all our interests combined.'

"And then," whispered the Irishman, seeing that I still eagerly listened, "give your ear to one of his moments of direct vision. Note its simplicity, and the authority of its conviction:

"'On a certain spring morning I went out to walk. The fields were green, the birds sang, the dew glistened, the smoke was rising, here and there a man appeared; a light as of transfiguration lay on all things. It was only a little bit of the earth; it was only a moment of her existence; and yet as my look embraced her more and more it seemed to me not only so beautiful an idea, but so true and clear a fact, that she is an angel, an angel so rich and fresh and flower-like, and yet going her round in the skies so firmly and so at one with herself, turning her whole living face to Heaven, and carrying me along with her into that Heaven, that I asked myself how the opinions of men could ever have so spun themselves away from life as to deem the earth only a dry clod, and to seek for angels above it or about it in the emptiness of the sky,—only to find them nowhere.'"

Fire-engines, clanging as with a hurrying anger through the night, broke in upon his impassioned sentences; the shouts of the men drowned his last words....

Life became very wonderful inside those tight, confining walls, for the spell and grandeur of the whole conception lifted the heart. Even if belief failed, in the sense of believing—a shilling, it succeeded in the sense of believing—a symphony. The invading beauty swept about us both. Here was a glory that was also a driving power upon which any, but a man half dead could draw for practical use. For the big conceptions fan the will. The little pains of life, they make one feel, need not kill true joy, nor deaden effort.

"Come," said O'Malley softly, interrupting my dream of hope and splendor, "let us walk together through the Park to your place. It is late, and you, I know, have to be up early in the morning ... earlier than I."

And presently we passed the statue of Achilles and got our feet upon the turf beyond—a little bit of living planet in the middle of the heavy smothering London town. About us, over us, within us, stirred the awe of that immense idea. Upon that bit of living, growing turf, we passed toward the Marble Arch, treading, as it were, the skin of a huge Body—the physical expression of a grand angelic Being, alive, sentient, conscious. Conscious, moreover, of our little separate individual selves who walked ... a Being who cared; who felt us; who knew, understood, and—loved us as a mother her own offspring.... "To whom men could pray as they pray to their saints."

The conception, even thus dimly and confusedly adumbrated, brought a new sense of life—terrific and eternal. All living things upon the earth's surface were emanations of her mighty central soul, all—from the gods and fairies of olden time who knew it, to the men and women of Today who have forgotten it.

The gods—!

Were these then projections of her personality—aspects and facets of her divided self—emanations now withdrawn? Latent in her did they still exist as moods or Powers—true, alive, everlasting, but unmanifest? Still knowable to simple men and to Children of Nature?

Was this the giant truth that Stahl had built on Fechner?

Everything about us seemed to draw together into an immense and towering configuration that included trees and air and the sweep of open park—the looming and overwhelming beauty of one of these very gods survived—Pan, the eternal and the splendid ... a mood of the Earth-life, a projection clothed with the light of stars, the cloudy air, the passion of the night, the thrill of an august, extended Mood.

And the others were not so very far behind—those other little parcels of Earth's Consciousness the Greeks and early races, the simple, primitive, childlike peoples of the dawn, divined the existence of, and labeled "gods" ... and worshipped ... so as to draw their powers into themselves by ecstasy and vision ...

Could, then, worship now still recall them? Was the attitude of even one true worshipper's heart the force necessary to touch that particular aspect of the mighty total Consciousness of Earth, and call forth those ancient forms of beauty? Could it be that this idea—the idea of "the gods"—was thus forever true and vital...? And might they be known and felt in the heart if not actually in some suggested form?

I only know that as we walked home past the doors of that dingy Paddington house where Terence O'Malley kept his dusty books and papers and so to my own quarters, these things he talked about dropped into my mind with a bewildering splendor to stay forever. His words I have forgotten, or how he made such speculations worth listening to at all. Yet, I hear them singing in my blood as though of yesterday; and often when that conflict comes 'twixt duty and desire that makes life sometimes so vain and bitter, the memory comes to lift with strength far greater than my own. The Earth can heal and bless.

XVIII

Slowly, taking life easily, the little steamer puffed its way across the Ionian Sea. The pyramid of Etna, bluer even than the sky, dominated the western horizon long after the heel of Italy had faded, then melted in its turn into the haze of cloud and distance. No other sails were visible.

With the passing of Calabria spring had leaped into the softness of full summer, and the breezes were gentle as those that long ago fanned the cheeks and hair of Io, beloved of Zeus, as she flew southwards toward the Nile. The passengers, less lovely than that fair daughter of Argos, and with the unrest of thinner adventure in their blood, basked lazily in the sun; but the sea was not less haunted for those among them whose hearts could travel. The Irishman at any rate slipped beyond the confines of the body, viewing that ancient scene as she had done, from above. His widening consciousness expanded to include it.

Cachalots spouted; dolphins danced, as though still to those wild flutes of Dionysus; porpoises rolled beneath the surface of the transparent waves, diving below the vessel's sides but just in time to save their shiny noses; and all day long, ignoring the chart upon the stairway walls, the tourists turned their glasses eastwards, searching for a first sight of Greece.

O'Malley, meanwhile, trod the decks of a new ship. For him now sea and sky were doubly peopled. The wind brought messages of some divine deliverance approaching slowly, the heat of that pearly, shining sun warmed centers of his being that hitherto the world kept chill. The land toward which the busy steamer moved he knew, of course, was but the shell from which the inner spirit of beauty once vivifying it had long since passed away. Yet it remained a clue. That ancient loveliness, as a mood of the earth's early consciousness, was buried, not destroyed. Eternally it still flamed somewhere. And long before the days of Greece, he knew, it had existed in yet fuller and more complete manifestation: that earliest, vastly splendid Mood of the earth's soul, too mighty for any existence that the history of humanity can recall, and too remote for any but the most daringly imaginative minds even to conceive. The Urwelt Mood, as Stahl himself admitted, even while it called to him, was a reconstruction that to men today could only seem—dangerous.

And his own little Self, guided by the inarticulate stranger, was being led at last toward its complete recapture.

Yet, while he crawled slowly with the steamer over a tiny portion of the spinning globe, feeling that at the same time he crawled toward a spot upon it where access would be somehow possible to this huge expression of her first Life—what was it, phrased timidly as men phrase big thoughts today, that he really believed? Even in our London talks, intimate as they were, interpreted too by gesture, facial expression, and silence, his full meaning evaded precise definition. "There are no words, there are no words," he kept saying, shrugging his shoulders and stroking his untidy hair. "In me, deep down, it all lies clear and plain and strong; but language cannot seize a mode of life that throve before language existed. If you cannot catch the picture from my thoughts, I give up the whole dream in despair." And in his written account, owing to its strange formlessness, the result was not a little bewildering.

Briefly stated, however—that remnant, at least, which I discover in my own mind when attempting to tell the story to others—what he felt, believed, lived, at any rate while the adventure lasted, was this:—

That the Earth, as a living, conscious Being, had known visible projections of her consciousness similar to those projections of our own personality which the advanced psychologists of today now envisage as possible; that the simple savagery of his own nature, and the poignant yearnings derived from it, were in reality due to his intimate closeness to the life of the Earth; that, whereas in the body the fulfillment of these longings was impossible, in the spirit he might yet know contact with the soul of the planet, and thus experience their complete satisfaction. Further, that the portion of his personality which could thus enter this heaven of its own subjective construction, was that detachable portion Stahl had spoken of as being "malleable by desire and longing," leaving the body partially and temporarily sometimes in sleep, and, at death, completely. More,—that the state thus entered would mean a quasi-merging back into the life of the Earth herself, of which he was a partial expression.

This closeness to Nature was today so rare as to be almost unrecognized as possible. Its possession constituted its owner what the doctor called a "Cosmic Being"—a being scarcely differentiated from the life of the Earth Spirit herself—a direct expression of her life, a survival of a time before such expressions had separated away from her and become individualized as human creatures. Moreover, certain of these earliest manifestations or projections of her consciousness, knowing in their huge shapes of fearful yet simple beauty a glory of her own being, still also survived. The generic term of "gods" might describe their status as interpreted to the little human power called Imagination.

This call to the simple life of primal innocence and wonder that had ever brimmed the heart of the Irishman, acknowledged while not understood, might have slumbered itself away with the years among modern conditions into atrophy and denial, had he not chanced to encounter a more direct and vital instance of it even than himself. The powerfully-charged being of this Russian stranger had summoned it forth. The mere presence of this man quickened and evoked this faintly-stirring center in his psychic being that opened the channel of return. Speech, as any other explanation, was unnecessary. To resist was still within his power. To accept and go was also open to him. The "inner catastrophe" he feared need not perhaps be insuperable or permanent.

"Remember," the doctor had said to him at the end of that last significant conversation, "this berth in my stateroom is freely at your disposal till Batoum." And O'Malley, thanking him, had shaken off that restraining hand upon his arm, knowing that he would never make use of it again.

For the Russian stranger and his son had somehow made him free.

Between that cabin and the decks, he spent his day. Occasionally he would go below to report progress, as it were, by little sentences which he divined would be acceptable, and at the same time gave expression to his own growing delight. The boy, meanwhile, was everywhere, playing alone like a wild thing; one minute in the bows, hat off, gazing across the sea beneath a shading hand, and the next leaning over the stern-rails to watch the churning foam that drove them forwards. At regular intervals he, too, rushed to the cabin and brought communications to his parent.

"Tomorrow at dawn," observed the Irishman, "we shall see Cape Mattapan rising from the sea. After that, Athens for a few hours; then coasting through the Cyclades, close to the mainland often." And glancing over to the berth, while pretending to be busy with his steamer-trunk, he saw the great smile of happiness break over the other's face like a sunrise....

For it was clear to him that with the approach to Greece, a change began to come over his companions. It was noticeable chiefly in the father. The joy that filled the man, too fine and large to be named excitement, passed from him in radiations that positively seemed to carry with them a physical extension. This, of course, was purely a clairvoyant effect upon the mind—O'Malley's divining faculty visualized the spiritual traits of the man's dilating Self. But, nevertheless, the truth remained that—somehow he increased. He grew; became interiorly more active, alive, potent; and of this singular waxing of the inner spirit something passed outwards and stood with rare dignity about his very figure.

And this manifestation of themselves was due to that expansion of the inner life caused by happiness. The little point of their personalities they showed normally to the world was but a single facet, a tip as it were of their whole selves. More lay within, beyond. As with the rest of the world, a great emotion stimulated and summoned it forth into activity nearer the surface. Clearly, for these two Greece symbolized a point of departure of a great hidden passion. Something they expected lay waiting for them there. Guidance would come thence.

And, by reflection perhaps as much as by direct stimulation, the same change made itself felt in himself. Joy caught him—the joy of a home-coming, long deferred....

At the same time, the warning of Dr. Stahl worked in him, if subconsciously only. He showed this by mixing more with the other passengers. He chatted with the Captain, who was as pleased with his big family as though he had personally provided the weather that made them happy; with the Armenian priest, who was eager to show that he had read "a much of T'ackeray and Kipling; and especially with the boasting Moscow merchant, who by this time "owned" the smoking-room and imposed his verbose commonplaces upon one and all with authoritative self-confidence in six languages—a provincial mind in full display. The latter in particular held him to a normal humanity; his atmosphere breathed the wholesome thickness of the majority of humankind—ordinary, egoistic, with the simplicity of the uninspiring sort. The merchant acted upon him as a sedative, and that day the Irishman took him in large doses, allopathically, for his talk formed an admirable antidote to the stress of that other burning excitement that, according to Stahl, threatened to disintegrate his personality.

Though hardly in the sense he intended, the fur-merchant was entirely delightful—engaging as a child; for, among other marked qualities, he possessed the unerring instinct of the snob which made him select for his friends those whose names or position might glorify his banal insignificance—and his stories were vivid pictorial illustrations of this useful worldly faculty. O'Malley listened with secret delight, keeping a grave face and dropping in occasional innocent questions to heighten the color or increase the output. Others in the circle responded in kind, feeling the same chord vibrating in themselves. Even the priest, like a repeating-gun, continually discharged his little secret pride that Byron had occupied a room in that Venetian monastery where he lived; and at last O'Malley himself was conscious of an inclination to report his own immense and recently discovered kinship with a greater soul and consciousness than his own. After all, he reflected with a deep thrill while he listened, the desire ot the snob was but a crude and simple form of the desire of the mystic:—to lose one's little self in a Self which is greater!

Then, weary of them all and their minute personal interests, he left the smoking-room and joined the boy again, running absurd races with him from stern to bow, playing hide-and-seek among the decks, even playing shuffle-board together. They sweated in the blazing sun and watched the dance of the sea; caught the wind in their faces with a shout of joy, or with pointing fingers followed the changing outlines of the rare, soft clouds that sailed the world of blue above them. There was no speech between them, and both felt that other things, invisible, swift, and spirit-footed, whose home is just beyond the edge of life as the senses report life, played wildly with them. The smoking-room then, with its occupants so greedy for the things that money connotes—the furs, champagne, cigars, and heavy possessions that were symbols of the personal aggrandizement they sought and valued—seemed to the Irishman like a charnel-house where those about to die sat making inventories in blind pride of the things they must leave behind.

It was, indeed, a contrast of Death and Life. For beside him, with that playing, silent boy, coursed the power of transforming loveliness which had breathed over the world before her surface knew this swarming race of men. The life of the Earth knew no need of outward acquisition, possessing all things so completely in herself. And he—he was her child—O glory! Joy passing belief!

"Oh!" he cried once with passion, turning to the fair-haired figure of youth who stood with him in the bows, meeting the soft wind,—"Oh, to have heard the trees whispering together in the youth of the world, and felt one of the earliest winds that ever blew across the cooling seas!"

And the boy, not understanding the words, but responding with a perfect naturalness to the emotion that drove them forth, seized his hand and with an extraordinarily free motion as of flying, raced with him down the decks, happy, laughing, hair loose over his face, and with a singular action of the shoulders as though he somehow—cantered. O'Malley remembered his vision of the Flying Shapes....

Toward the evening, however, the boy disappeared, keeping close to his father's side, and after dinner both retired early to their cabin.

And the ship, meanwhile, drew ever nearer to the haunted land.

XIX

"Privacy is ignorance."

—JOSIAH ROYCE

Somewhat after the manner of things suffered in vivid dreams, where surprise is numbed and wonder becomes the perfect password, the Irishman remembers the sequence of little events that filled the following day.

Yet his excitement held nothing of the vicious fling of fever; it was spread over the entire being rather than located hotly in the brain and blood alone; and it "derived," as it were, from tracts of his personality usually unstirred, atrophied indeed in most men, that connected him as by a delicate network of feelers with Nature and the Earth. He came gradually to feel them, as a man in certain abnormal conditions becomes conscious of the bodily processes that customarily go on in himself without definite recognition.

Stahl could have told him, had he cared to seek the information, that this fringe of wider consciousness, stretching to the stars and winds and earth, was the very part that had caused his long unrest and yearning—the part that knew the Earth as mother and sought the sweet and savage freedom of what he called with the poverty of modern terms—primitive. The channels leading toward a state of Cosmic Consciousness, one with the Earth Life, were being now flushed and sluiced by the forces emanating from the persons of his new companions.

And as this new state slowly usurped command, the readjustment of his spiritual economy thus involved, caused other portions of himself to sink into temporary abeyance. While it alarmed him, it was too delicious to resist. He made no real attempt to resist. Yet he knew full well that the portion sinking thus out of sight was what folk with such high pride call Reason, Judgment, Common Sense!

In common with animal, bird, and insect life, all intimately close to Nature, he began to feel as realities those subtle currents of the Earth's personality by which the seals know direction in the depths of a thousand-mile sea, by which the homing pigeons blaze trails through space, birds fly south, the wild bees know their pathways, and all simple life, from the Red Indian to the Red Ant, acknowledges the viewless guidance of the mother's enveloping heart. The cosmic life ran through his being, lighting signals, offering service, more—claiming leadership.

With it, however, came no loss of individuality, but rather a powerful increase of life by means of which for the first time he dreamed of a fuller existence which should eventually harmonize and combine the ancient simplicity of soul that claimed the Earth, with the modern complexity which, indulged alone, rendered the world so ugly and insignificant…! He experienced an immense, driving push upon what Bergson has called the élan vital of his being.

The opening charge of his new discovery, however, was more than disconcerting, and it is not surprising that he lost his balance. Its attack and rush were overwhelming. Thus, it was a kind of exalted speculative wonder lying behind his inner joy that caused his mistakes. He had imagined, for instance, that the first sight of Greece would bring some climax of revelation, making clear to what particular type of early life the spirits of his companions conformed; more, that they would then betray themselves to one and all for what they were in some effort to escape, in some act of unrestraint, something, in a word, that would explain themselves to the world of passengers, and focus them upon the doctor's microscope forever.

Yet when Greece showed her first fair rim of outline, his companions still slept peacefully in their bunks. The anticipated dénouement did not appear. Nothing happened. It was not the mere sight of so much land lying upon the sea's cool cheek that could prove vital in an adventure of such a kind. For the adventure remained spiritual. O'Malley had merely confused two planes of consciousness. As usual, he saw the thing "whole" in that extraordinary way to which his imagination alone held the key and hence his error.

Yet the moment has ever remained for him one of vital, stirring splendor, significant as life or death. He remembers that he was early on deck and saw the dawn blow up softly from behind the islands with a fresh, salt wind that blew at the same time like music into his very heart. Golden clear it rose; and just below, like the petals of some vast, archetypal flower that gave birth, the low blue hills of coast and island opened magically into blossom. The rocky cliffs of Mattapan slipped past; the smooth, bare slopes of the ancient shore-line followed; treeless peaks and shoulders, abrupt precipices, summits and ridges all exquisitely rosy and alive. He had seen Greece before, yet never thus, and the emotion that invaded every corner of his larger consciousness lay infinitely deeper than any mere pseudo-classical thrill he had known in previous years. He saw it, felt it, knew it from within, instead of as a spectator from without. This dawn-mood of the Earth was also his own; and upon his spirit, as upon her blue-crowned hills, lay the tide of highlight with its delicate swift blush. He saw it with her—through one of her opened eyes.

The hot hours the steamer lay in the Piraeus Harbor were wearisome, the noise of loading and unloading cargo worse even than at Catania. While the tourist passengers hurried fussily ashore, carrying guidebooks and cameras, to chatter among the ruined temples, he walked the decks alone, dreaming his great dream, conscious that he spun through leagues of space with the great Being who more and more possessed him. Beyond the shipping and the masts collected there from all the ports of the Mediterranean and the Levant, he watched the train puffing slowly to the station that lay in the shadow of Theseus' Temple, but his eyes at the same tune strained across the haze toward Eleusis Bay, and while his ears caught the tramping feet of the long Torchlight Procession, some power of his remoter consciousness divined the forms of hovering gods, expressions of his vast Mother's personality with which, in worship, this ancient people had believed it possible to merge themselves. The significant truths that lay behind the higher Mysteries degraded since because forgotten and misinterpreted, trooped powerfully down into his mind. For the supreme act of this profound cult, denied by a grosser age that seeks to telephone to heaven, deeming itself thereby "advanced," lay in the union of the disciple with his god, the god he worshipped all his life, and into whose Person he slipped finally at death by a kind of marriage rite.

"The gods!" ran again through his mind with passion and delight, as the letter of his early studies returned upon him, accompanied now for the first time by the in-living spirit that interpreted them. "The gods!—Moods of her giant life, manifestations of her spreading Consciousness pushed outwards, Powers of life and truth and beauty…!"

* * * * *

And, meanwhile, Dr. Stahl, sometimes from a distance, sometimes coming close, kept over him a kind of half-paternal, half-professional attendance, the Irishman accepting his ministrations without resentment, almost with indifference.

"I shall be on deck between two and three in the morning to see the comet," the German observed to him casually toward evening as they met on the bridge. "We may meet perhaps—"

"All right, doctor; it's more than possible," replied O'Malley, realizing how closely he was being watched.

In his mind at the moment another sentence ran, the thought growing stronger and stronger within him as the day declined:

"It will come tonight—come as an inner catastrophe not unlike that of death! I shall hear the call—to escape...."

For he knew, as well as if it had been told to him in so many words, that the sleep of his two companions all day was in the nature of a preparation. The fluid projections of themselves were all the time active elsewhere. Their bodies heavily slumbered; their spirits were out and alert. Summoned forth by those strange and radiant evocative forces that even in the dullest minds "Greece" stirs into life, they had temporarily escaped. Again, he saw those shapes of cloud and wind moving with swift freedom over the long, bare hills. Again, and again the image returned. With the night a similar separation of the personality might come to himself too. Stahl's warning passed in letters of fire across his inner sight. With a relief that yet contained uneasiness he watched his shambling figure disappear down the stairway. He was alone.

XX

"To everything that a man does he must give his undivided attention or his Ego. When he has done this, thoughts soon arise in him, or else a new method of apprehension miraculously appears....

"Very remarkable it is that through this play of his personality man first becomes aware of his specific freedom, and that it seems to him as though he awaked out of a deep sleep as though he were only now at home in the world, and as if the light of day were breaking now over his interior life for the first time.... The substance of these impressions which affect us we call Nature, and thus Nature stands in an immediate relationship to those functions of our bodies which we call senses. Unknown and mysterious relations of our body allow us to surmise unknown and mysterious correlations with Nature, and therefore Nature is that wondrous fellowship into which our bodies introduce us, and which we learn to know through the mode of its constitutions and abilities."

—NOVALIS, Disciples at Saïs. Translated by U.C.B.

And so, at last, the darkness came, a starry darkness of soft blue shadows and phosphorescent sea out of which the hills of the Cyclades rose faint as pictures of floating smoke and a wind might waft away like flowers to the sky.

The plains of Marathon lay far astern, blushing faintly with their scarlet tamarisk blossoms. The strange purple glow of sunset upon Hymettus had long since faded. A hush grew over the sea, now a marvelous cobalt blue. The earth, gently sleeping, manifested dreamily. Into the subconscious state passed one half of her huge, gentle life.

The Irishman, responding to the eternal spell of her dream-state, experienced in quite a new way the magic of her Night-Mood. He found it more difficult than ever to realize as separate entities the little things that moved about through the upper surface of her darkness. Wings of silver, powerfully whirring, swept his soul onwards to another place—toward Home.

And the two worlds intermingled oddly. These little separate "outer things" going to and fro busily became as symbols more or less vital, more or less transparent. They varied according to their simplicity. Some of them were channels that led directly where he was going; others, again, had lost all connection with their vital source and center of existence. To the former belonged the sailors, children, the tired birds that rested on the ship as they journeyed northwards, swallows, doves, and little travelers with breasts of spotted yellow that nested in the rigging; even, in a measure, the gentle, brown-eyed priest; but to the latter, the noisy, vulgar, beer-drinking tourists, and, especially, the fur-merchant.... Stahl, interpreter and intermediary, hovered between—incarnate compromise.

Escaping from everybody, at length, he made his way into the bows; there, covered by the stars, he waited. And the thing he waited for—he felt coming over him with a kind of massive sensation as little local as heat or cold—was that disentanglement of a part of his personality from the rest against which Stahl had warned him. That portion of his complex personality in which resided desire and longing, matured during these many years of poignant nostalgia, was now slowly and deliberately loosening out from the parent center. It was the vehicle of his Urwelt yearnings; and the Urwelt was about to draw it forth. The Call was on its way.

Hereabouts, then, near the Isles of Greece, lay a channel to the Earth's far youth, a channel for some reason still unclosed. His companions knew it; he, too, had half divined it. The increased psychic activity of all three as they approached Greece seemed explained. The sign—would it be through hearing, sight, or touch?—would shortly come that should convince.

That very afternoon Stahl had said—"Greece will betray them," and he had asked: "Their true form and type?" And for answer the old man did an expressive thing, far more convincing than words: he bent forwards and downwards. He made as though to move a moment on all fours.

O'Malley remembered the brief and vital scene now. The word, however, persistently refused to come into his mind. Because the word was really inadequate, describing but partially a form and outline symbolically of far more,—a measure of Nature and Deity alike.

And so, as a man dreading the entrance to a great adventure that he yet desires, the Irishman waited there alone beneath the cloud of night.... Soft threads of star-gold, trailing the sea, wove with the darkness a veil that hid from his eyes the world of crude effects. All memory of the casual realities of modern life that so distressed his soul fled far away. The archetypal world, soul of the Earth, swam close about him, enormous and utterly simple. He seemed alone in some hollow of the night which Time had overlooked, and where the powers of sea and air held him in the stretch of their gigantic, changeless hands. In this hollow lay the entrance to the channel down which he presently might flash back to that primal Garden of the Earth's first beauty—her Golden Age... down which, at any rate, the authoritative Call he awaited was to come.... "Oh! what a power has white simplicity!"

Wings from the past, serene and tranquil, bore him toward this ancient peace where echoes of life's brazen clash today could never enter. Ages before Greece, of course, it had flourished, yet Greece had caught some flying remnant ere it left the world of men, and for a period had striven to renew its life, though by poetry but half believed. Over the vales and hills of Hellas this mood had lingered bravely for a while, then passed away forever … and those who dreamed of its remembrance remain homeless and lonely, seeking it ever again in vain, lost citizens, rejected by the cycles of vainer life and action that succeeded.

The Spirit of the Earth, yes, whispered in his ears as he waited covered by the night and stars. She called him, as though across all the forests on her breast the long, sweet winds went whispering his name. Lying there upon the coils of thick and tarry rope, the Urwelt caught him back with her splendid passion. Currents of Earth life, quasi-deific, gentle as the hands of little children, tugged softly at this loosening portion of his Self, urging his very lips, as it were, once more to the mighty Mother's breasts. Again, he saw those cloud-like shapes careering over long, bare hills … and almost knew himself among them as they raced with streaming winds … free, ancient comrades among whom he was no longer alien and outcast, including his two companions of the steamer. The early memory of the Earth became his own; as a part of her, he shared it too.

The Urwelt closed magnificently about him. Vast shapes of power and beauty, other than human, once his comrades thus, but since withdrawn because denied by a pettier age, moved up, huge and dim, across the sham barriers of time and space, singing the great Earth-Song of welcome in his ears. The whisper grew awfully…. The Spirit of the Earth flew close and called upon him with a shout…!

Then, out of this amazing reverie, he woke abruptly to the consciousness that someone was approaching him stealthily, yet with speed, through the darkness. With a start he sat up, peering about him. There was dew on his clothes and hair. The stars he saw had shifted their positions.

He heard the surge of the water from the vessel's bows below. The line of the shore lay close on either side. Overhead he saw the black threads of rigging, quivering with the movement of the ship; the swaying mast-head light; the dim, round funnels; the confused shadows where the boats swung—and nearer, moving between the ropes and windlasses, this hurrying figure whose approach had disturbed him in his gorgeous dream.

And O'Malley divined at once that, though in one sense a portion of his dream, it belonged outwardly to the same world as this long dark steamer that trailed after him across the sea. A piece of his vision, as it were, had broken off and remained in the cruder world wherein his body lay upon these tarry ropes. The boy came up and stood a moment by his side in silence, then, stooping to the level of his head, he spoke:—

"Come," he said in low tones of joy; "come! We wait a long time for you already!"

The words, like music, floated over the sea, as O'Malley took the outstretched hand and suffered himself to be led quickly toward the lower deck. He walked at first as in a dream continued after waking; more than once it seemed as though they stepped together from the boards and moved through space toward the line of peaked hills that fringed the steamer's course so close. For through the salt night air ran a perfume that suggested flowers, earth, and woods, and there seemed no break in the platforms of darkness that knit sea and shore to the very substance of the vessel.

XXI

The lights in the saloon were out, the smoking-room empty, the passengers in bed. The ship seemed entirely deserted. Only, on the bridge, the shadow of the first officer paced quietly to and fro. Then, suddenly, as they approached the stern, O'Malley discerned anther figure, huge and motionless, against the background of phosphorescent foam; and at the first glance it was exactly as though he had detached from the background of his mind one of those Flying Outlines upon the hills—and caught it there, arrested visibly at last.

He moved along, fairly sure of himself, yet with a tumult of confused sensations, as if consciousness were transferring itself now more rapidly to that portion of him which sought to escape.

Leaning forward, in a stooping posture over the bulwarks, wrapped in the flowing cape he sometimes wore, the man's back and shoulders married so intimately with the night that it was hard to determine the dividing line between the two. So much more of the deck behind him, and of the sky immediately beyond his neck, was obliterated than by any possible human outline. Whether owing to obliquity of disturbed vision, tricks of shadow, or movement of the vessel between the stars and foam, the Irishman saw these singular emanations spread about him into space. He saw them this time directly. And more than ever before they seemed in some way right and comely—true. They were in no sense monstrous; they reported beauty, though a beauty cloaked in power.

And, watching him, O'Malley felt that this loosening portion of himself, as once before in the little cabin, likewise began to grow and spread. Within some ancient fold of the Earth's dream-consciousness they both lay caught. In some mighty Dream of her planetary Spirit, dim, immense, slow-moving, they played their parts of wonder. Already they lay close enough to share the currents of her subconscious activities. And the dream, as she turned in her vast, spatial sleep, was a dream of a time long gone.

Here, amid the loneliness of deserted deck and night, this illusion of bulk was more than ever before outwardly impressive, and as he yielded to the persuasion of the boy's hand, he was conscious of a sudden wild inclination to use his own arms and legs in a way he had never before known or dreamed of, yet that seemed curiously familiar. The balance and adjustment of his physical frame sought to shift and alter; neck and shoulders, as it were, urged forward; there came a singular pricking in the loins, a rising of the back, a thrusting up and outwards of the chest. He felt that something grew behind him with a power that sought to impel or drive him in advance and out across the world at a terrific gait; and the hearing of his ears became of a sudden intensely acute. While his body moved ordinarily, he knew that a part of him that was not body moved—otherwise, that he neither walked, ran, nor stepped upon two feet, but—galloped. The motion proclaimed him kin with the flying shapes upon the hills. At the heart of this portion which sought to detach itself from his central personality—which, indeed, seemed already half escaped—he cantered.

The experience lasted but a second—this swift, free motion of the escaping Double—then passed away like those flashes of memory that rise and vanish again before they can be seized for examination. He shook himself free of the unaccountable obsession, and with the effort of returning to the actual present, the passing-outwards was temporarily checked. And it was then, just as he held himself in hand again, that glancing sideways, he became aware that the boy beside him had, like his parent, also changed—grown large and shadowy with a similar suggestion of another splendid outline. The extension already half accomplished in himself and fully accomplished in the father, was in process of accomplishment in the smaller figure of the son. Clothed in the emerged true shape of their inner being they slowly revealed themselves. It was as bewildering as watching death, and as stern and beautiful.

For the boy, still holding his hand, loped along beside him as though the projection that emanated from him, grown almost physical, were somehow difficult to manage.

In the moment of nearer, smaller consciousness that yet remained to him, O'Malley recalled the significant pantomime of Dr. Stahl two days before in the cabin. It came with a rush of fire. The warning operated; his caution instantly worked. He dropped the hand, let the clinging fingers slip from his own, overcome by something that appalled. For this, surely, was the inner catastrophe that he dreaded, the radical internal dislocation of his personality that involved—death. The thing that had happened, or was happening to these other two, was on the edge of fulfillment in himself—before he was either ready or had decided to accept it.

At any rate he hesitated; and the hesitation, shifting his center of consciousness back into his brain, checked and saved him. A confused sense of forces settling back within himself followed; a kind of rush and scuttle of moods and powers: and he remained temporarily master of his being, recovering balance and command. Twice already—in that cabin-scene, as also on the deck when Stahl had seized him—the moment had come close. Now, again, had he kept hold of the boy's grasp, that inner transformation, which should later become externalized, must have completed itself.

"No, no!" he tried to cry aloud, "for I'm not yet ready!" But his voice rose scarcely above a whisper. The decision of his will, however, had produced the desired result. The "illusion," so strangely born, had passed, at any rate for the time. He knew once more the glory of the steadfast stars, realized that he walked normally upon a steamer's deck, heard with welcome the surge of the sea below, and felt the peace of this calm southern night as they coasted with two hundred sleeping tourists between the islands and the Grecian mainland.... He remembered the fur-merchant, the Armenian priest, the Canadian drummer....

It seemed his feet half tripped, or at least that he put out a hand to steady himself against the ship's long roll, for the pair of them moved up to the big man's side with a curious, rushing motion that brought them all together with a mild collision. And the boy laughed merrily, his laughter like singing half completed. O'Malley remembers the little detail, because it serves to show that he was still in a state of intensified consciousness, far above the normal level. It was still "like walking in my sleep or acting out some splendid dream," as he put it in his written version. "Half out of my body, if you like, though in no sense of the words at all half out of my mind!"

XXII

What followed he relates with passion, half confused. Without speaking the big Russian turned his head by way of welcome, and O'Malley saw that the proportions of it were magnificent like a fragment of the night and sky. Though too dark to read the actual expression in the eyes, he detected their gleam of joy and splendor.

The whole presentment of the man was impressive beyond any words that he could find. Massive, yet charged with swift and alert vitality, he reared there through the night, his inner self now toweringly manifested. At any other time, and without the preparation already undergone, the sight might almost have terrified; now it only uplifted. For in similar fashion, though lesser in degree, because the mold was smaller, and hesitation checked it, this very transformation had been going forward within himself.

The three of them leaned there upon the rails, rails oddly dwindled now to the size of a toy steamer, while thus the spirit of the dreaming Earth swam round and through them, awful in power, yet at the same time gentle, winning, seductive as wildflowers in the spring. And it was this delicate, hair-like touch of delight, magical with a supreme and utterly simple innocence, that made the grandeur of the whole experience still easily manageable, and terror in it all unknown.

The Irishman stood on the outside, toward the vessel's stern, next him the father, beyond, the boy. They touched. A current like a river in flood swept through all three.

He, too, was caught within those visible extensions of their personalities; all again, caught within the consciousness of the Earth. Across the sea they gazed together in silence—waiting.

It was the Oro passage, where the mainland hills on the west and the Isle of Tenos on the east draw close together, and the steamer passes for several miles so near to Greece that the boom of surf upon the shore is audible. That night, however, the sea lay too still for surf; it whispered softly in its sleep; and in its sleep, too, listened. They heard its multitudinous rush of voices as the surge below raced by—a giant frieze in which the phosphorescence painted dancing forms and palely luminous faces. Unsubstantial shapes of foam held hands in continuous array below the waves, lit by soft-sea-lanterns strung together along the steamer's sides.

Yet it was not these glimmering shapes the three of them watched, thus intently silent. The lens of yearning focused not in sight. Down the great channel at whose opening they stood, leading straight to the Earth's old central heart, the message of communion would not be a visual one. The sensitive fringe of their stretched personalities, contacting thus actually the consciousness of the planet-soul, would quiver to a reaction of another kind. This point of union, already affected, would presently report itself, unmistakably, yet not to the eyes. The increased acuteness of the Irishman's hearing—a kind of interior hearing—quickly supplied the key. It was that all three—listened.

Some primitive sound of Earth would presently vibrate through their extended beings with an authoritative sweet thunder not to be denied. By a Voice, a Call, the Earth would tell them that she heard; that lovingly she was aware of their presence in her heart. She would call them, with the voice of one of their own kind.

How strange it all was! Enormous in conception, enormous in distance, scope, stretch! Yet so tiny, intimate, sweet! And this vast splendor was to report itself by one of the insignificant little channels by which men, locked in cramped physical bodies, interpret the giant universe—a trivial sense-impression! That so terrible a communication could reach the soul via the quivering of a wee material nerve was on a par with that other grave splendor—that God can exist in the heart of a child.

Thus, dimly, yet with an authority that shakes the soul, may little human hearts divine the Immensities that travel with a thunder of great glory close about their daily life. Through regions of their subliminal consciousness, which transcends the restricted physical expression of it called personality as the moisture of the world transcends a drop of water, deific presences pass grandly to and fro.

For here, to this wild-hearted Irishman with the forbidden strain of the Urmensch in his blood, came the sharp and instant revelation that the Consciousness is not contained skin-tight around the body. It spread enormously about him, remote, extended; and in some distant tract of it this strange occurrence took place. The idea of distance and extension, of course, were merely intellectual concepts, like that of Time. For what happened, it happened near and close, beside, within his actual physical person. That physical person, with its brain, however, he realized, was but a fragment of his total Self. A broken piece of the occurrence filtered through from beyond and fell upon the deck at his feet. The rest he divined, seeing it whole. Only the little bit, however, has he found the language to describe.

And that for which all three listened was already on the way. Forever it had been "happening," yet only reached them now because they were ready and open to it. Events upon the physical plane, he grasped, represented the last feeble expression of things that had happened interiorly with a vaster power long ago—and are ever happening still. This Sound they listened for, coming from the Spirit of the Earth, lay ever close to men's ears, divinely sweet and splendid. It seemed born somewhere in the heart of the blue gloom that draped the hills of Greece. Thence, across the peaked mountains, stretched the immense pipe of starry darkness that carried it toward them as along a channel. Made possible of approach by the ancient passion of beauty that Greece once knew, it ran down upon the world into their hearts, direct from the Being of the Earth.

With a sudden rush, it grew nearer, swelling with a draught of sound that sucked whole spaces of sky and sea and stars with it. It emerged. They heard, all three.

Above the pulse and tremble of the steamer's engines, above the surge and gurgle of the sea, a cry swept toward them from the shore. Long-drawn, sweetly-penetrating, yet with some strident accent of power and command, this voice of Earth rushed upon them over the quiet water—then died away again among the mountains and the night. Its passage through the sky was torrential. The whole pouring flood of it dipped back with abrupt swiftness into silence. The Irishman understood that but an echo of its main volume had come through.

A deep, convulsive movement ran over the great body at his side, and at once communicated itself to the boy beyond. Father and son straightened up abruptly as though the same force lifted both; then stretched down and forwards over the bulwarks. They seemed to shake themselves free of something. Neither spoke. Something utterly overwhelming lay in that moment. For the cry was at once of enchanting sweetness, yet with a deep and dreadful authority that overpowered. It invited the very soul.

A moment of silence followed, and the cry was then repeated, thinner, fainter, already further away. It seemed withdrawn, sunk more deeply into the night, higher up, too, floating away northwards into remoter vales and glens that lay beyond the shore-line. Though still a single cry, there were distinct breaks of utterance in it this time, as of words. It was, of a kind—speech: a Message, a Summons, a Command that somehow held entreaty at its heart.

And this time the appeal in it was irresistible. Father and son started forwards as though deliberately pulled; while from himself shot outwards that loosening portion of his being that all the evening had sought release. The vehicle of his yearnings, passionately summoned, leaped to the ancient call of the Earth's eternally young life. This vital essence of his personality, volatile as air and fierce as lightning, flashed outwards from its hidden prison where it lay choked and smothered by the weights and measures of modern life. For the beauty and splendor of that far voice wrung his very heart and set it free. He knew a quasi-physical wrench of detachment. A wild and tameless glory fused the fastenings of ages.

Only the motionless solidity of the great figure beside him prevented somehow the complete escape and made him understand that the Call just then was not for all three of them, especially not for himself. The parent rose beside him, massive and stable, secure as the hills which were his true home, and the boy broke suddenly into happy speech which was wild and singing.

He looked up swiftly into his parent's steady visage.

"Father!" he cried in tones that merged half with the wind, half with the sea, "it is his voice! Chiron calls—!" His eyes shone like stars, his young face was alight with joy and passion.—"Go, father, you, or—"

He stopped an instant, catching the Irishman's eyes upon his own across the form between them.

"—or you!" he added with a laughter of delight; "you go!"

The big figure straightened up, standing back a pace from the rails. A low sound rolled from him that was like an echo of thunder among hills. With slow, laborious distinctness it broke off into fragments that were words, with great difficulty uttered, but with a final authority that rendered them command.

"No," O'Malley heard, "you—first. And—carry word—that we—are—on the way." Staring out across the sea and sky he boomed it deeply. "You—first. We—follow—!" And the speech seemed to flow from the entire surface of his body rather than from the lips alone. The sea and air mothered the syllables. Thus, might the Night herself have spoken.

Chiron! The word, with its clue of explanation, flamed about him with a roar. Was this, then, the type of cosmic life to which his companions, and himself with them, inwardly approximated...?

The same instant, before O'Malley could move a muscle to prevent it, the boy climbed the rails with an easy, vaulting motion that was swift yet oddly spread, and dropped straight down into the sea. He fell; and as he fell it was as if the passage through the air drew out a part of him again like smoke. Whether it was due to the flying cloak, or to some dim wizardry of the shadows, there grew over him an instantaneous transformation of outline that was far more marked than anything before. For as the steamer drew onwards, and the body thus passed in its downward flight close beneath O'Malley's eyes, he saw that the boy was making the first preparatory motions of swimming,—movements, however, that were not the horizontal sweep of a pair of human arms, but rather the vertical strokes of a swimming animal. He pawed the air.

The surprise of the whole unexpected thing came upon him with a crash that brought him back effectually again into himself. That part of him, already half emerged in similar escape, now flashed back sheath-like within him. The inner catastrophe he dreaded while desiring it, had not yet completed itself.

He heard no splash, for the ship was high out of the water, and the place where the body met the sea already lay far astern; but when the momentary arrest of his faculties had passed and he found his voice to cry for help, the father turned upon him like a lion and clapped a great, encompassing hand upon his mouth.

"Quiet!" his deep voice boomed. "It is well—and he—is—safe."

And across the huge and simple visage ran an expression of such supreme happiness, while in his act and gesture lay such convincing power, that the Irishman felt himself overborne and forced to acknowledge another standard of authority that somehow made the whole thing right. To cry "man overboard," to stop the ship, throw life-buoys and the rest, was not only unnecessary, but foolish. The boy was safe; it was well with him; he was not "lost"...

"See," said the parent's deep voice, breaking in upon his thoughts as he drew him to one side with a certain vehemence, "See!"

He pointed downwards. And there, between them, half in the scuppers, against their very feet, lay the huddled body upon the deck, the arms outstretched, the face turned upwards to the stars.

* * * * *

The bewilderment that followed was like the confusion which exists between two states of consciousness when the mind passes from sleep to waking, or vice versa. O'Malley lost that power of attention which enables a man to concentrate on details sufficiently to recall their exact sequence afterwards with certainty.

Two things, however, stood out and he tells them briefly enough: first, that the joy upon the father's face rendered an offer of sympathy ludicrous; secondly, that Dr. Stahl was again upon the scene with a promptness which proved him to have been close at hand all the time.

It was between two and three in the morning, the rest of the passengers asleep still, but Captain Burgenfelder and the first officer appeared soon after and an orderly record of the affair was drawn up formally. The depositions of the father and of himself were duly taken down in writing, witnessed, and all the rest.

The scene in the doctor's cabin remains vividly in his mind: the huge Russian standing by the door—for he refused a seat—incongruously smiling in contrast to the general gravity, his mind obviously brought by an effort of concentration to each question; the others seated round the desk some distance away, leaving him in a space by himself; the scratching of the doctor's pointed pen; the still, young outline underneath the canvas all through the long pantomime, lying upon a couch at the back where the shadows gathered thickly. And then the gust of fresh wind that came in with a little song as they opened the door at the end, and saw the crimson dawn reflected in the dewy, shining boards of the deck. The father, throwing the Irishman a significant and curious glance, was out to join it on the instant.

Syncope, produced by excitement, cause unknown, was the scientific verdict, and an immediate burial at sea the parent's wish. As the sun rose over the highlands of Asia Minor it was carried into effect.

But the father's eyes followed not the drop. They gazed with rapt, intent expression in another direction where the shafts of sunrise sped across the sea toward the glens and dales of distant Pelion. At the sound of the plunge, he did not even turn his eyes. He pointed, gathering O'Malley somehow into the gesture, across the Ægean Sea to where the shores of north-western Arcadia lay below the horizon, raised his arms with a huge sweep of welcome to the brightening sky, then turned and went below without a single word.

For a few minutes, puzzled and perhaps a little awed, the group of sailors and ship's officers remained standing with bared heads, then disappeared silently in their turn, leaving the decks to the sunrise and the wind.

XXIII

But O'Malley did not immediately return to his own cabin; he yielded to Dr. Stahl's persuasion and dropped into the armchair he had already occupied more than once, watching his companion's preparations with the lamp and coffeepot.

With his eyes, that is, he watched, staring, as men say, absent-mindedly; for the fact was, only a little bit of him hovered there about his weary physical frame. The rest of him was off somewhere else across the threshold—subliminal: below, with the Russian, beyond with the traveling spirit of the boy; but the major portion, out deep in space, reclaimed by the Earth.

So, at least, it felt; for the circulation of blood in his brain ran low and physical sensation there was almost none. The driving impulse upon the outlying tracts of consciousness usually submerged had been tremendous.

"That time," he heard Stahl saying in an oddly distant voice from across the cabin, "you were nearly—out—"

"You heard? You saw it all?" he murmured as in half-sleep. For it was an effort to focus his mind even upon simple words.

The reply he hardly caught, though he felt the significant stare of the man's eye upon him and divined the shaking of his head. His life still pulsed and throbbed far away outside his normal self. Complete return was difficult. He felt all over: with the wind and hills and sea, all his little personal sensations tucked away and absorbed into Nature. In the Earth he lay, pervading her whole surface, still sharing her vaster life. With her he moved, as with a greater, higher, and more harmonious creation than himself. In large measure the cosmic instincts still swept these quickened fringes of his deep subconscious personality.

"You know them now for what they are," he heard the doctor saying at the end of much else he had entirely missed. "The father will be the next to go, and then—yourself. I warn you before it is too late. Beware! And—resist!"

His thoughts, and with them those subtle energies of the soul that are the vehicles of thought, followed where the boy had gone. Deep streams of longing swept him. The journey of that spirit, so singularly released, drew half his forces after it. Thither the bereaved parent and himself were also bound; and the lonely incompleteness of his life lay wholly now explained. That cry within the dawn, though actually it had been calling always, had at last reached him; hitherto he had caught only misinterpreted echoes of it. From the narrow body it had called him forth. Another moment and he would have known complete emancipation; and never could he forget that glorious sensation as the vital essence tasted half release. Next time the process should complete itself, and he would—go!

"Drink this," he heard abruptly in Stahl's grating voice, and saw him cross the cabin with a cup of steaming coffee. "Concentrate your mind now upon the things about you here. Return to the present. And tell me, too, if you can bring yourself to do so," he added, stooping over him with the cup, "a little of what you experienced. The return, I know, is pain. But try—try—"

"Like a little bit of death, yes," murmured the Irishman. "I feel caught again and caged—small." He could have wept. This ugly little life!

"Because you've tasted a moment of genuine cosmic consciousness and now you feel the limitations of normal personality," Stahl added, more soothingly. He sat down beside him and sipped his own coffee.

"Dispersed about the whole earth I felt, deliciously extended and alive," O'Malley whispered with a faint shiver as he glanced about the little cabin, noticing the small windows and shut door. "Upholstery" oppressed him. "Now I'm back in prison again."

There was silence for a moment. Then presently the doctor spoke, as though he thought aloud, expecting no reply.

"All great emotions," he said in lowered tones, "tap the extensions of the personality we now call subconscious, and a man in anger, in love, in ecstasy of any kind is greater than he knows. But to you has come, perhaps, the greatest form of all—a definite and instant merging with the being of the Earth herself. You reached the point where you *felt* the spirit of the planet's life. You almost crossed the threshold—your extension edged into her own. She bruised you, and you knew—"

"'Bruised'?" he asked, startled at the singular expression into closer hearing.

"We are not 'aware' of our interior," he answered, smiling a little, "until something goes wrong, and the attention is focused. A keen sensation—pain—and you become aware. Subconscious processes then become consciously recognized. I bruise your lung for instance; you become conscious of that lung for the first time and feel it. You gather it up from the general subconscious background into acute personal consciousness. Similarly, a word or mood may sting and stimulate some phase of your consciousness usually too remote to be recognized. Last night—regions of your extended Self, too distant for most men to realize their existence at all, contacted the consciousness of the Earth herself. She bruised you, and *via* that bruise caught you up into her greater Self. You experienced a genuine cosmic reaction."

O'Malley listened, though hardly to the actual words. Behind the speech, which was in difficult German for one thing, his mind heard the rushing past of this man's ideas. They moved together along the same stream of thought, and the Irishman knew that what he thus heard was true, at any rate, for himself. And at the same time, he recognized with admiration the skill with which this scientific mystic of a *Schiffsarzt* sought to lead him back into the safer regions of his normal state. Stahl did not now oppose or deny. Catching the wave of the Celt's experience, he let his thought run sympathetically with it, alongside, as it were, guiding gently and insinuatingly down to earth again.

And the result justified this cunning wisdom; O'Malley returned to the common world by degrees. For it was enchanting to find his amazing adventure explained even in this partial, speculative way. Who else among his acquaintances would have listened at all, much less admitted its possibility?

"But, why in particular *me*?" he asked. "Can't everybody know these cosmic reactions you speak of?" It was his intellect that asked the foolish question. His whole Self knew the answer beforehand.

"Because" replied the doctor, tapping his saucer to emphasize each word, "in some way you have retained an almost unbelievable simplicity of heart—an innocence singularly undefiled—a sort of primal, spontaneous innocence that has kept you clean and open. I venture even to suggest that shame, as most men know it, has never come to you at all."

The words sank down into him. Passing the intellect that would have criticized, they nested deep within where the intuition knew them true. Behind the clumsy language that is, he caught the thought.

"As if I were a saint!" he laughed faintly.

Stahl shook his head. "Rather, because you live detached," he replied, "and have never identified your Self with the rubbish of life. The channels in you are still open to these tides of larger existence. I wish I had your courage."

"While others—?"

The German hesitated a moment. "Most men," he said, choosing his words with evident care, "are too grossly organized to be aware that these reactions of a wider consciousness can be possible at all. Their minute normal Self they mistake for the whole, hence denying even the experiences of others. 'Our actual personality may be something considerably unlike that conception of it which is based on our present terrestrial consciousness—a form of consciousness suited to, and developed by, our temporary existence here, *but not necessarily more than a fraction of our total self*. It is quite credible that our entire personality is never terrestrially manifest.'" Obviously he quoted. The Irishman had read the words somewhere. He came back more and more into the world—correlated, that is, the subconscious with the conscious.

"Yet consciousness apart from the brain is inconceivable," he interposed, more to hear the reply than to express a conviction.

Whether Stahl divined his intention or not, he gave no sign.

"'We cannot say with any security that the stuff called brain is the only conceivable machinery which mind, and consciousness are able to utilize though it is true that we know no other.'" The last phrase he repeated: "'though it is true that we know no other.'"

O'Malley sank deeper into his chair, making no reply. His mind clutched at the words "too grossly organized," and his thoughts ran back for a moment to his daily life in London. He pictured his friends and acquaintances there; the men at his club, at dinner parties, in the parks, at theatres; he heard their talk—shooting—destruction of exquisite life; horses, politics, women, and the rest; yet good, honest, lovable fellows all. But how did they breathe in so small a world at all? Practical-minded specimens of the greatest civilization ever known! He recalled the heavy, dazed expression on the faces of one or two to whom he had sometimes dared to speak of those wider realms that were so familiar to himself....

"'Though it is true that we know no other,'" he heard Stahl repeating slowly as he looked down into his cup and stirred the dregs.

Then, suddenly, the doctor rose and came over to his side. His eyes twinkled, and he rubbed his hands vigorously together as he spoke. He laughed.

"For instance, I have no longer now the consciousness of that coffee I have just swallowed," he exclaimed, "yet, if it disagreed with me, my consciousness of it would return."

"The abnormal states you mean are a symptom of disorder then?" the Irishman asked, following the analogy.

"At present, yes," was the reply, "and will remain so until their correlation with the smaller conscious Self is better understood. These belligerent Powers of the larger Consciousness are apt to overwhelm as yet. That time, perhaps, is coming. Already a few here and there have guessed that the states we call hysteria and insanity, conditions of trance, hypnotism, and the like, are not too satisfactorily explained." He peered down at his companion. "If I could study your Self at close quarters for a few years," he added significantly, "and under various conditions, I might teach the world!"

"Thank you!" cried the Irishman, now wholly returned into his ordinary self. He could think of nothing else to say, yet he meant the words and gave them vital meaning. He moved across to another chair. Lighting a cigarette, he puffed out clouds of smoke. He did not desire to be caught again beneath this man's microscope. And in his mind he had a sudden picture of the speculative and experimenting doctor being "requested to sever his connection" with the great Hospital for the sake of the latter's reputation. But Stahl, in no way offended, was following his own thoughts aloud, half speaking to himself.

"... For a being organized as you are, more active in the outlying tracts of consciousness than in the centers lying nearer home,—a being like yourself, I say, might become aware of Other Life and other personalities even more advanced and highly organized than that of the Earth."

A strange excitement came upon him, making his eyes shine. He walked to and fro, O'Malley watching him, a touch of alarm mingled with his interest.

"And to think of the great majority that denies because they are—dead!" he cried. "Smothered! Undivining! Living in that uninspired fragment which they deem the whole! Ah, my friend,"—and he came abruptly nearer—"the pathos, the comedy, the pert self-sufficiency of their dull pride, the crass stupidity and littleness of their denials, in the eyes of those like us who have actually known the passion of the larger experience—! For all this modern talk about a Subliminal Self is woven round a profoundly significant truth, a truth newly discovered and only just beginning to be understood. We are much greater than we know, and there is a vast subconscious part of us. But what is more important still, there is a super-consciousness as well. The former represents what the race has discarded; it is past; but the latter stands for what it reaches out to in the future. The perfect man you dream of perhaps is he who shall eventually combine the two, for there is, I think, a vast amount the race has discarded unwisely and prematurely. It is of value and will have to be recovered. In the subconsciousness it lies secure and waiting. But it is the super-consciousness that you should aim for, not the other, for there lie those greater powers which so mysteriously wait upon the call of genius, inspiration, hypnotism, and the rest."

"One leads, though, to the other," interrupted O'Malley quickly. "It is merely a question of the swing of the pendulum?"

"Possibly," was the laconic reply.

"They join hands, I mean, behind my back, as it were."

"Possibly."

"This stranger, then, may really lead me forward and not back?"

"Possibly," again was all the answer that he got.

For Stahl had stopped short, as though suddenly aware that he had said too much, betraying himself in the sudden rush of interest and excitement. The face for a moment had seemed quite young, but now the flush faded, and the light died out from his eyes. O'Malley never understood how the change came about so quickly, for in a moment, it seemed, the doctor was calm again, quietly lighting one of his black cigars over by the desk, peering at him half quizzingly, half mockingly through the smoke.

"So, I urge you again," he was saying, as though the rest had been some interlude that the Irishman had half imagined, "to proceed with the caution of this sane majority, the caution that makes for safety. Your friend, as I have already suggested to you, is a direct expression of the cosmic life of the earth. Perhaps, you have guessed by now, the particular type and form. Do not submit your inner life too completely to his guidance. Contain your Self—and resist—while it is yet possible."

And while he sat on there, sipping hot coffee, half listening to the words that warned of danger while at the same time they cunningly urged him forwards, it seemed that the dreams of childhood revived in him with a power that obliterated this present day—the childhood, however, not of his mere body, but of his spirit, when the world herself was young.... He, too, had dwelt in Arcady, known the free life of splendor and simplicity in some Saturnian Reign; for now, this dream but half remembered, half believed, though eternally yearned for—dream of a Golden Age untouched by Time, still there, still accessible, still inhabited, was actually coming true.

It surely was that old Garden of innocence and joy where the soul, while all unvexed by a sham and superficial civilization of the mind, might yet know growth—a realm half divined by saints and poets, but to the gross majority forgotten or denied.

The Simple Life! This new interpretation of it at first overwhelmed. The eyes of his soul turned wild with glory; the passion that o'er-runs the world in desolate places was his; his, too, the strength of rushing rivers that coursed their parent's being. He shared the terror of the mountains and the singing of the sweet Spring rains. The spread wonder of the woods of the world lay imprisoned and explained in the daily hurry of his very blood. He understood, because he felt, the power of the ocean tides; and, flitting to and fro through the tenderer regions of his extended Self, danced the fragrance of all the wildflowers that ever blew. That strange allegory of man, the microcosm, and earth, the macrocosm, became a sudden blazing reality. The feverish distress, unrest, and vanity of modern life was due to the distance men had traveled from the soul of the world, away from large simplicity into the pettier state they deemed so proudly progress.

Out of the trans liminal depths of this newly awakened Consciousness rose the pelt and thunder of these magical and enormous cosmic sensations—the pulse and throb of the planetary life where his little

Self had fringed her own. Those untamed profundities in himself that walked alone, companionless among modern men, suffering an eternal nostalgia, at last knew the approach to satisfaction. For when the "inner catastrophe" completed itself and escape should come—that transfer of the conscious center across the threshold into this vaster region stimulated by the Earth—all his longings would be housed at last like homing birds, nested in the gentle places his yearnings all these years had lovingly built for them—in a living Nature! The fever of modern life, the torture and unrest of a false, external civilization that trained the brain while it still left wars and baseness in the heart, would drop from him like the symptoms of some fierce disease. The god of speed and mechanism that ruled the world today, urging men at ninety miles an hour to enter a Heaven where material gain was only a little sublimated and not utterly denied, would pass for the nightmare that it really was. In its place the cosmic life of undifferentiated simplicity, clean and sweet and big, would hold his soul in the truly everlasting arms.

And that little German doctor, sitting yonder, enlightened yet afraid, seeking an impossible compromise—Stahl could no more stop his going than a fly could stop the rising of the Atlantic tides.

Out of all this tumult of confused thought and feeling there rose then the silver face of some forgotten and passionate loveliness. Apparently it reached his lips, for he heard his own voice murmuring outside him somewhere across the cabin:—

"The gods of Greece—and of the world—"

Yet the instant words clothed it, the flashing glory went. The idea plunged back out of sight—untranslatable in language. Thrilled and sad, he lay back in his chair, watching the doctor and trying to focus his mind upon what he was saying. But the lost idea still dived and reared within him like a shining form, yet never showing more than this radiant point above the surface. The passion and beauty of it...! He tried no more to tie a label of modern words about its neck. He let it swim and dive and leap within him uncaught. Only he understood better why, close to Greece, his friends had betrayed their inner selves, and why for the lesser of the two, whose bodily cage was not yet fully clamped and barred by physical maturity, escape, or return rather, had been possible, nay, had been inevitable.

XXIV

Stahl, he remembers, had been talking for a long time. The general sense of what he said reached him, perhaps, but certainly not many of the words. The doctor, it was clear, wished to coax from him the most intimate description possible of his experience. He put things crudely in order to challenge criticism, and thus to make his companion's reason sit in judgment on his heart. If this visionary Celt would let his intellect pass soberly and dissectingly upon these flaming states of wider consciousness he had touched, the doctor would have data of real value for his own purposes.

But this discriminating analysis was precisely what the Irishman found impossible. His soul was too "dispersed" to concentrate upon modern terms and phrases. These in any case dealt only with the fragments of Self that manifested through brain and body. The rest could be felt only, never truly described. Since the beginning of the world such transcendental experiences had never been translatable in the language of "common" sense; and today, even, when a few daring minds sought a laborious classification, straining the resources of psychology, the results were little better than a rather enticing and suggestive confusion.

In his written account, indeed, he gives no proper report of what Stahl tried to say. A gaping hiatus appears in the manuscript, with only asterisks and numbers that referred to pages of his tumbled notebooks. Following these indications, I came across the skeletons of ideas which perhaps were the raw material, so to say, of these crude and speculative statements that the German poured out at him across that cabin—blocks of exaggeration he flung at him, in the hope of winning some critical and intelligible response. Like the structure of some giant fairy-tale they read—some toppling scaffolding that needed reduction in scale before it could be focused for normal human sight.

"Nature" was really alive for those who believed—and worshipped; for worship was that state of consciousness which opens the sense and provides the channel for this singular interior realization. In very desolate and lonely places, unsmothered and unstained by men as they exist today, such expressions of the Earth's stupendous, central vitality were still possible.... The "Russian" himself was some such fragment, some such cosmic being, strayed down among men in a form outwardly human, and the Irishman had in his own wild, untamed heart those same very tender and primitive possibilities which enabled him to know and feel it.

In the body, however, he was fenced off—without. Only by the disentanglement of his primitive self from the modern development which caged it, could he recover this strange lost Eden and taste in its fullness the mother-life of the planetary consciousness which called him back. This dissociation might be experienced temporarily as a subliminal adventure; or permanently—in death.

Here, it seemed, was a version of the profound mystical idea that a man must lose his life to find it, and that the personal self must be merged in a larger one to know peace—the incessant, burning nostalgia that dwells in the heart of every religion known to men: escape from the endless pain of futile personal ambitions and desires for external things that are unquenchable because never possible of satisfaction. It had never occurred to him before in so literal and simple a form. It explained his sense of kinship with the earth and nature rather than with men....

There followed, then, another note which the Irishman had also omitted from his complete story as I found it—in this MS. that lay among the dust and dinginess of the Paddington back-room like some flaming gem in a refuse heap. It was brief but pregnant—the block of another idea, Fechner's apparently, hurled at him by the little doctor.

That, just as the body takes up the fact of the bruised lung into its own general consciousness, lifting it thereby from the submerged, unrealized state; and just as our human consciousness can be caught up again as a part of the earth's; so, in turn, the Planet's own vast personality is included in the collective consciousness of the entire Universe—all steps and stages of advance to that final and august Consciousness of which they are fragments, projections, manifestations in Time—GOD.

And the immense conception, at any rate, gave him a curious, flashing clue to that passionate inclusion which a higher form of consciousness may feel for the countless lesser manifestations below it and so to that love for humanity as a whole that saviors feel....

Yet, out of all this deep flood of ideas and suggestions that somehow poured about him from the mind of this self-contradictory German, alternately scientist and mystic, O'Malley emerged with his own smaller and vivid personal delight that he would presently himself—escape: escape under the guidance of the big Russian into some remote corner of his own extended Being, where he would enjoy a quasi-merging with the Earth-life and know subjectively at least the fruition of all his yearnings.

The doctor had phrased it once that a part of him fluid, etheric or astral, malleable by desire, would escape and attain to this result. But, after all, the separation of one portion of himself from the main personality could only mean being conscious it: another part of it—in a division usually submerged.

As Stahl so crudely put it, the Earth had bruised him. He would know in some little measure the tides of her own huge life, his longings, loneliness, and nostalgia explained and satisfied. He would find that fair old Garden. He might even know the lesser gods.

* * * * *

That afternoon at Smyrna the matter was officially reported, and so officially done with. It caused little enough comment on the steamer. The majority of the passengers had hardly noticed the boy at all, much less his disappearance; and while many of them landed there for Ephesus, still more left the ship next day at Constantinople.

The big Russian, though he kept mostly to his own cabin, was closely watched by the ship's officers, and O'Malley, too, realized that he was under observation. But nothing happened; the emptied steamer pursued her quiet way, and the Earth, unrealized by her teeming freight so busy with their tiny personal aims, rushed forwards upon her glorious journey through space.

O'Malley alone realized her presence, aware that he rushed with her amid a living universe. But he kept his new sensations to himself. The remainder of the voyage, indeed, across the Black Sea via Samsoun and Trebizond, is hazy in his mind so far as practical details are concerned, for he found himself in a dreamy state of deep peace and would sometimes sit for hours in reverie, only reminded of the present by certain pricks of annoyance from the outer world. He had returned, of course, to his own stateroom, yet felt in such close sympathy with his companion that no outward expression by way of confidence or explanation was necessary. In their Subconsciousness they were together and at one.

The pricks of annoyance came, as may be expected, chiefly from Dr. Stahl, and took the form of variations of "I told you so." The man was in a state of almost anger, caused half by disappointment, half by unsatisfied curiosity. His cargo of oil and water would not mix, yet he knew not which to throw overboard; here was another instance where facts refused to tally with the beliefs dictated by sane reason; where the dazzling speculations he played with threatened to win the day and destroy the compromise his soul loved.

The Irishman, however, did not resent his curiosity, though he made no attempt to satisfy it. He allowed him to become authoritative and professional, to treat him somewhat as a patient. What could it matter to him, who in a few hours would land at Batoum and go off with his guide and comrade to some place where—? The thought he could never see completed in words, for he only knew that the fulfillment of the adventure would take place—somewhere, somehow, somewhen—in that space within the soul of which external space is but an image and a figure. What takes place in the mind and heart are alone the true events; their outward expression in the shifting and impermanent shapes of matter is the least real thing in all the world. For him the experience would be true, real, authoritative—fact, in the deepest sense of the word. Already he saw it "whole."

Faith asks no travelers' questions—exact height of mountains, length of rivers, distance from the sea, precise spelling of names, and so forth. He felt—the quaint and striking simile is in the written account—like a man hunting for a pillar-box in a strange city—absurdly difficult to find, as though purposely concealed by the authorities amid details of street and houses to which the eye is unaccustomed, yet really close at hand all the time....

But at Trebizond, a few hours before Batoum, Dr. Stahl in his zealous attentions went too far; for that evening he gave his "patient" a sleeping-draught in his coffee that caused him to lie for twelve hours on the cabin sofa, and when at length he woke toward noon, the Customs officers had been aboard since nine o'clock, and most of the passengers had already landed.

Among them, leaving no message, the big Russian had also gone ashore. And, though Stahl may have been actuated by the wisest and kindest motives, he was not quite prepared for the novel experience with which it provided him—namely, of hearing an angry Irishman saying rapidly what he thought of him in a stream of eloquent language that lasted nearly a quarter of an hour without a break!

XXV

Although Batoum is a small place, and the trains that leave it during the day are few enough, O'Malley knew that to search for his friend by the methods of the ordinary detective was useless. It would have been also wrong. The man had gone deliberately, without attempting to say good-bye—because, having come together in the real and inner sense, real separation was not possible. The vital portion of their beings, thought, feeling, and desire, were close and always would be. Their bodies, busy at different points of the map among the casual realities of external life, could make no change in that. And at the right moment they would assuredly meet again to begin the promised journey.

Thus, at least, in some fashion peculiarly his own, was the way the Irishman felt; and this was why, after the first anger with his German friend, he resigned himself patiently to the practical business he had in hand.

The little incident was characteristically revealing and shows how firmly rooted in his imaginative temperament was the belief, the unalterable conviction rather, that his life operated upon an outer and an inner plane simultaneously, the one ever reacting upon the other. It was as if he were aware of two separate sets of faculties, subtly linked, one carrying on the affairs of the physical man in the "practical" world, the other dealing with the spiritual economy in the subconscious. To attend to the latter alone was to be a useless dreamer among men, unpractical, unbalanced; to neglect it wholly for the former was to be crassly limited, but half alive; to combine the two in effective co-operation was to achieve that high level of a successful personality, which some perhaps term genius, some prophet, and others, saint. It meant, at any rate, to have sources of inspiration within oneself.

Thus, he spent the day completing what was necessary for his simple outfit and put up for the night at one of the little hotels that spread their tables invitingly upon the pavement, so that dinner may be enjoyed in full view of one of the most picturesque streams of traffic it is possible to see.

The sultry, enervating heat of the day had passed, and a cool breeze came shorewards over the Black Sea. With a box of thin Russian cigarettes before him he lingered over the golden Kakhetian wine and watched the crowded street. Knowing enough of the language to bargain smartly for his room, his pillows, sheets, and samovar, he yet could scarcely compass conversation with the strangers about him. Of Russian proper, besides, he heard little; there was a Babel of many tongues, Armenian, Turkish, Georgian, explosive phrases of Swanetian, soft gliding Persian words, and the sharp or guttural exclamations of the big-voiced, giant fellows, all heavily armed, who belonged to the bewildering tribes that dwelt among the mountains beyond. Occasionally came a broken bit of French or German; but they strayed in, lost and bizarre, as fragments from some distant or forgotten world.

Down the pavement, jostling his elbows, strode the constant, gorgeous procession of curious, wild, barbaric faces, bearded, with hooked noses, flashing eyes, burkas flowing; cartridge-belts of silver and ivory gleaming across chests in the glare of the electric light; bashliks of white, black, and yellow wool upon the head, increasing the stature; evil-looking Black Sea knives stuck in most belts, rifles swung across great supple shoulders, long swords trailing; Turkish gypsies, dark and furtive-eyed, walking softly in leather slippers—of endless and fascinating variety, many colored and splendid, it all was. From time to time a droschky with two horses, or a private carriage with three, rattled noisily over the cobbles at a reckless pace, stopping with the abruptness of a practiced skater; and officers with narrow belted waists like those of women, their full-skirted cloaks reaching half-way down high boots of shining leather, sprang out to pay the driver and take a vacant table at his side; and once or twice a body of soldiers, several hundred strong, singing the national songs with a full-throated vigor, hoarse, wild, somehow half terrible, passed at a swinging gait away into the darkness at the end of the street, the roar of their barbaric singing dying away in the distance by the sea where the boom of waves just caught it.

And O'Malley loved it all, and "thrilled" as he watched and listened. From his hidden self within something passed out and joined it. He felt the wild pulse of energetic life that drove along with the tumult of it. The savage, untamed soul in him leaped as he saw; the blood ran faster. Sitting thus upon the bank of the hurrying stream, he knew himself akin to the main body of the invisible current further out; it drew him with it, and he experienced a quickening of all his impulses toward some wild freedom that was mighty—clean—simple.

Civilian dress was rare, and noticeable when it came. The shipping agents wore black alpaca coats, white trousers, and modern hats of straw. A few ship's officers in blue, with official caps gold-braided, passed in and out like men without a wedding garment, as distressingly out of the picture as tourists in check knickerbockers and nailed boots moving through some dim cathedral aisle. O'Malley recognized one or two from his own steamer and turned his head the other way. It hurt. He caught himself thinking, as he saw them, of Stock Exchanges, two-penny-tubes, Belgravia dinner parties, private views, "small and earlies," musical comedy, and all the rest of the dismal and meager program. These harmless little modern uniforms were worse than ludicrous, for they formed links with the glare and noise of the civilization he had left behind, the smeared vulgarity of the big cities where men and women live in their possessions, wasting life in that worship of external detail they call "progress"...

A well-known German voice crashed through his dream.

"Already at the wine! These Caucasian vintages are good; they really taste of grapes and earth and flowers. Yes, thanks, I'll join you for a moment if I may. We only lie three days in port and are glad to get ashore."

O'Malley called for a second glass and passed the cigarettes.

"I prefer my black cigars, thank you," was the reply, lighting one. "You push on tomorrow, I suppose? Kars, Tiflis, Erzerum or somewhere a little wilder in the mountains, eh?"

"Toward the mountains, yes," the Irishman said. Dr. Stahl was the only person he could possibly have allowed to sit next him at such a time. He had quite forgiven him now, and though at first he felt no positive welcome, the strange link between the two men quickly asserted itself and welded them together in that odd harmony they knew in spite of all differences. They could be silent together, too, without distress or awkwardness, sure test that at least some portion of their personalities fused.

And for a long time, they remained silent, watching the surge and movement of the old, old types about them. They sipped the yellow wine and smoked. The stars came out; the carriages grew less; from far away floated a deep sonorous echo now and then of the soldiers singing by their barracks. Sometimes a steamer hooted. Cossacks swung by. Often some wild cry rang out from a side street. There were heavy, unfamiliar perfumes in the air. Presently Stahl began talking about the Revolution of a few years before and the scenes of violence he had witnessed in these little streets, the shooting, barricades, bombs thrown into passing carriages, Cossacks charging down the pavements with swords drawn, shouting and howling. O'Malley listened with a part of his mind at any rate. The rest of him was much further away.... He was up among the mountain fastnesses.

Already, it seemed, he knew the secret places of the mist, the lair of every running wind....

Two tall mountain tribesmen swaggered past close to their table; the thick grey burkas almost swept their glasses. They walked magnificently with easy, flowing stride, straight from the hips.

"The earth here," said O'Malley, taking advantage of a pause in the other's chatter, "produces some splendid types. Look at those two; they make one think of trees walking—blown along bodily before a wind." He watched them with admiration as they swung off and disappeared among the crowd.

Dr. Stahl, glancing keenly at him, laughed a little.

"Yes," he said; "brave, generous fellows too as a rule, who will shoot you for a pistol that excites their envy yet give their life to save one of their savage dogs. They're still—natural," he added after a moment's hesitation; "still unspoiled. They live close to Nature with a vengeance. Up among the Ossetians on the high saddles you'll find true Pagans who worship trees, sacrifice blood, and offer bread and salt to the nature-deities."

"Still?" asked O'Malley, sipping his wine.

"Still," replied Stahl, following his example.

Over the glasses' rims their eyes met. Both smiled, though neither quite knew why. The Irishman, perhaps, was thinking of the little city clerks he knew at home, pigeon-breasted, pale-faced, under-sized. One of these big men, so full of rushing, vigorous life, would eat a dozen at a sitting.

"There's something here the rest of the world has lost," he murmured to himself. But the doctor heard him.

"You feel it?" he asked quickly, his eyes brightening. "The awful, primitive beauty—?"

"I feel—something, certainly," was the cautious answer. He could not possibly have said more just then; yet it seemed as though he heard far echoes of that voice that had been first borne to his ears across the blue Ægean. In the gorges of these terrible mountains, it surely sounded still. These men must know it too.

"The spell of this strange land will never leave you once you've felt it," pursued the other quietly, his voice deepening. "Even in the towns here—Tiflis, Kutais—I have felt it. Hereabouts is the cradle of the human race, they say, and the people have not changed for thousands of years. Some of them you'll find"—he hunted for a word, then said with a curious, shrugging gesture, "terrific."

"Ah—" said the Irishman, lighting a fresh cigarette from the dying stump so clumsily that the trembling of the hand was noticeable.

"And akin most likely," said Stahl, thrusting his face across the table with a whispering tone, "to that—man—who—tempted you."

O'Malley did not answer. He drank the liquid golden sunshine in his glass; his eyes lifted to the stars that watched above the sea; between the surge of human figures came a little wind from the grim, mysterious Caucasus beyond. He turned all tender as a child, receiving as with a shock of sudden strength and sweetness a thousand intimate messages from the splendid mood of old Mother-Earth who here expressed herself in such a potent breed of men and mountains.

He heard the doctor's voice still speaking as from a distance though:—

"For here they all grow with her. They do not fight her and resist. She pours freely through them; there is no opposition. The channels still lie open; ... and they share her life and power."

"That beauty which the modern world has lost," repeated the other to himself, lingering over the words, and wondering why they expressed so little of what he really meant.

"But which will never—*can* never come again," Stahl completed the sentence. There was a wistful, genuine sadness in his voice and eyes, and the sympathy touched the inflammable Celt with fire. It was ever thus with him. The little man opposite, with the ragged beard, and the bald, domed head gleaming in the electric light, had laid a card upon the table, showing a bit of his burning heart. The generous Irishman responded like a child, laying bare himself. So hungry was he for comprehension.

"Men have everywhere else clothed her fair body with their smothering, ugly clothing and their herded cities," he burst out, so loud that the Armenian waiter sidled up, thinking he called for wine.

"But here she lies naked and unashamed, sweet in divinity made simple. By Jove! I tell you, doctor, it burns and sweeps me with a kind of splendid passion that drowns my little shame-faced personality of the twentieth century. I could run out and worship—fall down and kiss the grass and soil and sea—!"

He drew back suddenly like a wounded animal; his face turned scarlet, as though he knew himself convicted of a hysterical outburst. Stahl's eyes had changed even as he spoke the flaming words that struggled so awkwardly to seize his mood of rapture—a thought the Earth poured through him for a moment. The bitter, half-mocking smile lay in them, and on the lips the cold and critical expression of the other Stahl, skeptic and science-man. A revulsion of feeling caught them both. But to O'Malley came the thought that once again he had been drawn—was being coaxed for examination beneath the microscope.

"The material here," Stahl said presently, with the calm tones of a dispassionate diagnosis, "is magnificent as you say, uncivilized without being merely savage, untamed, yet far from crude barbarism. When the progress of the age gets into this land the transformation will be grand. When Russia lets in culture, when modern improvements have developed her resources and trained the wild human forces into useful channels...."

He went on calmly by the yard, till it was all the Irishman could do not to dash the wine-glass in his face.

"Remember my words when you are up in the lonely mountains," he concluded at length, smiling his queer sardonic smile, "and keep yourself in hand. Put on the brakes when possible. Your experience will thus have far more value."

"And you," replied O'Malley bluntly, so bluntly it was almost rudeness, "go back to Fechner, and try to save your compromising soul before it is too late—"

"Still following those lights that do mislead the morn," Stahl added gently, breaking into English for a phrase he apparently loved. They laughed and raised their glasses.

A long pause came which neither cared to break. The streets were growing empty, the personality of the mysterious little Black Sea port folding away into the darkness. The wilder element had withdrawn behind the shuttered windows. There came a murmur of the waves, but the soldiers no longer sang. The droschkys ceased to rattle past. The night flowed down more thickly from the mountains, and the air, moist with that malarial miasma which makes the climate of this reclaimed marsh whereon Batoum is built so unhealthy, closed unpleasantly about them. The stars died in it.

"Another glass?" suggested Stahl. "A drink to the gods of the Future, and till we meet again, on your return journey, eh?"

"I'll walk with you to the steamer," was the reply. "I never care for much wine. And the gods of the Future will prefer my usual offering, I think—imaginative faith."

The doctor did not ask him to explain. They walked down the middle of the narrow streets. No one was about, nor were there lights in many windows. Once or twice from an upper story came the faint twanging of a balalaika against the drone of voices, and occasionally they passed a little garden where figures outlined themselves among the trees, with the clink of glasses, laughter of men and girls, and the glowing tips of cigarettes.

They turned down toward the harbor where the spars and funnels of the big steamers were just visible against the sky, and opposite the unshuttered window of a shop—one of those modern shops that oddly mar the town with assorted German tinware, Paris hats, and oleographs indiscriminately mingled—Stahl stopped a moment and pointed. They moved up idly and looked in. From the shadows of the other side, well hidden, an armed patrol eyed them suspiciously, though they were not aware of it.

"It was before a window like this," remarked Stahl, apparently casually, "that I once in Tiflis overheard two mountain Georgians talking together as they examined a reproduction of a modern picture—Böcklin's 'Centaur.' They spoke in half whispers, but I caught the trend of what they said. You know the picture, perhaps?"

"I've seen it somewhere, yes," was the short reply. "But what were they saying?" He strove to keep his voice commonplace and casual like his companion's.

"Oh, just discussing it together, but with a curious stretched interest," Stahl went on. "One asked, 'What does it say?' and pointed to the inscription underneath. They could not read. For a long time, they stared in silence, their faces grave and half afraid. 'What is it?' repeated the first one, and the other, a much older man, heavily bearded and of giant build, replied low, 'It's what I told you about'; there was awe in his tone and manner; 'they still live in the big valley of the rhododendrons beyond—' mentioning some lonely uninhabited region toward Daghestan; 'they come in the spring, and are very swift and roaring....You must always hide. To see them is to die. But they cannot die; they are of the mountains. They are older, older than the stones. And the dogs will warn you, or the horses, or sometimes a great sudden wind, though you must never shoot.' They stood gazing in solemn wonder for minutes...till at last, realizing that their silence was final, I moved away. There were manifestations of life in the mountains, you see, that they had seen and knew about—old forms akin to that picture apparently."

The patrol came out of his shadows, and Stahl quickly drew his companion along the pavement.

"You have your passport with you?" he asked, noticing the man behind them.

"It went to the police this afternoon. I haven't got it back yet." O'Malley spoke thickly, in a voice he hardly recognized as his own. How much he welcomed that casual interruption of the practical world he could never explain or tell. For the moment he had felt like wax in the other's hands. He had dreaded searching questions and felt unspeakably relieved. A minute more and he would have burst into confession.

"You should never be without it," the doctor added. "The police here are perfect fiends and can cause you endless inconvenience."

O'Malley knew it all, but gladly seized the talk and spun it out, asking innocent questions while scarcely listening to the answers. They distanced the patrol and neared the quays and shipping. In the darkness of the sky a great line showed where the spurs of the Lesser Caucasus gloomed huge and solemn to the East and West. At the gangway of the steamer, they said good-bye. Stahl held the Irishman's hand a moment in his own.

"Remember, when you know temptation strong," he said gravely, though a smile was in the eyes, "the passwords that I now give you: Humanity and Civilization."

"I'll try."

They shook hands warmly enough.

"Come home by this steamer if you can," he called down from the deck. "And keep to the middle of the road on your way back to the hotel. It's safer in a town like this." O'Malley divined the twinkle in his eyes as he said it. "Forgive my many sins," he heard finally, "and when we meet again, tell me your own...." The darkness took the sentence. But the word the Irishman took home with him to the little hotel was the single one—Civilization: and this, owing to the peculiar significance of intonation and accent with which this bewildering and self-contradictory being had uttered it.

XXVI

He walked along the middle of the street as Stahl had advised. He would have done so in any case, unconsciously, for he knew these towns quite as well as the German did. Yet he did not walk alone. The entire Earth walked with him, and personal danger was an impossibility. A dozen ruffians might attack him, but none could "take" his life.

How simple it all seemed, yet how utterly beyond the reach of intelligible description to those who have never felt it—this sudden surge upwards, downwards, all around and about of the vaster consciousness amid which the sense of normal individuality seemed but a tiny focused point. That loss of personality he first dreaded as an "inner catastrophe" appeared to him now for what it actually was—merely an extinction of some phantasmal illusion of self into the only true life. Here, upon the fringe of this wonder-region of the Caucasus, the spirit of the Earth still manifested as of old, reached out lovingly to those of her children who were simple enough to respond, ready to fold them in and heal them of the modern, racking fevers which must otherwise destroy them.... The entire sky of soft darkness became a hand that covered him and stroked him into peace; the perfume that wafted down that narrow street beside him was the single, enveloping fragrance of the whole wide Earth herself; he caught the very murmur of her splendid journey through the stars. The certitude of some state of boundless being flamed, roaring and immense, about his soul....

And when he reached his room, a little cell that shut out light and air, he met that sinister denial of the simple life which, for him at least, was the true Dweller on the Threshold. Crashing into it he choked, as it were, and could have cried aloud. It gripped and caught him by the throat—the word that Stahl—Stahl who understood even while he warned and mocked and hesitated himself—had flung so tauntingly upon him from the decks—Civilization.

Upon his table lay by chance—the Armenian hotel-keeper had evidently unearthed it for his benefit—a copy of a London halfpenny paper, a paper that feeds the public with the ugliest details of all the least important facts of life by the yard, inventing others when the supply is poor. He read it over vaguely, with a sense of cold distress that was half pain, half nausea. Somehow it stirred his sense of humor; he returned slowly to his normal, littler state. But it was not the contrast which made him smile; rather was it the chance juxtaposition of certain of the contents; for on the page facing the accounts of railway accidents, of people burned alive, explosions, giant strikes, crumpled air-men and other countless horrors which modern inventions offered upon the altar of feverish Progress, he read a complacently boastful leader that extolled the conquest of Nature men had learned by speed. The ability to pass from one point to another across the skin of the globe in the least possible time was a sign of the development of the human soul.

The pompous flatulence of the language touched bathos. He thought of the thousands who had read both columns and preened themselves upon that leader. He thought how they would pride themselves upon the latest contrivance for speeding their inert bodies from one point to another "annihilating distance"; upon being able to get from suburbia to the huge shops that created artificial wants, then filled them; from the pokey villas with their wee sham gardens to the dingy offices; from dark airless East End rooms to countless factories that pour out semi fraudulent, unnecessary wares upon the world, explosives and weapons to destroy another nation, or cheapjack goods to poison their own—all in a few minutes less than they could do it the week before.

And then he thought of the leisure of the country folk and of those who knew how to be content without external possessions, to watch the sunset and the dawn with hearts that sought realities, sharing the noble slowness of the seasons, the gradual growth of flowers, trees, and crops, the unhurried dignity of Nature's grand procession, the repose-in-progress of the Mother-Earth.

The calmness of the unhastening Earth once more possessed his soul in peace. He hid the paper, watching the quiet way the night beyond his window buried it from sight...

And through that open window came the perfume and the mighty hand of darkness slowly. It seemed to this imaginative Irishman that he caught a sound of awful laughter from the mountains and the sea, a laughter that brought, too, a wave of sighing—of deep and old-world sighing.

And before he went to sleep he took an antidote in the form of a page from that book that accompanied all his travels, a book which was written wholly in the open air because its message refused to come to the heart of the inspired writer within doors, try as he would, the "sky especially containing for me the key, the inspiration—"

And the fragment that he read expressed a little bit of his own thought and feeling. The seer who wrote it looked ahead, naming it "After Civilization," whereas he looked back. But they saw the same vision; the confusion of time was nothing:—

In the first soft winds of spring, while snow yet lay on the ground—
Forth from the city into the great woods wandering,
Into the great silent white woods where they waited in their beauty and majesty

For man their companion to come:
There, in vision, out of the wreck of cities and civilizations,
Slowly out of the ruins of the past

Out of the litter and muck of a decaying world,
Lo! even so I saw a new life arise.
O sound of waters, jubilant, pouring, pouring—O hidden song in the hollows!
Secret of the Earth, swelling, sobbing to divulge itself!
Slowly, building, lifting itself up atom by atom,
Gathering itself round a new center—or rather round the world old center once more revealed—
I saw a new life, a new society, arise.
Man I saw arising once more to dwell with Nature;
(The old old story—the prodigal son returning, so loved,
The long estrangement, the long entanglement in vain things)—
The child returning to its home—companion of the winter woods once more—
Companion of the stars and waters—hearing their words at first-hand (more than all science ever taught)—
The near contact, the dear dear mother so close—the twilight sky and the young tree-tops against it;
The few needs, the exhilarated radiant life—the food and population question giving no more trouble;
No hurry more, no striving one to over-ride the other:
 … man the companion of Nature.
Civilization behind him now—the wonderful stretch of the past;
Continents, empires, religions, wars, migrations—all gathered up in him;
The immense knowledge, the vast winged powers—to use or not to use—…

And as he fell asleep at length it seemed there came a sound of hushed huge trampling underneath his window, and that when he rose to listen, his big friend from the steamer led him forth into the darkness, that those shapes of Cloud and Wind he now so often saw, companioned them across the heights of the night toward some place in the distant mountains where light and flowers were, and all his dream of years most exquisitely fulfilled.…

He slept. And through his sleep there dropped the words of that old tribesman from the wilderness: "They come in the spring... and are very swift and roaring. They are older, older than the stones. They cannot die... they are of the mountains, and you must hide."

But the dream-consciousness knows no hiding; and though memory failed to report with detail in the morning, O'Malley woke refreshed and blessed, knowing that companionship awaited him, and that once he found the courage to escape completely, the Simple Life of Earth would claim him in full consciousness.

Stahl with his little modern "Intellect" was no longer there to hinder and prevent.

XXVII

"Far, very far, steer by my star,
Leaving the loud world's hurry and clamor,
In the mid-sea waits you, maybe,
The Isles of Glamour, where Beauty reigns.
From coasts of commerce and myriad-marted
Towns of traffic by wide seas parted,
Past shoals unmapped and by reefs uncharted,
The single-hearted my isle attains.

"Each soul may find faith to her mind,
Seek you the peace of the groves Elysian,
Or the ivy twine and the wands of vine,
The Dionysian, Orphic rite?
To share the joy of the Maenad's leaping
In frenzied train thro' the dusk glen sweeping,
The dew-drench'd dance and the star-watch'd sleeping,
Or temple keeping in vestal white?

"Ye who regret suns that have set,
Lo, each god of the ages golden,
Here is enshrined, ageless and kind,

Unbeholden the dark years through.
Their faithful oracles yet bestowing,
By laurels whisper and clear streams flowing,
Or the leafy stir of the Gods' own going,
In oak trees blowing, may answer you!"

—From PEREGRINA'S SONG

For the next month Terence O'Malley possessed his soul in patience; he worked, and the work saved him. That is to say it enabled him to keep what men call "balanced." Stahl had—whether intentionally or not he was never quite certain—raised a tempest in him. More accurately, perhaps, he had called it to the top, for it had been raging deep down ever since he could remember or had begun to think.

That the earth might be a living, sentient organism, though too vast to be envisaged as such by normal human consciousness, had always been a tenet of his imagination's creed. Now he knew it true, as a dinner-gong is true. That deep yearnings, impossible of satisfaction in the external conditions of ordinary life, could know subjective fulfillment in the mind, had always been for him poetically true, as for any other poet: now he realized that it was literally true for some outlying tract of consciousness usually inactive, termed by some trans liminal. Spiritual nostalgia provided the channel, and the transfer of consciousness to this outlying tract, involving, of course, a trance condition of the usual self, indicated the way—that was all.

Again, his mystical temperament had always seen objects as forces which from some invisible center push outwards into visible shape—as bodies: bodies of trees, stones, flowers, men, women, animals; and others but partially pushed outwards, still invisible to limited physical sight at least, either too huge, too small, or too attenuated for vision. Whereas now, as a result of Stahl and Fechner combined, it flamed into him that this was positively true; more—that there was a point in his trans liminal consciousness where he might "contact" these forces before they reached their cruder external expression as bodies. Nature, in this sense, had always been for him alive, though he had allowed himself the term by a long stretch of poetic sympathy; but now he knew that it was actually true, because objects, landscapes, humans, and the rest, were verily aspects of the collective consciousness of the Earth, moods of her spirit, phases of her being, expressions of her deep, pure, passionate "heart"—projections of herself.

He pondered lingeringly over this. Common words revealed their open faces to him. He saw the ideas behind language, saw them naked. Repetition had robbed them of so much that now became vital, like Bible phrases that too great familiarity in childhood kills for all subsequent life as meaningless. His eyes were opened perhaps. He took a flower into his mind and thought about it; really thought; meditated lovingly. A flower was literally projected by the earth so far as its form was concerned. Its roots gathered soil and earth-matter, changing them into leaves and blossoms; its leaves again, took of the atmosphere, also a part of the earth. It was projected by the earth, born of her, fed by her, and at "death" returned into her. But this was its outward and visible form only. The flower, for his imaginative mind, was a force made visible as literally as a house was a force the mind of the architect made visible. In the mind, or consciousness of the Earth this flower first lay latent as a dream. Perhaps, in her consciousness, it nested as that which in us corresponds to a little thought.... And from this he leaped, as the way ever was with him, to bigger "projections"—trees, atmosphere, clouds, winds, some visible, some invisible, and so to a deeper yet simpler comprehension of Fechner's thundering conception of human beings as projections. Was he, then, literally, a child of the Earth, mothered by the whole magnificent planet...? All the world akin—that seeking for an eternal home in every human heart explained...? And were there—had there been rather—these other, vaster projections Stahl had adumbrated with his sudden borrowed stretch of vision—forces, thoughts, moods of her hidden life invisible to sight, yet able to be felt and known interiorly?

That "the gods" were definitely knowable Powers, accessible to any genuine worshipper, had ever haunted his mind, thinly separated only from definite belief: now he understood that this also had been true, though only partially divined before. For now, he saw them as the rare expressions of the Earth's in the morning of her life. That he might ever come to know them close made him tremble with a fearful joy, the idea flaming across his being with a dazzling brilliance that brought him close to that state of consciousness termed ecstasy. And that in certain unique beings, outwardly human like his friend, there might still survive some primitive expression of the Earth-Soul, lesser than the gods, and intermediate as it were, became for him now a fact—wondrous, awe-inspiring, even holy, but still a fact that he could grasp.

He had found one such; and Stahl, by warnings that fought with an urging invitation at the same time, had confirmed it.

It was singular, he reflected, how worship had ever turned for him a landscape or a scene enchantingly alive. Worship, he now understood, of course invited "the gods," and was the channel through which their manifestation became possible to the soul. All the gods, then, were accessible in this interior way, but Pan especially—in desolate places and secret corners of a wood.... He remembered dimly the Greek idea of worship in the Mysteries: that the worshipper knew actual temporary union with his deity in ecstasy, and at death went permanently into his sphere of being. He understood that worship was au fond a desire for loss of personal life—hence its subtle joy; and a fear lest it be actually accomplished—whence its awe and wonder.

Some glorious, winged thing moved now beside him; it held him by the hand. The Earth possessed him; and the whole adventure, so far as he can make it plain, was an authoritative summons to the natural, Simple Life.

For the next month, therefore, O'Malley, unhurrying, blessed with a deeper sense of happiness than he had ever known before, dismissed the "tempest" from his surface consciousness, and set to work to gather the picturesque impressions of strange places and strange peoples that the public liked to read about in occasional letters of travel. And by the time May had passed into June he had moved up and down the Caucasus, observing, learning, expanding, and gathering in the process through every sense—through the very pores of his skin almost—draughts of a new and abundant life that is to be had there merely for the asking.

That modification of the personality which comes even in cities to all but the utterly hidebound—so that a man in Rome finds himself not quite the same as he was in London or in Paris a few days before—went forward in him on a profounder scale than anything he had known hitherto. Nature fed stimulated and called him with a passionate intimacy that destroyed all sense of loneliness, and with a vehement directness of attack that simply charged him to the brim with a new joy of living. His vitality, powers, even his physical health, stood at their best and highest. The country laid its spell upon him, in a word; and if he expresses it thus with some intensity it was because life came to him so. His record is the measure of his vision. Those who find exaggeration in it merely confess thereby their own smaller capacity of living.

Here, as he wandered to and fro among these proud, immense, secluded valleys, through remote and untamed forests, and by the banks of wild rivers that shook their flying foam across untrodden banks, he wandered at the same time deeper and ever deeper into himself, toward a point where he lost touch with all that constituted him "modern," or held him captive in the spirit of today. Nearer and ever nearer he moved into some tremendous freedom, some state of innocence and simplicity that, while gloriously unrestrained, yet knew no touch of license. Dreams had whispered of it; childhood had fringed its frontiers; longings had even mapped it faintly to his mind. But now he breathed its very air and knew it face to face. The Earth surged wonderfully about him.

With his sleeping-bag upon a small Caucasian horse, a sack to hold his cooking things, a pistol in his belt, he wandered thus for days, sleeping beneath the stars, seeing the sunset and the dawn, drenched in new strength and wonder all the time. Here he touched deeper reaches of the Earth that spoke of old, old things, that were still young because they knew not change. He walked in the morning of the world, through her primal fire and dew, when all was a first and giant garden.

The advertised splendors of other lands, even of India, Egypt, and the East, seemed almost vulgar beside this country that had somehow held itself aloof, unstained and clean. The civilization of its little towns seemed but a coated varnish that an hour's sun would melt away; the railway, crawling along the flanks of the great range, but a ribbon of old iron pinned on that, with the first shiver of those giant sides, would split and vanish.

Here, where the Argonauts once landed, the Golden Fleece still shone o' nights in the depths of the rustling beech woods; along the shores of that old Phasis their figures might still be seen, tall Jason in the lead, erect and silvery, passing o'er the shining, flowered fields upon their quest of ancient beauty. Further north from this sunny Colchian strand rose the peak of Kasbek, gaunt and desolate pyramid of iron, "sloping through five great zones of climate," whence the ghost of Prometheus still gazed down from his "vast frozen precipice" upon a world his courage would redeem. For somewhere here was the cradle of the human race, fair garden of some Edened life before the "Fall," when the Earth sang for joy in her first, golden youth, and her soul expressed itself in mighty forms that remain for lesser days but a faded hierarchy of visioned gods.

A living Earth went with him everywhere, with love that never breathed an alarm. It seemed he felt her very thoughts within himself—thoughts, however that now no longer married with a visible expression as shapes.

Among these old world tribes and peoples with their babble of difficult tongues, wonder and beauty, terror and worship, still lay too deeply buried to have as yet externalized themselves in mental forms as legend, myth, and story. In the blood ran all their richness undiluted. Life was simple, fully charged with an immense delight. At home little cocksure writers in little cocksure journals, pertly modern and enlightened, might dictate how far imaginative vision and belief could go before they overstepped the limits of an artificial schedule; but here "everything possible to be believed was still an image of truth," and the stream of life flowed deeper than all mere intellectual denials.

A little out of sight, but thinly veiled, the powers that in this haunted corner of the earth, too strangely neglected, pushed outwards into men and trees, into mountains, flowers, and the rest, were unenslaved and intensely vital. In his blood O'Malley knew the primal pulses of the world.

It was irresistibly seductive. Whether he slept with the Aryan Ossetians upon the high ridges of the central range, or shared the stone huts of the mountain Jews, unchanged since Bible days, beyond the Suram heights, there came to all his senses the message of that Golden Age his longings ever sought—the rush and murmur of the *Urwelt* calling.

And so it was, about the first week in June that lean, bronzed, and in perfect physical condition, this wandering Irishman found himself in a little Swanetian hamlet beyond Alighir, preparing with a Georgian peasant-guide to penetrate yet deeper into the mountain recesses and feed his heart with what he found of loneliness and beauty.

This region of Imerethia, bordering on Mingrelia, is smothered beneath an exuberance of vegetation almost tropical, blue and golden with enormous flowers, tangled with wild vines, rich with towering soft beech woods, and finally, in the upper sections, ablaze with leagues of huge rhododendron trees in blossom that give whole mountain-sides the aspect of a giant garden, flowering amid peaks that even dwarf the Alps. For here the original garden of the world survives, run wild with pristine loveliness. The prodigality of Nature is bewildering, almost troubling. There are valleys, rarely entered by the foot of man, where monstrous lilies, topping a man on foot and even reaching to his shoulder on horseback, have suggested to botanists in their lavish luxuriance a survival of the original flora of the world. A thousand flowers he found whose names he had never heard of their hues and forms as strangely lovely as those of another planet. The grasses alone in scale and mass were magnificent. While, in and out of all this splendor, less dense and voluminous only than the rhododendron forests, ran scattered lines of blazing yellow—the crowding clusters of azalea bushes that scented the winds beyond belief.

Beyond this region of extravagance in size and color, there ran immense bare open slopes of smooth turf that led to the foot of the eternal snowfields, with, far below, valleys of prodigious scale and steepness that touched somehow with disdain all memory of other mountain ranges he had ever known.

And here it was this warm June evening—June 15th it was—while packing his sack with cheese and maize-flour in the dirty yard of a so-called "post-house," more hindered than helped by his Georgian guide, that he realized the approach of a familiar, bearded figure. The figure emerged. There was a sudden clutch and lift of the heart ... then a rush of wild delight. There stood his Russian steamer-friend, part of the scale and splendor, as though grown out of the very soil. He occupied in a flash the middle of the picture. He gave it meaning. He was part of it, exactly as a tree or big grey boulder were part of it.

XXVIII

"Seasons and times; Life and Fate—all are remarkably rhythmic, metric, regular throughout. In all crafts and arts, in all machines, in organic bodies, in our daily occupations everywhere there is rhythm, meter, accent, melody. All that we do with a certain skill unnoticed, we do rhythmically. There is rhythm everywhere; it insinuates itself everywhere. All mechanism is metric and rhythmic. There must be more in it than this. Is it merely the influence of inertia?"

—NOVALIS, Translated by U.C.B.

Notwithstanding the extent and loneliness of this wild country, coincidence seemed in no way stretched by the abrupt appearance; for in a sense, it was not wholly unexpected. There had been certain indications that the meeting again of these two was imminent. The Irishman had never doubted they would meet. But something more than mere hints or warnings, it seemed, had prepared him.

The nature of these warnings, however, O'Malley never fully disclosed. Two of them he told to me by word of mouth, but there were others he could not bring himself to speak about at all. Even the two he mentioned do not appear in his written account. His hesitation is not easy to explain, unless it be that language collapsed in the attempt to describe occurrences so remote from common experience. This may be so, although he grappled not unsuccessfully with the rest of the amazing adventure. At any rate I could never coax from him more than the confession that there *were* other things that had brought him hints. Then came a laugh, a shrug of the shoulders, an expression of confused bewilderment in eyes and manner and—silence.

The two he spoke of I report as best I can. On the roof of that London apartment-house where so many of our talks took place beneath the stars and to the tune of bustling modern traffic, he told them to me. Both were consistent with his theory that he was becoming daily more active in some outlying portion of his personality—knowing experiences in a region of extended consciousness stimulated so powerfully by his strange new friend.

Both, moreover, brought him one and the same conviction that he was no longer—alone. For some days past he had realized this. More than his peasant guide accompanied him. He was both companioned and—observed.

"A dozen times," he said, "I thought I saw him, and a dozen times I was mistaken. But my mind looked for him. I knew that he was somewhere close." He compared the feeling to that common experience of the streets when a friend, not known to be near, or even expected, comes abruptly into the thoughts, so that numberless individuals may trick the sight with his appearance before he himself comes suddenly down the pavement. His approach has reached the mind before his mere body turns the corner. "Something in me was aware of his approach," he added, "as though his being were sending out feelers in advance to find me. They reached me first, I think"—he hesitated briefly, hunting for a more accurate term he could not find—"in dream."

"You dreamed that he was coming, then?"

"It came first in dream," he answered, "only when I woke the dream did not fade; it passed over into waking consciousness, so that I could hardly tell where the threshold lay between the two. And, meanwhile, I was always expecting to see him at every turn of the trail almost; a little higher up the mountain, behind a rock, or standing beside a tree, just as in the end I actually did see him. Long before he emerged in this way, he had been close about me, guiding, waiting, watching."

He told it as a true thing he did not quite expect me to believe. Yet, in a sense, *his* sense, I could and did believe it. It was so wholly consistent with the tenor of his adventure and the condition of abnormal receptivity of mind. For his stretched consciousness was in a state of white sensitiveness whereon the tenderest mental force of another's thought might well record its signature. Acutely impressionable he was all over. Physical distance was of as little, or even of less, account to such forces as it is to electricity.

"But it was more than the Russian who was close," he added quietly with one of those sentences that startled me into keen attention. "He was there—with others—of his kind."

And then, hardly pausing to take breath, he plunged, as his manner was, full tilt into the details of this first experience that thrilled my hedging soul with an astonishing power of conviction. As always when his heart was in the words, the scenery about us faded and I lived the adventure with him. The cowled and hooded chimneys turned to trees, the stretch of dim star-lit London Park became a deep Caucasian vale, the thunder of the traffic was the roaring of the snow-fed torrents. The very perfume of strange flowers floated in the air.

They had been in their blankets, he and his peasant guide, for hours, and a moon approaching the full still concealed all signs of dawn, when he woke out of deep sleep with the odd sensation that it was only a part of him that woke. One portion of him was in the body, while another portion was elsewhere, manifesting with ease and freedom in some state or region whither he had traveled in his sleep—where, moreover, he had not been alone.

And close about him in the trees was—movement. Yes! Through and between the scattered trunks he saw it still.

With eyes a little dazed, the active portion of his brain perceived this processing movement passing to and fro across the glades of moonlight beneath the steady trees. For there was no wind. The shadows of the branches did not stir. He saw swift running shapes, vigorous yet silent, hurrying across the network of splashed silver and pools of black in some kind of organized movement that was circular and seemed not due to chance. Arranged it seemed and ordered, like the regulated revolutions of a set and whirling measure.

Perhaps twenty feet from where he lay was the outer fringe of what he discerned to be this fragment of some grand gamboling dance or frolic; yet discerned but dimly, for the darkness combined with his uncertain vision to obscure it.

And the shapes, as they sped across the silvery patchwork of the moon, seemed curiously familiar. Beyond question he recognized and knew them. For they were akin to those shadowy emanations seen weeks ago upon the steamer's after-deck, to that "messenger" who climbed from out the sea and sky, and to that form the spirit of the boy assumed, set free in death. They were the flying outlines of Wind and Cloud he had so often glimpsed in vision, racing over the long, bare, open hills—at last come near.

In the moment of first waking, when he saw them clearest, he declares with emphasis that he *knew* the father and the boy were among them. Not so much that he saw them actually for recognition, but rather that he felt their rushing presences; for the first sensation on opening his eyes was the conviction that both had passed him close, had almost touched and called him. Afterwards he searched in vain among the flying forms that swept in the swift succession of their leaping dance across the silvery pathways. While varying in size all were so similar.

His description of them is confused a little, for he admits that he could never properly focus them in steady sight. They slipped with a melting swiftness under the eye; the moment one seemed caught in vision it passed on further and the next was in its place. It was like following a running wave-form on the sea. He says, moreover, that while erect and splendid, their backs and shoulders seemed prolonged in hugeness as though they often crouched to spring; they seemed to paw the air; and that a faint delicious sound to which they kept obedient time and rhythm, held that same sweetness which had issued from the hills of Greece, blown down now among the trees from very far away. And when he says, "blown down among the trees," he qualifies this phrase as well, because at the same time it came to him that the sound also rose up from underneath the earth, as if the very surface of the ground ran shaking with a soft vibration of its own. Some marvelous dream it might have been in which the forms, the movement, and the sound were all thrown up and outwards from the quivering surface of the Earth itself.

Yet, almost simultaneously with the first instant of waking, the body issued its call of warning. For, while he gazed, and before time for the least reflection came, the Irishman experienced this dislocating conviction that he himself was taking part in the whirling gambol even while he lay and watched it, and that in this way the sense of division in his personality was explained. The fragment of himself within the brain watched some other more vital fragment—some projection of his consciousness detached and separate—playing yonder with its kind beneath the moon.

This sense of a divided self was not new to him, but never before had he known it so distinct and overwhelming. The definiteness of the division, as well as the importance and vitality of the separated portion, were arrestingly novel. It felt as though he were completely out, or to such a degree, at least, that the fraction left behind with the brain was at first only just sufficient for him to recognize his body at all.

Yonder with these others he felt the wind of movement pass along his back, he saw the trees slip by and knew the very contact of the ground between the leaps. His movements were natural and easy, light as air and fast as wind; they seemed automatic, impelled by something mighty that directed and contained them. He knew, too, the sensation that others pressed behind him and passed before, slipped in and out, and that through the whole wild urgency of it he yet could never make an error. More—he knew that these shifting forms had been close and dancing about him for a time not measurable merely by the hours of a single night, that in a sense they were always there though he had but just discovered them. His earlier glimpses had been a very partial divination of a truth, immense and beautiful, that now dawned quite gorgeously upon him all complete.

The whole world danced. The Universe was rhythmical as well as metrical.

For this amazing splendor showed itself in a flash-like revelation to the freed portion of his consciousness, and he knew it irresistibly because he himself shared it. Here was an infinite joy, naked and unashamed, born of the mighty Mother's heart and life, a joy which, in its feebler, lesser manifestations, trickles down into human conditions, though still spontaneously even then, so pure its primal urgency, as—dancing.

The entire experience, the entire revelation, he thinks, can have occupied but a fraction of a second, but it seemed to smite the whole of his being at once with the conviction of a supreme authority. And close behind it came, too, that other sister expression of a spontaneous and natural expression, equally rhythmical—the impulse to sing. He could have sung aloud. For this puissant and mysterious rhythm to which all moved was greater than any little measure of their own. Surging through them, it came from outside and beyond, infinitely greater than themselves, springing from something of which they were, nevertheless, a living portion. From the body of the Earth, it came direct—it was in fact a manifestation of her own vibrating life. The currents of the Earth pulsed through them.

"And then," he says, "I caught this flaming thought of wonder, though so much of it faded instantly upon my full awakening that I can only give you the merest suggestion of what it was."

He stood up beside me as he said it, spreading his arms, as so often when he was excited, to the sky. I caught the glow of his eyes, and in his voice was passion. He spoke unquestionably of something he had intimately known, not as men speak of even the vividest dreams but of realities that have burned the heart and left their trails of glory.

"Science has guessed some inkling of the truth," he cried, "when it declares that the ultimate molecules of matter are in constant vibratory movement one about another, even upon the point of a needle. But I saw—*knew*, rather, as if I had always known it, sweet as summer rain, and close in me as love—that the whole Earth with all her myriad expressions of life moved to this primal rhythm as of some divine dancing."

"Dancing?" I asked, puzzled.

"Rhythmical movement call it then," he replied. "To share the life of the Earth is to dance and sing in a huge abundant joy! And the nearer to her great heart, the more natural and spontaneous the impulse—the instinctive dancing of primitive races, of savages and children, still artless and untamed; the gamboling of animals, of rabbits in the meadows and of deer unwatched in forest clearings—you know naturalists have sometimes seen it; of birds in the air—rooks, gulls, and swallows; of the life within the sea; even of gnats in the haze of summer afternoons. All life simple enough to touch and share the enormous happiness of her deep, streaming, personal Being, dances instinctively for very joy—obedient to a greater measure than they know.... The natural movement of the great Earth-Soul is rhythmical. The very winds, the swaying of trees and flowers and grasses, the movement of the sea, of water running through the fields with silver feet, of the clouds and edges of the mist, even the trembling of the earthquakes,—all, all respond in sympathetic motions to this huge vibratory movement of her great central pulse. Ay, and the mountains too, though so vastly scaled their measure that perhaps we only know the pauses in between and think them motionless.... The mountains rise and fall and change; our very breathing, first sign of stirring life, even the circulation of our blood, bring testimony; our speech as well—inspired words are ever rhythmical, language that pours into the poet's mind from something greater than himself. And not unwisely, but in obedience to a deep instinctive knowledge was dancing once—in earlier, simpler days—a form of worship. You know, at least, how rhythm in music and ceremonial uplifts and cleans and simplifies the heart toward the greater life.... You know, perhaps, the Dance of Jesus...."

The words poured from him with passion, yet always uttered gently with a smile of joy upon the face. I saw his figure standing over me, outlined against the starry sky; and, deeply stirred, I listened with delight and wonder. Rhythm surely lies behind all expression of life. He was on the heels of some simple, dazzling verity though he phrased it wildly. But not a tenth part of all he said could I recapture afterwards for writing down. The steady, gentle swaying of his body I remember clearly, and that somewhere or other in the stream of language, he made apt reference to the rhythmical swaying of those who speak in trance, or know some strange, possessing gust of inspiration.

The first and natural expression of the Earth's vitality lies in a dancing movement of purest joy and happiness—that for me is the gist of what remains. Those near enough to Nature feel it. I myself remembered days in spring ... my thoughts, borne upon some sweet emotion, traveled far....

"And not of the Earth alone," he interrupted my dreaming in a voice like singing, "but of the entire Universe. The spheres and constellations weave across the fields of ether the immense old rhythm of their divine, eternal dance...!"

Then, with a disconcerting abruptness, and a strange little wayward laugh as of apology for having let himself so freely go, he sat down beside me with his back against the chimney-stack. He resumed more quietly the account of this particular adventure that lay 'twixt dream and waking:

All that he described had happened in a few seconds. It flashed, complete, authoritative and vivid, then passed away. He knew again the call and warning of his body—to return. For this consciousness of being in two places at once, divided as it were against himself, brought with it the necessity for decision. With which portion should he identify himself? By an act of will, it seemed, a choice was possible.

And with it, then, came the knowledge that to remain "out" was easier than to return. This time, to come back into himself would be difficult.

The very possibility seemed to provide the shock of energy necessary for overcoming it; the experience alarmed him; it was like holding an option upon living—like a foretaste of death. Automatically, as it were, these loosened forces in him answered to the body's summons. The result was immediate and singular; one of these Dancing outlines separated itself from the main herd, approached with a sudden silent rush, enveloped him for a second of darkness and confusion, losing its shape completely on the way, and then merged into his being as smoke slips in and merges with the structure of a tree.

The projected portion of his personality had returned. The sense of division was gone. There remained behind only the little terror of the weak flesh whose summons had thus brought it back.

The same instant he was fully awake—the night about him empty of all but the silver dreaming of the moon among the shadows. Beside him lay the sleeping figure of his companion, the bashlik of lamb's wool drawn closely down about the ears and neck, and the voluminous black burka shrouding him from feet to shoulders. A little distance away the horse stood, munching grass. Again, he noted that there was no wind, and the shadows of the trees lay motionless upon the ground. The air smelt sweet of forest, soil, and dew.

The experience—it seemed now—belonged to dreaming rather than to waking consciousness, for there was nothing about him to confirm it outwardly. Only the memory remained—that, and a vast, deep-coursing, subtle happiness. The smaller terror that he felt was of the flesh alone, for the flesh ever instinctively fought against such separation. The happiness, though, contained and overwhelmed the fear.

Yes, only the memory remained, and even that fast fading. But the substance of what had been, passed into his inmost being: the splendor of that would remain forever, incorporated with his life. He had shared in this brief moment of extended consciousness some measure of the Mother's cosmic being, simple as sunshine, unrestrained as wind, complete and satisfying. Its natural expression was rhythmical, a deep, pure joy that drove outwards even into little human conditions as dancing and singing. He had known it, too, with companions of his kind…

Moreover, though no longer visible or audible, it still continued somewhere close. He was blessedly companioned all the time—and watched. *They* knew him one of themselves—these brother expressions of her cosmic life—these *Urwelt* beings that Today had no external, bodily forms. They waited, knowing well that he would come. Fulfillment beckoned surely just beyond…

XXIX

"… And then suddenly,—
While perhaps twice my heart was dutiful
To send my blood upon its little race—

I was exalted above surety,
And out of Time did fall."

—LASCELLES ABERCROMBIE, Poems and Interludes

This, then, was one of the "hints" by which O'Malley knew that he was not alone and that the mind of his companion was stretched out to find him. He became aware after it of a distinct guidance, even of direction as to his route of travel. The "impulse came," as one says, to turn northwards, and he obeyed it without more ado. For this "dream" had come to him when camped upon the slopes of Ararat, further south toward the Turkish frontier, and though all prepared to climb the sixteen-thousand-foot summit, he changed his plans, dismissed the local guide, and turned back for Tiflis and the Central Range. In the wilder, lonelier mountains, he felt strongly, was where he ought to be.

Another man, of course, would have dismissed the dream or forgotten it while cooking his morning coffee; but, rightly or wrongly, this divining Celt accepted it as real. He held an instinctive belief, that in dreams of a certain order the forces that drive behind the soul at a given moment, may reveal themselves to the subconscious self, becoming authoritative in proportion as they are sanely encouraged and interpreted. They dramatize themselves in scenes that are open to intuitive interpretation. And O'Malley, it seems, possessed, like the Hebrew prophets of old, just that measure of judgment and divination which go to the making of a true clear-vision.

Packing up kit and dunnage, he crossed the Georgian Military Route on foot to Vladikavkaz, and thence with another horse and a Mohammedan Georgian as guide, Rostom by name, journeyed *via* Alighir and Oni up a side valley of unforgettable splendor toward an Imerethian hamlet where they meant to lay-in supplies for a prolonged expedition into the uninhabited wilderness.

And here, the second occurrence he told me of took place. It was more direct than the first, yet equally strange; also, it brought a similar authority—coming first along the deep mysterious under paths of sleep—sleep, that short cut into the subconscious.

They were camped among low boxwood trees, a hot dry night, wind soft and stars very brilliant, when the Irishman turned in his sleeping-bag and abruptly woke. This time there was no dream—only the certainty that something had wakened him deliberately. He sat up, almost with a cry. It was exactly as though he heard himself called by name and recognized the voice that spoke it. He looked quickly round. Nothing but the crowding army of the box-trees was visible, some bushy and round, others straggling in their outline, all whispering gently together in the night. Beyond ran the immense slopes, and far overhead he saw the gleaming snow on peaks that brushed the stars.

No one was visible. This time no flying figures danced beneath the moon. There was, indeed, no moon. Something, however, he knew had come up close and touched him, calling him from the depths of a profound and tired slumber. It had withdrawn again, vanished into the night. The strong certainty remained, though, that it lingered near about him still, trying to press forwards and outwards into some kind of objective visible expression that *included himself*. He had responded with an effort in his sleep, but the effort had been unsuccessful. He had merely waked ... and lost it.

The horse, tethered a few feet away, was astir and troubled, straining at the rope, whinnying faintly, and Rostom, the Georgian peasant, he saw, was already up to quiet it. A curious perfume passed him through the air—once, then vanished; unforgettable, however, for he had known it already weeks ago upon the steamer. And before the gardened woods about him smothered it with their richer smells of a million flowers and weeds, he recognized in it that peculiar pungent whiff of horse that had reached him from the haunted cabin. This time it was less fleeting—a fine, clean odor that he liked even while it strangely troubled him.

Kicking out of his blankets, he joined the man and helped to straighten out the tangled rope. Rostom spoke little Russian, and O'Malley's knowledge of Georgian lay in a single phrase, "Look sharp!" but with the aid of French the man had learned from shooting-parties, he gathered that someone had approached during the night and camped, it seemed, not far away above them.

Though unusual enough in so unfrequented a region, this was not necessarily alarming, and the first proof O'Malley had that the man experienced no ordinary physical fear was the fact that he had left both knife and rifle in his blankets. Hitherto, at the least sign of danger, he changed into a perfect arsenal; he invariably slept "in his weapons"; but now, even in the darkness, the other noted that he was unarmed, and therefore it was no attempt at horse-stealing or of assault upon themselves he feared.

"Who is it? What is it?" he asked, stumbling over the tangle of string-like roots that netted the ground. "Natives, travelers like ourselves, or—something else?" He spoke very low, as though aware that what had waked him still hovered close enough to overhear. "Why do you fear?"

And Rostom looked up a moment from stooping over the rope. He stepped a little nearer, avoiding the animal's hoofs. In a confused whisper of French and Russian, making at the same time the protective signs of his religion, he muttered a sentence of which the other caught little more than the unassuring word that something was about them close—something "*méchant*." This curious, significant word he used.

The whispered utterance, the manner that went with it, surely the dark and lonely setting of the little scene as well, served to convey the full suggestion of the adjective with a force the man himself could scarcely have intended. Something had passed by, not so much evil, wicked, or malign as strange and alien—uncanny. Rostom, a man utterly careless of physical danger, rising to it, rather, with delight, was frightened—in his soul.

"What do you mean?" O'Malley asked louder, with an air of impatience assumed. The man was on his knees, but whether praying, or merely struggling with the rope, was hard to see. "What is it you're talking about so foolishly?" He spoke with a confidence he hardly felt himself.

And the involved reply, spoken with lips against the earth, the head but slightly turned as he knelt, again smothered the words. Only the curious phrase came to him—"*de l'ancien monde—quelque-chose—*"

The Irishman took him by the shoulders. Not meaning actually to shake him, he yet must have used some violence, for the fact was that he did not like the answers and sought to deny some strong emotion in himself. The man stood up abruptly with a kind of sudden spring. The expression of his face was not easily divined in the darkness, but a gleam of the eyes was clearly visible. It may have been anger; it may have been terror; vivid excitement it certainly was.

"Something—old as the stones, old as the stones," he whispered, thrusting his dark bearded face unpleasantly close. "Such things are in these mountains.... *Mais oui! C'est moi qui vous le dis!* Old as the stones, I tell you. And sometimes they come out close—with sudden wind. *We* know!"

He stepped back again sharply and dropped upon his knees, bowing to the ground with flattened palms. He made a repelling gesture as though it was O'Malley's presence that brought the experience.

"And to see them is—to die!" he heard, muttered against the ground thickly. "To see them is to die!"

The Irishman went back to his sleeping-bag. Some strange passion of the man was deeply stirred; he did not wish to offend his violent beliefs and turn it against himself in a stupid, scrambling fight. He lay and waited. He heard the muttering of the deep voice behind him in the darkness. Presently it ceased. Rostom came softly back to bed.

"*He* knows; *he* warned me!" he whispered, jerking one hand toward the horse significantly, as they at length lay again side by side in their blankets and the stars shone down upon them from a deep black sky. "But, for the moment, they have passed, not finding us. No wind has come."

"Another—horse?" asked O'Malley suggestively, with a sympathy meant to quiet him.

But the peasant shook his head; and this time it was not difficult to divine the expression on his face even in the darkness. At the same moment the tethered animal again uttered a long whinnying cry, plaintive, yet of pleasure rather than alarm it seemed, which instantly brought the man again with a leap from the blankets to his knees. O'Malley did not go to help him; he stuffed the clothes against his ears and waited; he did not wish to hear the peasant's sentences.

And this pantomime went on at intervals for an hour or more, when at length the horse grew quiet, and O'Malley snatched moments of unrefreshing sleep. The night lay thick about them with a silence like the silence of the sky. The boxwood bushes ran together into a single sheet of black, the far peaks faded out of sight, the air grew keen and sharp toward the dawn on the wave of wind the sunrise drives before it round the world. But to and fro across the Irishman's mind as he lay between sleep and dozing ran the feeling that his friends were close, and that those dancing forms of cosmic life to which all three approximated had come near once more to summon him. He also knew that what the horse had felt was something far from terror. The animal instinctively had divined the presence of something to which it, too, was remotely kin.

Rostom, however, remained keenly on the alert, much of the time apparently praying. Not once did he touch the weapons that lay ready to hand upon the folded burka ... and when at last the dawn came, pale and yellow, through the trees, showing the outlines of the individual box and azalea bushes, he got up earlier than usual and began to make the fire for coffee. In the fuller light which soon poured swiftly over the eastern summits and dropped gold and silver into the tremendous valley at their feet, the men made a systematic search of the immediate surroundings, and then of the clearings and more open stretches beyond. In silence they made it. They found, however, no traces of another camping-party. And it was clear from the way they went about the search that neither expected to find anything. The ground was unbroken, the bushes undisturbed.

Yet still, both knew. That "something" which the night had brought and kept concealed, still hovered closely about them.

And it was at this scattered hamlet, consisting of little more than a farm of sorts and a few shepherds' huts of stone, where they stopped two hours later for provisions, that O'Malley looked up thus suddenly and recognized the figure of his friend. He stood among the trees a hundred yards away. At first the other thought he was a tree—his stalwart form the stem, his hair and beard the branches—so big and motionless he stood between the other trunks. O'Malley saw him for a full minute before he understood. The man seemed so absolutely a part of the landscape, a giant detail in keeping with the rest—a detail that had suddenly emerged.

The same moment a great draught of wind, rising from the depths of the valley below, swept overhead with a roaring sound, shaking the beech and box trees and setting all the golden azalea heads in a sudden agitation. It passed as swiftly as it came. The peace of the June morning again descended on the mountains.

It was broken by a wild, half-smothered cry,—a cry of genuine terror.

For O'Malley had turned to Rostom with some word that here, in this figure, lay the explanation of the animal's excitement in the night, when he saw that the peasant, white as chalk beneath the tangle of black hair that covered his face, had stopped dead in his tracks. His mouth was open, his arms upraised to shield; he was staring fixedly in the same direction as himself. The next instant he was on his knees, bowing and scraping toward Mecca, groaning, hiding his eyes with both hands. The sack he held had toppled over; the cheese and flour rolled upon the ground; and from the horse came that long-drawn whinnying of the night.

There was a momentary impression—entirely in the Irishman's mind, of course, -that the whole landscape veiled a giant, rushing movement that passed across it like a wave. The surface of the earth, it seemed, ran softly quivering, as though that wind had stirred response together with the trembling of the million leaves … before it settled back again to stillness. It passed in the flash of an eyelid. The earth lay tranquil in repose.

But, though the suddenness of the stranger's arrival might conceivably have startled the ignorant peasant, with nerves already overwrought from the occurrence of the night, O'Malley was not prepared for the violence of the man's terror as shown by the immediate sequel. For after several moments' prayer and prostration, with groans half smothered against the very ground, he sprang impetuously to his feet again, turned to his employer with eyes that gleamed wildly in that face of chalk, cried out—the voice thick with the confusion of his fear—"It is the Wind! *They* come; from the mountains *they* come! Older than the stones they are. Save yourself.... Hide your eyes … fly…!"—and was gone. He went like a deer. He waited neither for food nor payment but flung the great black burka round his face—and ran.

And to O'Malley, bereft of all power of movement as he watched in complete bewilderment, one thing seemed clear: the man went in this extraordinary fashion because he was afraid of something he had *felt*, not seen. For as he ran with wild and leaping strides, he did not run away from the figure. He took the direction straight toward the spot where the stranger still stood motionless as a tree. So, close he passed him that he almost have brushed his very shoulder. He did not see him.

The last thing the Irishman noted was that in his violence the man had dropped the yellow bashlik from his head. O'Malley saw him stoop with a flying rush to pick it up. He seemed to catch it as it fell.

And then the big figure moved. He came slowly forward from among the trees, his hands outstretched in greeting, on his great visage a shining smile of welcome that seemed to share the sunrise. In that moment for the Irishman all was forgotten as though unknown, unseen, save the feelings of extraordinary happiness that filled him to the brim.

XXX

"The poets are thus liberating gods. The ancient British bards had for the title of their order, 'Those who are free throughout the world.' They are free, and they make free. An imaginative book renders us much more service at first, by stimulating us through its tropes, than afterward, when we arrive at the precise sense of the author. I think nothing is of any value in books, excepting the transcendental and extraordinary. If a man is inflamed and carried away by his thought, to that degree that he forgets the authors and the public, and heeds only this one dream, which holds him like an insanity, let me read his paper, and you may have all the arguments and histories and criticism."

—EMERSON

To criticize, deny, perhaps to sneer, is not very difficult or uncommon function of the mind, and the story as I first heard him tell it, lying there in the grass beyond the Serpentine that summer evening, roused in me, I must confess, all of these very ordinary faculties. Yet, as I listened to his voice that mingled with the rustle of the poplars overhead, and watched his eager face and gestures, it came to me dimly that a man's mistakes may be due to his attempting bigger things than his little critic ever dreamed perhaps. And gradually I shared the vision that this unrhyming poet by my side had somehow lived out in action.

Inner experience for him was ever the reality—not the mere forms or deeds that clothe it in partial physical expression.

There was no question, of course, that he had actually met this big, inarticulate Russian on the steamer; that Stahl's part in the account was unvarnished; that the boy had fallen on the deck from heart disease; and that, after an interval, chance had brought O'Malley and the father together again in this valley of the Central Caucasus. All that was as literal as the superstitious terror of the Georgian peasant. Further, that the Russian possessed precisely those qualities of powerful sympathy with the other's hidden longings which the subtle-minded Celt had been so quick to appropriate—this, too, was literal enough. Here, doubtless, was the springboard whence he leaped into the stream of this quasi-spiritual adventure with an eagerness of fine, whole-hearted belief which must make this dull world a very wonderful place indeed to those who know it; for it is the visioned faculty of correlating the commonest event with the procession of august Powers that pass ever to and fro behind life's swaying curtain, and of divining in the most ordinary of yellow buttercups the golden fires of a dropped star.

Again, for Terence O'Malley there seemed no definite line that marked off one state of consciousness from another, just as there seems no given instant when a man passes actually from sleep to waking, from pleasure to pain, from joy to grief. There is, indeed, no fixed threshold between the states of normal and abnormal consciousness. In this stranger he imagined a sense of companionship that by some magic of alchemy transformed his deep loneliness into joy and satisfied his passionate yearnings by bringing their subjective fulfillment within range. To have found acceptance in his sight was thus a revolutionary fact in his existence. While a part of my mind may have labeled it all as creative imagination, another part recognized it as plainly true—because his being lived it out without the least denial.

He, at any rate, was not inventing; nor ever knew an instant's doubt. He simply told me what had happened. The discrepancies—the omissions in his written account especially—were simply due, I feel, to the fact that his skill in words was not equal to the depth and brilliance of the emotions that he experienced. But the fact remains: he did experience them. His fairy tale convinced.

His faith had made him whole—one with the Earth. The sense of disunion between his outer and his inner self was gone.

And now, as these two began their journey together into the wilder region of these stupendous mountains, O'Malley says he realized clearly that the change he had dreaded as an "inner catastrophe" simply would mean the complete and final transfer of his consciousness from the "without" to the "within." It would involve the loss only of what constituted him a person among the external activities of the world today. He would lose his life to find it. The deeper self thus quickened by the stranger must finally assert its authority over the rest. To join these Urwelt beings and share their eternal life of beauty close to the Earth herself, he must shift the center. Only thus could he enter the state before the "Fall"—that ancient Garden of the World-Soul, walled-in so close behind his daily life—and know deliverance from the discontent of modern conditions that so distressed him.

To do this temporarily, perhaps, had long been possible to him—in dream, in reverie, in those imaginative trances when he almost seemed to leave his body altogether; but to achieve it permanently was something more than any such passing disablement of the normal self. It involved, he now saw clearly, that which he had already witnessed in the boy: the final release of his Double in so-called death.

Thus, as they made their way northwards, nominally toward the mighty Elbruz and the borders of Swanetia, the Irishman knew in his heart that they in reality came nearer to the Garden long desired, and to those lofty Gates of horn and ivory that hitherto he had never found—because he feared to let himself go. Often he had camped beneath the walls, had smelt the flowers, heard the songs, and even caught glimpses of the life that moved so gorgeously within. But the Gates themselves had never shone for him, even against the sky of dream, because his vision had been clouded by alarm. They swung, it had seemed to him before, in only one direction—for those who enter: he had always hesitated, lost his way, returned.... And many, like him, make the same mistake. Once in, there need be no return, for in reality the walls spread outwards and—enclose the entire world.

Civilization and Humanity, the man of smaller vision had called out to him as passwords to safety. Simplicity and Love, he now discovered, were the truer clues. His big friend in silence taught him. Now he knew.

For in that little hamlet their meeting had taken place—in silence. No actual speech had passed. "You go—so?" the Russian conveyed by a look and by a movement of his whole figure, indicating the direction; and to the Irishman's assenting inclination of the head, he made an answering gesture that merely signified compliance with a plan already known to both. "We go together then." And, there and then, they started, side by side.

The suddenness of this concerted departure only seemed strange afterwards when O'Malley looked back upon it, for at the time it seemed as inevitable as being obliged to swim once the dive is taken. He stood upon a pinnacle whence lesser details were invisible; he knew a kind of exaltation—of loftier vision. Small facts that ordinarily might fill the day with trouble sank below the horizon then. He did not even notice that they went without food, horse, or blankets. It was reckless, unrestrained, and utterly unhindered, this free setting-forth together. Thus, he might have gone upon a journey with the wind, the sunshine, or the rain. Departure with a thought, a dream, a fancy could not have been less unhampered.

The only detail of his outer world that lingered—and that, already sinking out of sight like a stone into deep water—was the image of the running peasant. For a moment he recalled the picture. He saw the man in the act of stooping after the fallen bashlik. He saw him seize it, lift it to his head again. But the picture was small—already very far away. Before the bashlik actually reached the head, the detail dipped into mist and vanished....

XXXI

It was spring—and the flutes of Pan played everywhere. The radiance of the world's first morning shone undimmed. Life flowed and sang and danced, abundant and untamed. It bathed the mountains and that sky of stainless blue. It bathed him too. Dipped, washed, and shining in it, he walked the Earth as she lay radiant in her early youth. The crystal presence of her everlasting Spring flew laughing through a world of light and flowers—flowers that none could ever pluck to die, light that could never fade to darkness within walls and roofs.

All day they wound easily, as though on winged feet, through the steep belt of box and beech woods, and in sparkling brilliant heat across open spaces where the azaleas shone; a cooling wind, fresh as the dawn, seemed ever to urge them forwards. The country, for all its huge scale and wildness, was park-like; the giant, bushy trees wore an air of being tended by the big winds that ran with rustling music among their waving foliage. Between the rhododendrons were avenues of turf, broad-gladed pathways, yet older than the moon, from which a thousand gardeners of wind and dew had gone but a moment before to care for others further on. Overall brimmed up some primal, old-world beauty of a simple life—some immemorial soft glory of the dawn.

Closer and closer, deeper and deeper, ever swifter, ever more direct, O'Malley passed down toward the heart of his mother's being. Along the tenderest pathways of his inner being, so wee, so soft, so simple that for most men they lie ignored or overgrown, he slipped with joy a little nearer—one stage perhaps—toward Reality.

Pan "blew in power" across these Caucasian heights and valleys.

Sweet, sweet, sweet, O Pan!
Piercing sweet by the river!
Blinding sweet, O great god Pan!
The sun on the hill forgot to die,
And the lilies revived, and the dragon-fly
Came back to dream on the river

In front his big leader, no longer blundering clumsily as on that toy steamer with the awkward and lesser motion known to men, pressed forward with a kind of giant sure supremacy along paths he knew, or rather over a trackless, pathless world which the great planet had charted lovingly for his splendid feet. That wind, blowing from the depths of valleys left long since behind, accompanied them wisely. They heard not the faint horns of Elfland faintly blowing, but the blasts of the *Urwelt* trumpets growing out of the still distance, nearer, ever nearer. For leagues below the beech woods poured over the enormous slopes in a sea of soft green foam, and through the meadow spaces they saw the sweet nakedness of running water and listened to its song. At noon they rested in the greater heat, sleeping beneath the shadow of big rocks; and sometimes traveled late into the night, when the stars guided them, and they knew the pointing of the winds. The very moonlight then, that washed this lonely world with silver, sheeting the heights of snow beyond, was friendly, half divine ... and it seemed to O'Malley that while they slept they were watched and cared for—as though Others who awaited had already come halfway out to meet them.

And ever more and more, the passion of his happiness increased; he knew himself complete, fulfilled, made whole. It was as though his Self were passing outwards into hundreds of thousands and becoming countless as the sand. He was everywhere; in everything; shining, singing, dancing.... With the ancient woods he breathed; slipped with the streams down the still darkened valleys; called from each towering summit to the Sun; and flew with all the winds across the immense, untrodden slopes. About him lay this whole spread being of the flowered Caucasus, huge and quiet, drinking in the sunshine at its leisure. But it lay also *within* himself, for his expanding consciousness included and contained it. Through it—this early potent Mood of Nature—he passed toward the Soul of the Earth within, even as a child, caught by a mood of winning tenderness in its mother, passes closer to the heart that gave it birth. Some central love enwrapped him. He knew the surrounding power of everlasting arms.

XXXII

"Inward, ay, deeper far than love or scorn,
Deeper than bloom of virtue, stain of sin,
Rend thou the veil and pass alone within,
Stand naked there and know thyself forlorn.
Nay! in what world, then, spirit, vast thou born?
Or to what World-Soul art thou entered in?
Feel the Self fade, feel the great life begin.
With Love re-rising in the cosmic morn.
The Inward ardor yearns to the inmost goal;
The endless goal is one with the endless way;
From every gulf the tides of Being roll,
From every zenith burns the indwelling day,
And life in Life has drowned thee and soul in Soul;
And these are God and thou thyself art they."

—F.W.H. MYERS.

From "A Cosmic Outlook"

The account of what followed simply swept me into fairyland, yet a Fairyland that is true because it lives in every imaginative heart that does not dream itself shut off from the Universe in some wee compartment all alone.

If O'Malley's written account, and especially his tumbled notebooks, left me bewildered and confused, the fragments that he told me brought this sense of an immense, sweet picture that actually existed. I caught small scenes of it, set in some wild high light. Their very incoherence conveyed the gorgeous splendor of the whole better than any neat ordered sequence could possibly have done.

Climax, in the story-book meaning, there was none. The thing flowed round and round forever. A sense of something eternal wrapped me as I listened; for his imagination set the whole adventure out of time and space, and I caught myself dreaming too. "A thousand years in His sight"—I understood the old words as refreshingly new—might be a day. Thus, felt that monk, perhaps, for whose heart a hundred years had passed while he listened to the singing of a little bird.

My practical questions—it was only at the beginning that I was dull enough to ask them—he did not satisfy, because he could not. There was never the least suggestion of the artist's mere invention.

"You really felt the Earth about and in you," I had asked, "much as one feels the presence of a friend and living person?"

"Drowned in her, yes, as in the thoughts and atmosphere of someone awfully loved." His voice trembled a little as he said it.

"So, speech unnecessary?"

"Impossible—fatal," was the laconic, comprehensive reply, "limiting destructive even."

That, at least, I grasped: the pitifulness of words before that love by which self goes wholly lost in the being of another, adrift yet cared for, gathered all wonderfully in.

"And your Russian friend—your leader?" I ventured, haltingly.

His reply was curiously illuminating:—

"Like some great guiding Thought within her mind—some flaming motif—interpreting her love and splendor—leading me straight."

"As you felt at Marseilles, a clue—a vital clue?" For I remembered the singular phrase he had used in the notebook.

"Not a bad word," he laughed; "certainly, as far as it goes, not a wrong one. For he—it—was at the same time within me. We merged, as our life grew and spread. We swept things along with us from the banks. We were in a flood together," he cried. "We drew the landscape with us!"

The last words baffled me; I found no immediate response. He pushed away the plates on the table before us, where we had been lunching in the back room of a dingy Soho restaurant. We now had the place to ourselves. He drew his chair a little nearer.

"Don't ye see—our journey also was within," he added abruptly.

The pale London sunlight came through the window across chimneys, dreary roofs, and courtyards. Yet where it touched his face it seemed at once to shine. His voice was warm and eager. I caught from him, as it were, both heat and light.

"You moved actually, though, over country—?"

"While at the same time we moved within, advanced, sank deeper," he returned; "call it what you will. Our condition moved. There was this correspondence between the two. Over her face we walked, yet into her as well. We 'traveled' with One greater than ourselves, both caught and merged in her, in utter sympathy with one another as with herself..."

This stopped me dead. I could not pretend more than a vague sympathetic understanding with such descriptions of a mystical experience. Nor was it clear, did he expect it of me. Even his own heart was troubled, and he knew he spoke of things that only few may deal with sanely, still fewer hear with patience.

But, oh, that little room in Greek Street smelt of forests, dew, and dawn as he told it,—that dear wayward Child of Earth! For "his voice fell, like music that makes giddy the dim brain, faint with intoxication of keen joy." I watched those delicate hands he spread about him through the air, the tender, sensitive lips, the light blue eyes that glowed. I noted the real strength in the face,—a sort of nobility it was—his shabby suit of grey, his tie never caught properly in the collar, the frayed cuffs, and the enormous boots he wore even in London—"policeman boots" as we used to call them with a laugh.

So vivid was the picture that he painted! Almost, it seemed, I knew myself the pulse of that eternal Spring beneath our feet, beating in vain against the suffocating weight of London's bricks and pavements laid by civilization—the Earth's delight striving to push outwards into visible form as flowers. She flashed some scrap of meaning thus into me, though blunted on the way, I fear, and crudely paraphrased.

Yes, as he talked across the airless gloom of that little back room, in some small way I caught the splendor of his vision. Behind the words, I caught it here and there. My own wee world extended. My being stretched to understand him and to net in fugitive fragments the scenes of wonder that he knew completely.

Perhaps his larger consciousness fringed my own to "bruise" it, as he claimed the Earth had done to him, so that I glimpsed in tinier measure an experience that in himself blazed whole and thundering. It was, I must admit, exalting and invigorating, if a little breathless; and the return to streets and omnibuses painful—a descent to ugliness and disappointment. For things I can hardly understand now, even in my own descriptions of them, seemed at the time quite clear—or clear-ish at any rate. Whereas normally I could never have compassed them at all.

It taught me: that, at least, I know. In some spiritual way I quickened to the view that all great teaching really comes in some such curious fashion—via a temporary stretching or extension of the "heart" to receive it. The little normal self is pushed aside to make room, even to the point of loss, in order to contain it. Later, the consciousness contracts again. But it has expanded—and there has been growth. Was this, I wondered, perhaps what mystics speak of when they say the personal life must slip aside, be trampled on, submerged, before there can be room for the divine Presences...?

At any rate, as he talked there over coffee that grew cold and cigarette smoke that made the air yet thicker than it naturally was, his words conveyed with almost grandeur of conviction this reality of a profound inner experience. I shared in some faint way its truth and beauty, so that when I saw it in his written form I marveled to find the thing so thin and cold and dwindled. The key his personal presence supplied, of guidance and interpretation, of course was gone.

XXXIII

"Why, what is this patient entrance into Nature's deep resources
But the child's most gradual learning to walk upright without bane?
When we drive out, from the cloud of steam, majestical white horses,
Are we greater than the first men who led black ones by the mane?"

—E.B. BROWNING

The "Russian" led.

O'Malley styled him thus to the end for want of a larger word, perhaps—a word to phrase the inner and the outer. Although the mountains were devoid of trails, he seemed always certain of his way. An absolute sense of orientation possessed him; or, rather, the whole earth became a single pathway. Her being, in and about their hearts, concealed no secrets; he knew the fresh, cool water-springs as surely as the corners where the wild honey gathered. It seemed as natural that the bees should leave them unmolested, giving them freely of their store, as that the savage dogs in the aouls or villages, they passed so rarely now, should refrain from attack. Even the peasants shared with them some common, splendid life. Occasionally they passed an Ossetian on horseback, a rifle swung across his saddle, a covering burka draping his shoulders and the animal's haunches in a single form that seemed a very outgrowth of the mountains. But not even a greeting was exchanged. They passed in silence; often very close, as though they did not see these two on foot. And once or twice the horses reared and whinnied, while their riders made the signs of their religion.... Sentries they seemed. But for the password known to both, they would have stopped the travelers. In these forsaken fastnesses mere unprotected wandering means death. Yet to the happy Irishman there never came a thought of danger or alarm. All was a portion of himself, and no man can be afraid of his own hands or feet. Their convoy was immense, invisible, a guaranteed security of the vast Earth herself. No little personal injury could pass so huge defense.

Others, armed with a lesser security of knives and guns and guides, would assuredly have been turned back, or had they shown resistance, would never have been heard to tell the tale. Dr. Stahl and the fur-merchant, for instance—

But such bothering little thoughts with their hard edges no longer touched reality; they spun away and found no lodgment; they were—untrue; false items of some lesser world unrealized.

For, in proportion as he fixed his thoughts successfully on outward and physical things, the world wherein he now walked grew dim: he missed the path, stumbled, saw trees and flowers indistinctly, failed to hear properly the call of birds and wind, to feel the touch of sun; and, most unwelcome of all,—was aware that his leader left him, dwindling in size, dropping away somehow among shadows far behind or far ahead.

The inversion was strangely complete: what men called solid, real, and permanent he now knew as the veriest shadows of existence, fleeting, unsatisfactory, false.

Their dreary make-believe had all his life oppressed him. He now knew why. Men, driving their forces outwards for external possessions had lost the way so utterly. It truly was amazing. He no longer quite understood how such feverish strife was possible to intelligent beings: the fur-merchant, the tourists, his London friends, the great majority of men and women he had known, pain in their hearts and weariness in their eyes, the sad strained faces, the furious rush to catch a little pleasure they deemed joy. It seemed like some wild senseless game that madness plays. He found it difficult to endow them, one and all, with any sense of life. He saw them groping in thick darkness, snatching with hands of shadow at things of even thinner shadow, all moving in a wild and frantic circle of artificial desires, while just beyond, absurdly close to many, blazed this great living sunshine of Reality and Peace and Beauty. If only they would turn—and look within—!

In fleeting moments these sordid glimpses of that dark and shadow-world still afflicted his outer sight—the nightmare he had left behind. It played like some gloomy memory through a corner of consciousness not yet wholly disentangled from it. Already he burned to share his story with the world...! A few he saw who here and there half turned, touched by a flashing ray—then rushed away into the old blackness as though frightened, not daring to escape. False images thrown outward by the intellect prevented. Stahl he saw ... groping; a soft light of yearning in his eyes ... a hand outstretched to push the shadows from him, yet ever gathering them instead.... Men he saw by the million, youth still in their hearts, yet slaving in darkened trap-like cages not merely to earn a competency but to pile more gold for things not really wanted; faces of greed round gambling-tables; the pandemonium of Exchanges; even fair women, playing Bridge through all a summer afternoon—the strife and lust and passion for possessions degrading every heart, choking the channels of simplicity.... Over the cities of the world, he heard the demon Civilization sing its song of terror and desolation. Its music of destruction shook the nations. He saw the millions dance. And mid the bewildering ugly thunder of that sound few could catch the small, sweet voice played by the Earth upon the little Pipes of Pan... the fluting call of Nature to the Simple Life—which is the Inner.

For now, as he moved closer to the Earth, deeper ever deeper into the enfolding moods of her vast collective consciousness, he drew nearer to the Reality that satisfies. He approached that center where outward activity is less, yet energy and vitality far greater—because it is at rest. Here he met things halfway, as it were, en route for the outer physical world where they would appear later as "events," but not yet emerged, still alive and breaking with their undischarged and natural potencies. Modern life, he discerned, dealt only with these forces when they had emerged, masquerading at the outer rim of life as complete embodiments, whereas actually they are but partial and symbolic expressions of their eternal prototypes behind. And men today were busy at this periphery only, touch with the center lost, madly consumed with the unimportant details that concealed the inner glory. It was the spirit of the age to mistake the outer shell for the inner reality. He at last understood the reason of his starved loneliness amid the stupid uproar of latter-day life, why he distrusted "Civilization," and stood apart. His yearnings were explained. His heart dwelt ever in the Golden Age of the Earth's first youth, and at last—he was coming home.

Like mud settling in dirty water, the casual realities of that outer life all sank away. He grew clear within, one with the primitive splendor, beauty, grace of a fresh world. Over his inner self, flooding slowly the passages and cellars, those subterranean ways that honeycomb the dim-lit foundations of personality, this tide of power rose. Filling chamber after chamber, melting down walls and ceiling, eating away divisions softly and irresistibly, it climbed in silence, merging all moods and disunion of his separate Selves into the single thing that made him comprehensible to himself and able to know the Earth as Mother. He saw himself whole; he knew himself divine. A strange tumult as of some ecstasy of old remembrance invaded him. He dropped back into a more spacious scale of time, long long ago when a month might be a moment, or a thousand years pass round him as a single day....

The qualities of all the Earth lay too, so easily contained within himself. He understood that old legend by which man the microcosm represents and sums up Earth, the macrocosm in himself, so that Nature becomes the symbol and interpreter of his inner being. The strength and dignity of the trees he drew into himself; the power of the wind was his; with his unwearied feet ran all the sweet and facile swiftness of the rivulets, and in his thoughts the graciousness of flowers, the wavy softness of the grass, the peace of open spaces and the calm of that vast sky. The murmur of the Urwelt was in his blood, and in his heart the exaltation of her golden Mood of Spring.

How, then, could speech be possible, since both shared this common life? The communion with his friend and leader was too profound and perfect for any stammering utterance in the broken, partial symbols known as language. This was done for them: the singing of the birds, the wind-voices, the rippling of water, the very humming of the myriad insects even, and rustling of the grass and leaves, shaped all they felt in some articulate expression that was right, complete, and adequate. The passion of the larks set all the sky to music, and songs far sweeter than the nightingales' made every dusk divine.

He understood now that laborious utterance of his friend upon the steamer, and why his difficulty with words was more than he could overcome.

Like a current in the sea, he still preserved identity yet knew the freedom of a boundless being. And meanwhile the tide was ever rising. With this singular companion he neared that inner realization which should reveal them as they were—Thoughts in the Earth's old Consciousness too primitive, too far away, too vital and terrific to be confined in any outward physical expression of the "civilized" world today.... The earth shone, glittered, sang, holding them close to the rhythm of her gigantic heart. Her glory was their own. In the blazing summer of the inner life they floated, happy, caught away, at peace ... emanations of her living Self.

* * * * *

The valleys far below were filled with mist, cutting them off literally from the world of men, but the beauty of the upper mountains grew more and more bewilderingly enticing. The scale was so immense, while the brilliant clearness of the air brought distance close before the eyes, altered perspective, and robbed "remote" and "near" of any definite meaning. Space fled away. It shifted here and there at pleasure, according as they felt. It was within them, not without. They passed, dispersed and swift about the entire landscape, a very part of it, diffused in terms of light and air and color, scattered in radiance, distributed through flowers, spread through the sky and grass and forests. Space is a form of thought. But they no longer "thought": they felt.... O, that prodigious, clean, and simple Feeling of the Earth! Love that redeems and satisfies! Power that fills and blesses! Electric strength that kills the germ of separateness, making whole! The medicine of the world!

For days and nights, it was thus—or was it years and minutes?—while they skirted the slopes and towers of the huge Dykh-Taou, and Elbrous, supreme and lonely in the heavens, beckoned solemnly. The snowy Kochtan-Taou rolled past, yet through, them; Kasbek superbly thundered; hosts of lesser summits sang in the dawn and whispered to the stars. And longing sank away—impossible.

"My boy, my boy, could you only have been with me...!" broke his voice across the splendid dream, bringing me back to the choking, dingy room I had forgotten. It was like a cry—a cry of passionate yearning.

"I'm with you now," I murmured, some similar rising joy half breaking in my breast. "That's something—"

He sighed in answer. "Something, perhaps. But I have got it always; it's all still part of me. Oh, oh! that I could give it to the world and lift the ache of all humanity…!" His voice trembled. I saw the moisture of immense compassion in his eyes. I felt myself swim out into universal being.

"Perhaps," I stammered half beneath my breath, "perhaps someday you may…!"

He shook his head. His face turned very sad.

"How should they listen, much less understand? Their energies drive outwards, and separation is their God. There is no 'money in it'…!"

XXXIV

"Oh! whose heart is not stirred with tumultuous joy when the intimate Life of Nature enters into his soul with all its plenitude, … when that mighty sentiment for which language has no other name than Love is diffused in him, like some powerful all-dissolving vapor; when he, shivering with sweet terror, sinks into the dusky, enticing bosom of Nature; when the meager personality loses itself in the overpowering waves of passion, and nothing remains but the focal point of the incommensurable generative Force, an engulfing vortex in the ocean?"

NOVALIS, Disciples at Saïs. Translated by U.C.B.

Early in the afternoon they left the bigger trees behind and passed into that more open country where the shoulders of the mountains were strewn with rhododendrons. These formed no continuous forest, but stood about in groups some twenty-five feet high, their rounded masses lighted on the surface with fires of mauve and pink and purple. When the wind stirred them, and the rattling of their stiff leaves was heard, it seemed as if the skin of the mountains trembled to shake out colored flames. The air turned radiant through a mist of running tints.

Still climbing, they passed along broad glades of turfy grass between the groups. More rapidly now, O'Malley says, went forward that inner change of being which accompanied the progress of their outer selves. So intimate henceforth was this subtle correspondence that the very landscape took the semblance of their feelings. They moved as "emanations" of the landscape. Each melted in the other, dividing lines all vanished.

Their union with the Earth approached this strange and sweet fulfillment.

And so it was that, though at this height the vestiges of bird and animal life were wholly gone, there grew more and more strongly the sense that, in their further depths and shadows, these ancient bushes screened Activities even more ancient than themselves. Life, only concealed because they had not reached its plane of being, pulsed everywhere about their pathway, immense in power, moving swiftly, very grand and very simple, and sometimes surging close, seeking to draw them in. More than once, as they moved through glade and clearing, the Irishman knew thrills of an intoxicating happiness, as this abundant, driving life brushed past him. It came so close, it glided before his eyes, yet still was viewless. It strode behind him and before, peered down through space upon him, lapped him about with the stir of mighty currents. The deep suction of its invitation caught his soul, urging the change within himself more quickly forward. Huge and delightful, he describes it, awful, yet bringing no alarm.

He was always on the point of seeing. Surely the next turning would reveal; beyond the next dense, tangled group would come—disclosure; behind that clustered mass of purple blossoms, shaking there mysteriously in the wind, some half-veiled countenance of splendor watched and welcomed! Before his face passed swift, deific figures, tall, erect, compelling, charged with this ancient, golden life that could never wholly pass away. And only just beyond the fringe of vision. Vision already strained upon the edge. His consciousness stretched more and more to reach them, while They came crowding near to let him know inclusion.

These projections of the Earth's old consciousness moved thick and soft about them, eternal in their giant beauty. Soon he would know, perhaps, the very forms in which she had projected them—dear portions of her streaming life the earliest races half divined and worshipped, and never quite withdrawn. Worship could still entice them out. A single worshipper sufficed. For worship meant retreat into the heart where still they dwelt. And he had loved and worshipped all his life.

And always with him, now at his side or now a little in advance, his leader moved in power, with vigorous, springing gestures like to dancing, singing that old tuneless song of the wind, happier even than himself.

The splendor of the *Urwelt* closed about them. They drew nearer to the Gates of that old Garden, the first Time ever knew, whose frontiers were not less than the horizons of the entire world. For this lost Eden of a Golden Age when "first God dawned on chaos" still shone within the soul as in those days of innocence before the "Fall," when men first separated themselves from their great Mother.

A little before sunset they halted. A hundred yards above the rhododendron forest, in a clear wide space of turf that ran for leagues among grey boulders to the lips of the eternal snowfields, they waited. Through a gap of sky, with others but slightly lower than himself, the pyramid of Kasbek, grim and towering, stared down upon them, dreadfully close though really miles away. At their feet yawned the profound valley they had climbed. Halfway into it, unable to reach the depths, the sun's last rays dropped shafts like rivers slanting. Already in soft troops the shadows crept downwards from the eastern-facing summits overhead.

Out of these very shadows Night drew swiftly down about the world, building with her masses of silvery architecture a barrier that rose to heaven. These two lay down beside it. Beyond it spread that shining Garden…only the shadow-barrier between.

With the rising of the moon this barrier softened marvelously, letting the star beams in. It trembled like a line of wavering music in the wind of night. It settled downwards, shaking a little, toward the ground, while just above them came a curving inwards like a bay of darkness, with overhead two stately towers, their outline fringed with stars.

"The Gateway...!" whispered something through the mountains.

It may have been the leader's voice; it may have been the Irishman's own leaping thought; it may have been merely a murmur from the rhododendron leaves below. It came sifting gently through the shadows. O'Malley knew. He followed his leader higher. Just beneath this semblance of an old-world portal which Time could neither fashion nor destroy, they lay upon the earth—and waited. Beside them shone the world, dressed by the moon in silver. The wind stood still to watch. The peak of Kasbek from his cloudy distance listened too.

For, floating upwards across the spaces came a sound of simple, old-time piping—the fluting music of a little reed. It drew near, stopped for a moment as though the player watched them; then, with a plunging swiftness, passed off through starry distance up among the darker mountains. The lost, forsaken Asian valley covered them. Nowhere were they extraneous to it. They slept. And while they slept, they moved across the frontiers of fulfillment.

The moon-blanched Gate of horn and ivory swung open. The consciousness of the Earth possessed them. They passed within.

XXXV

"For of old the Sun, our sire,
Came wooing the mother of men,
Earth, that was virginal then,
Vestal fire to his fire.
Silent her bosom and coy,
But the strong god sued and press'd;
And born of their starry nuptial joy
Are all that drink of her breast.

"And the triumph of him that begot,
And the travail of her that bore,
Behold they are evermore
As warp and weft in our lot.
We are children of splendor and flame,
Of shuddering, also, and tears.
Magnificent out of the dust we came,
And abject from the spheres.

"O bright irresistible lord!
We are fruit of Earth's womb, each one,
And fruit of thy loins, O Sun,
Whence first was the seed outpour'd.
To thee as our Father we bow,
Forbidden thy Father to see,
Who is older and greater than thou, as thou
Art greater and older than we."

—WILLIAM WATSON, "Ode in May"

Very slowly the dawn came. The sky blushed rose, trembled, flamed. A breath of wind stirred the vapors that far below sheeted the surface of the Black Sea. But it was still in that gentle twilight before the actual color comes that O'Malley found he was lying with his eyes wide open, watching the rhododendrons. He may have slept meanwhile, though "sleep," he says, involving loss of consciousness, seemed no right description. A sense of interval there was at any rate, a "transition-blank,"—whatever that may mean—he phrased it in the writing.

And, watching the rhododendron forest a hundred yards below, he saw it move. Through the dim light this movement passed and ran, here, there, and everywhere. A curious soft sound accompanied it that made him remember the Bible phrase of wind "going in the tops of the mulberry trees." Hushed, swift, elusive murmur, it passed about him through the dusk. He caught it next behind him and, turning, noticed groups upon the slopes,—groups that he had not seen the night before. These groups seemed also now to move; the isolated scattered clusters came together, merged, ran to the parent forest below, or melted just beyond the line of vision above.

The wind sprang up and rattled all the million leaves. That rattling filled the air, and with it came another, deeper sound like to a sound of tramping that seemed to shake the earth. Confusion caught him then completely, for it was as if the mountain-side awoke, rose up, and shook itself into a wild and multitudinous wave of life.

At first he thought the wind had somehow torn the rhododendrons loose from their roots and was strewing them with that tramping sound about the slopes. But the groups passed too swiftly over the turf for that, swept completely from their fastenings, while the tramping grew to a roaring as of cries and voices. That roaring had the quality of the voice that reached him weeks ago across the Ægean Sea. A strange, keen odor, too, that was not wholly unfamiliar, moved upon the wind.

And then he knew that what he had been watching all along were not rhododendrons at all, but living, splendid creatures. A host of others, moreover, large ones and small together, stood shadowy in the background, stamping their feet upon the turf, manes tossing in the early wind, in their entire mass awful as in their individual outline somehow noble.

The light spread upwards from the east. With a fire of terrible joy and wonder in his heart, O'Malley held his breath and stared. The luster of their glorious bodies, golden bronze in the sunlight, dazed the sight. He saw the splendor of ten hundred velvet flanks in movement, with here and there the uprising whiteness of a female outline that flashed and broke above the general mass like foam upon a great wave's crest—figures of incomparable grace and power; the sovereign, upright carriage; the rippling muscles upon massive limbs, and shoulders that held defiant strength and softness in exquisite combination. And then he heard huge murmurs of their voices that filled the dawn, aged by lost thousand years, and sonorous as the booming of the sea. A cry that was like singing escaped him. He saw them rise and sweep away. There was a rush of magnificence. They cantered—wonderfully. They were gone.

The roar of their curious commotion traveled over the mountains, dying into distance very swiftly. The rhododendron forest that had concealed their approach resumed its normal aspect, but burning now with colors innumerable as the sunrise caught its thousand blossoms. And O'Malley understood that during "sleep" he had passed with his companion through the gates of ivory and horn and stood now within the first Garden of the early world. All frontiers crossed, all barriers behind, he stood within the paradise of his heart's desire. The Consciousness of the Earth included him. These were early forms of life she had projected—some of the living prototypes of legend, myth, and fable—embodiments of her first manifestations of consciousness, and eternal, accessible to every heart that holds a true and passionate worship. All his life this love of Nature, which was worship, had been his. It now fulfilled itself. Merged by love into the consciousness of the Being loved, he felt her thoughts, her powers, and manifestations of life as his own.

In a flash, of course, this all passed clearly before him; but there was no time to dwell upon it. For the activity of his companion had likewise become suddenly tremendous. He had risen into complete revelation at last. His own had called him. He was off to join his kind.

The transformation came upon both of them, it seems, at once, but in that moment of bewilderment, the Irishman only realized it first in his leader.

For on the edge of the advancing sunlight first this Cosmic Being crouched, then rose with alert and springing movement, leaping to his feet in a single bound that propelled him with a stride of more than a man's two limbs. His great sides quivered as he shook himself. A roar, similar to that sound the distance already swallowed, rolled forth into the air. With head thrown back, chest forward, too, for all the backward slant of the mighty shoulders, he stood there, grandly outlined, pushing the wind before him. The great brown eyes shone with the joy of freedom and escape—a superb and regal transformation.

Urged by the audacity of his strange excitement, the Irishman obeyed an impulse that came he knew not whence. The single word sprang to his lips before he could guess its meaning, much less hold it back.

"Lapithae...!" he cried aloud; "Lapithae...!"

The stalwart figure turned with an awful spring as though it would trample him to the ground. A moment the brown eyes flamed with a light of battle. Then, with another roar, and a gesture that was somehow both huge and simple, he seemed to rise and paw the air. The next second this figure of the Urwelt, come once more into its own, bent down and forward, leaped wonderfully—then, cantering, raced away across the slopes to join his kind. He went like a shape of wind and cloud. The heritage of racial memory was his, and certain words remained still vividly evocative. That old battle with the Lapithae was but one item of the scenes of ancient splendor lying pigeon-holed in his mighty Mother's consciousness. The instant he had called, the Irishman himself lay caught in lost memory's tumultuous whirl. The lonely world about him seemed of a sudden magnificently peopled—sky, woods, and torrents.

He watched a moment the fierce rapidity with which he sped toward the mountains, the sound of his feet already merged in that other, vaster tramping, and then he turned—to watch himself. For a similar transformation was going forward in himself, and with the happiness of wild amazement he saw it. Already, indeed, it was accomplished. All white and shining lay the sunlight over his own extended form. Power was in his limbs; he rose above the ground in some new way; the usual little stream of breath became a river of rushing air he drew into stronger, more capacious lungs; likewise, his bust grew strangely deepened, pushed the wind before it; and the sunshine glowed on shaggy flanks agleam with dew that powerfully drove the ground behind him while he ran.

He ran, yet only partly as a man runs; he found himself shot forwards through the air, upright, yet at the same time upon all fours brandishing his arms he flew with a free, unfettered motion, traversing the surface of the mother's mind and body. Free of the entire Earth he was.

And as he raced to join the others, there passed again across his memory faintly—it was like the little memory of some physical pain almost—the picture of the boy who swam so strangely in the sea, the picture of the parent's curious emanations on the deck, and, lastly, of those flying shapes of cloud and wind his inner vision brought so often speeding over long, bare hills. This was the final fragment of the outer world that reached him....

He tore along the mountains in the dawn, the awful speed at last explained. His going made a sound upon the wind, and like the wind he raced. Far beyond him in the distance, he saw the shadow of that disappearing host spreading upon the valleys like a mist. Faintly still he caught their sound of roaring; but it was his own feet now that made that trampling as of hoofs upon the turf. The landscape moved and opened, gathering him in....

And, hardly had he gone, when there stole upon the place where he had stood, a sweet and simple sound of music—the little piping of a reed. It dropped down through the air, perhaps, or came from the forest edge, or possibly the sunrise brought it—this ancient little sound of fluting on those Pipes men call the Pipes of Pan....

XXXVI

"Here we but peak and dwindle
The clank of chain and crane,
The whirr of crank and spindle
Bewilder heart and brain;
The ends of our endeavor
Are wealth and fame,
Yet in the still Forever
We're one and all the same;

"Yet beautiful and spacious
The wise, old world appears.
Yet frank and fair and gracious
Outlaugh the jocund years.
Our arguments disputing,
The universal Pan
Still wanders fluting—fluting—
Fluting to maid and man.
Our weary well-a-waying
His music cannot still:

Come! let us go a-maying,
And pipe with him our fill."

—W.E. HENLEY

In a detailed description, radiant with a wild loveliness of some forgotten beauty, and of necessity often incoherent, the Irishman conveyed to me, sitting in that dreary Soho restaurant, the passion of his vision. With an astonishing vitality and a wealth of deep conviction it all poured from his lips. There was no halting and no hesitation. Like a man in trance, he talked and like a man in trance he lived it over again while imparting it to me. None came to disturb us in our dingy corner. Indeed, there is no quieter place in all London town than the back room of these eating-houses of the French Quarter between the hours of lunch and dinner. The waiters vanish, the "patron" disappears; no customers come in. But I know surely that its burning splendor came not from the actual words he used but was due to definite complete transference of the vision itself into my own heart. I caught the fire from his very thought. His heat inflamed my mind. Words, both in the uttered and the written version, dimmed it all distressingly.

And the completeness of the transference is proved for me by the fact that I never once had need to ask a question. I saw and understood it all as he did. And hours must have passed during the strange recital, for toward the close people came in and took the vacant tables, the lights were up, and grimy waiters clattered noisily about with plates and knives and forks, thrusting an inky carte du jour beneath our very faces.

Yet how to set it down I swear I know not. Nor he, indeed. The notebooks that I found in that old sack of Willesden canvas were a disgrace to any man who bid for sanity,—a disgrace to paper and pencil too!

All memory of his former life, it seems, at first, had fallen utterly away; nothing survived to remind him of it; and thus, he lost all standard of comparison. The state he moved in was too complete to admit of standards or of critical judgment. For these confine, imprison, and belittle, whereas he was free. His escape was unconditioned. From the thirty years of his previous living, no single fragment broke through. The absorption was absolute.

"I really do believe and know myself," he said to me across that spotted table-cloth, "that for the time I was merged into the being of another, a being immensely greater than myself. Perhaps old Stahl was right, perhaps old crazy Fechner; and it actually was the consciousness of the Earth. I can only tell you that the whole experience left no room in me for other memories; all I had previously known was gone, wiped clean away. Yet much of what came in its place is beyond me to describe and for a curious reason. It's not the size or splendor that prevent the telling, but rather the sublime simplicity of it all. I know no language today simple enough to utter it. Far behind words it lies, as difficult of full recovery as the dreams of deep sleep, as the ecstasy of the religious, elusive as the mystery of Kubla Khan or the Patmos visions of St. John. Full recapture, I am convinced, is not possible at all in words.

"And at the time it did not seem like vision; it was so natural; unstudied, unprepared, and ever there; spontaneous too and artless as a drop of water or a baby's toy. The natural is ever the unchanging. My God! I tell you, man, it was divine!"

He made about him a vehement sweeping gesture with his arm which emphasized more poignantly than speech the contrast he felt here where we sat—tight, confining walls, small stifling windows, chairs to rest the body, smothering roof and curtains, doors of narrow entrance and exit, floors to lift above the sweet surface of the soil,—all of them artificial barriers to shut out light and separate away from the Earth. "See what we've come to!" it said plainly. And it included even his clothes and boots and collar, the ridiculous hat upon the peg, the unsightly "brolly" in the dingy corner. Had there been room in me for laughter, I could well have laughed aloud.

* * * * *

For as he raced across that stretch of splendid mountainous Earth, watching the sunrise kiss the valleys and the woods, shaking the dew from his feet and swallowing the very wind for breath, he realized that other forms of life similar to his own were everywhere about him—also moving.

"They were a part of the Earth even as I was. Here she was crammed to the brim with them—projections of her actual self and being, crowded with this incomparable ancient beauty that was strong as her hills, swift as her running streams, radiant as her wildflowers. Whether to call them forms or thoughts or feelings, or Powers perhaps, I swear, old man, I know not. Her Consciousness through which I sped, drowned, lost, and happy, wrapped us all in together as a mood contains its own thoughts and feelings. For she was a Being—of sorts. And I was in her mind, mood, consciousness, call it what you best can. These other thoughts and presences I felt were the raw material of forms, perhaps—Forces that when they reach the minds of men must clothe themselves in form in order to be known, whether they be Dreams, or Gods, or any other kind of inspiration. Closer than that I cannot get.... I knew myself within her being like a child, and I felt the deep, eternal pull—to simple things."

* * * * *

And thus, the beauty of the early world companioned him, and all the forgotten gods moved forward into life. They hovered everywhere, immense and stately. The rocks and trees and peaks that half concealed them, betrayed at the same time great hints of their mighty gestures. Near him, they were, he moved toward their region. If definite sight refused to focus on them the fault was not their own but his. He never doubted that they could be seen. Yet, even thus partially, they manifested—terrifically. He was aware of their overshadowing presences. Sight, after all, was an incomplete form of knowing—a thing he had left behind—elsewhere. It belonged, with the other limited sense-channels, to some attenuated dream now all forgotten. Now he knew all over. He himself was of them.

"I am home!" it seems he cried as he ran cantering across the sunny slopes. "At last, I have found you! Home...!" and the stones shot wildly from his thundering tread.

A roar of windy power filled the sky, and far away that echoing tramping paused to listen.

"We have called you! Come...!"

And the forms moved down slowly from their mountainous pedestals; the woods breathed out a sigh; the running water sang; the slopes all murmured through their grass and flowers. For a worshipper, strayed from the outer world of the dead, stood within the precincts of their ancient temple. He had passed the Angel with the flaming sword those very dead had set there long ago. The Garden now enclosed him. He had found the heart of the Earth, his mother. Self-realization in the perfect union with Nature was fulfilled. He knew the Great Atonement.

* * * * *

The quiet of the dawn still lay upon the world; dew sparkled; the air was keen and fresh. Yet, in spite of all this vast sense of energy, this vigor and delight, O'Malley no longer felt the least goading of excitement. There was this animation and this fine delight; but craving for sensation of any kind, was gone. Excitement, as it tortured men in that outer world he had left, could not exist in this larger state of being for excitement is the appetite for something not possessed, magnified artificially till it has become a condition of disease. All that he needed was now contained within himself; he was at-ease; and, literally, that unrest which men miscall delight could touch him not nor torture him again.

If this were death—how exquisite!

And Time was not a passing thing, for it lay, he says, somehow in an ocean everywhere, heaped up in gulfs and spaces. It was as though he could help himself and take it. That morning, had he so wished, could last forever; he could go backwards and taste the shadows of the night again, or forward and bask in the glory of hot noon. There were no parts of things, and so no restlessness, no sense of incompleteness, no divisions.

This quiet of the dawn lay in himself, and, since he loved it, lay there, cool and sweet and sparkling for—years; almost—forever.

* * * * *

Moreover, while this giant form of Urwelt-life his inner self had assumed was new, it yet seemed somehow familiar. The speed and weight and power caused him no distress, there was no detail that he could not manage easily. To race thus o'er the world, keeping pace with an eternal dawn, was as simple as for the Earth herself to spin through space. His union with her was as complete as that. In every item of her being lay the wonder of her perfect form—a sphere. It was complete. Nothing could add to it.

Yet, while all recollection of his former, pettier self was gone, he began presently to remember—men. Though never in relation to himself, he retained dimly a picture of that outer world of strife and terror. As a memory of illness, he recalled it—dreadfully, a nightmare fever from which he had recovered, its horror already fading out. Cities and crowds, poverty, illness, pain and all the various terror of Civilization, robbed of the power to afflict, yet still hung hovering about the surface of his consciousness, though powerless to break his peace.

For the power to understand it vanished; no part of him knew sympathy with it; so clearly he now saw himself sharing the Earth, that a vague wonder filled him when he recalled the mad desires of men to possess external forms of things. It was amazing and perplexing. How could they ever have devised such wild and childish efforts—all in the wrong direction?

If that outer life were the real one how could any intelligent being think it worthwhile to live? How could any thinking man hold up his head and walk along the street with dignity if that was what he believed? Was a man satisfied with it worth keeping alive at all? What bigger scheme could ever use him? The direction of modern life today was diametrically away from happiness and truth.

Peace was the word he knew, peace and a singing joy.

* * * * *

He played with the Earth's great dawn and raced along these mountains through her mind. Of course, the hills could dance and sing and clap their hands. He saw it clearly. How could it be otherwise? They were expressions of her giant moods—what in himself were thoughts—phases of her ample, surging Consciousness....

He passed with the sunlight down the laughing valleys, spread with the morning wind above the woods, shone on the snowy peaks, and leaped with rushing laughter among the crystal streams. These were his swift and darting signs of joy, words of his singing as it were. His main and central being swung with the pulse of the Earth, too great for any telling.

He read the book of Nature all about him, yes, but read it singing. He understood how this patient Mother hungered for her myriad lost children, how in the passion of her summers she longed to bless them, to wake their high yearnings with the sweetness of her springs, and to whisper through her autumns how she prayed for their return…!

Instinctively he read the giant Page before him. For "every form in nature" is a symbol of an idea and represents a sign or letter. A succession of such symbols forms a language; and he who is a true child of nature may understand this language and know the character of everything. His mind becomes a mirror wherein the attributes of natural things are reflected and enter the field of his consciousness…. For man himself is but a thought pervading the ocean of mind."

Whether or not lie remembered these stammering yet pregnant words from the outer world now left behind, the truth they shadowed forth rose up and took him … and so he flowed across the mountains like a thing of wind and cloud, and so at length came up with the stragglers of that mighty herd of Urwelt life. He joined them in a river-bed of those ancient valleys. They welcomed him and took him to themselves.

* * * * *

For the particular stratum, as it were, of the Earth's enormous Collective Consciousness to which he belonged, or rather that part and corner in which he was first at home, lay with these lesser ancient forms. Although aware of far mightier expressions of her life, he could not yet readily perceive or join them. And this was easily comprehensible by the analogy of his own smaller consciousness. Did his own mind hold thoughts of various kinds that could not readily mingle? His thoughts of play and frolic, for instance, could not combine with the august and graver sentiments of awe and worship, though both could dwell together in the same heart. And here apparently, as yet, he only touched that frolicsome fringe of consciousness that knew these wild and playful lesser forms. Thus, while he was aware of other more powerful figures of wonder all about him, he never quite achieved their full recognition. The ordered, deeper strata of her Consciousness to which they belonged still lay beyond him.

Yet everywhere he fringed them. They haunted the entire world. They brooded hugely with a kind of deep magnificence that was like the slow brooding of the Seasons; they rose, looming and splendid, through the air and sky, proud, strong, and tragic. For, standing aloof from all the rest, in isolation, like dreams in a poet's mind, too potent for expression, they thus knew tragedy—the tragedy of long neglect and loneliness.

Seated on peak and ridge, rising beyond the summits in the clouds, filling the valleys, spread over watercourse and forest, they passed their life of lonely majesty—apart, their splendor too remote for him as yet to share. Long since had Earth withdrawn them from the hearts of men. Her lesser children knew them no more. But still through the deep recesses of her further consciousness they thundered and were glad… though few might hear that thunder, share that awful joy….

Even the Irishman—who in ordinary life had felt instinctively that worship, which is close to love and so to the union that love brings—even he, in this new-found freedom, only partially discerned their presences. He felt them now, these stately Powers men once called the gods but felt them from a distance; and from a distance, too, they saw and watched him come. He knew their gorgeous forms half dimmed by a remote and veiled enchantment; knew that they reared aloft like ancient towers, ruined by neglect and ignorance, starved and lonely, but still hauntingly splendid and engaging, still terrifically alive. And it seemed to him that sometimes their awful eyes flashed with the sunshine over slope and valley, and that wherever they rested flowers sprang to life.

Their closeness sometimes swept him like a storm, and then the entire herd with which he mingled would stand abruptly still, caught by a wave of awe and wonder. The host of them stood still upon the grass, their frolic held a moment, their voices hushed, only deep panting audible and the soft shuffling of their hoofs among the flowers. They bowed their splendid heads and waited—while a god went past them…. And through himself, as witness of the passage, a soft, majestic power also swept. With the lift of a hurricane, yet with the gentleness of dew, he felt the noblest in himself irresistibly evoked. It was gone again as soon as come. It passed. But it left him charged with a regal confidence and joy. As in the mountains a shower of snow picks out the highest peaks in white, tracing its course and pattern over the entire range, so in himself he knew the highest powers—aspirations, yearnings, hopes—raised into shining, white activity, and by these quickened splendors of his soul could recognize the nature of the god who came so close.

* * * * *

And, keeping mostly to the river-beds, they splashed in the torrents, played and leaped and cantered. From the openings of many a moist cave others came to join them. Below a certain level, though, they never went; the forests knew them not; they loved the open, windy heights. They turned and circulated as by a common consent, wheeling suddenly together as if a single desire actuated the entire mass. One instinct spread, as it were, among the lot, shared instantly, conveying to each at once the general impulse. Their movements in this were like those of birds whose flight in coveys obeys the order of a collective consciousness of which each single one is an item—expressions of one single Bird-Idea behind, distributed through all.

And O'Malley without questioning or hesitation obeyed, while yet he was free to do as he wished alone. To do as they did was the greatest pleasure, that was all.

For sometimes with two of them, one fully-formed, the other of lesser mold—he flew on little journeys of his own. These two seemed nearer to him than the rest. He felt he knew them and had been with them before. Their big brown eyes continually sought his own with pleasure. It almost seemed as if they had all three been separated long away from one another and had at last returned. No definite memory of the interval came back, however; the sea, the steamer, and the journey's incidents all had faded—part of that world of lesser insignificant dream where they had happened. But these two kept close to him; they ran and danced together....

The time that passed included many dawns and nights and also many noons of splendor. It all seemed endless, perfect, and serene. That anything could finish here did not once occur to him. Complete things cannot finish. He passed through seas and gulfs of glorious existence. For the strange thing was that while he only remembered afterwards the motion, play, and laughter, he yet had these other glimpses here and there of some ordered and progressive life existing just beyond. It lay hidden deeper within. He skimmed its surface; but something prevented his knowing it fully. And the limitation that held him back belonged, it seemed, to that thin world of trivial dreaming he had left behind. He had not shaken it off entirely. It still obscured his sight.

The scale and manner of this greater life faintly reached him, nothing more. It may be that he only failed to bring back recollection, or it may be that he did not penetrate deeply enough to know. At any rate, he recognized that this sudden occasional passing by of vast deific figures had to do with it, and that all this ocean of Earth's deeper Consciousness was peopled with forms of life that obeyed some splendid system of progressive ordered existence. To be gathered up in this one greater consciousness was not the end.... Rather was it merely the beginning....

Meantime he learned that here, among these lesser thoughts of the great Mother, all the Pantheons of the world had first their origin—the Greek, the Eastern, and the Northern too. Here all the gods that men have ever half divined, still ranged the moods of Her timeless consciousness. Their train of beauty, too, accompanied them.

* * * * *

I cannot half recall the streams of passionate description with which his words clothed these glowing memories of his vision. Great pictures of it haunt the background of my mind, pictures that lie in early mists, framed by the stars and glimmering through some golden, flowered dawn. Besides the huge outlines that stood breathing in the background like dark mountains, there flitted here and there strange dreamy forms of almost impossible beauty, slender as lilies, eyes soft and starry shining through the dusk, hair flying past them like a rain of summer flowers. Nymph-like they moved down all the pathways of the Earth's young mind, singing and radiant, spring blossoms in the Garden of her Consciousness.... And other forms, more vehement and ruder, urged to and fro across the pictures; crowding the movement; some playful and protean; some clothed as with trees, or air, or water; and others dark, remote, and silent, ranging her deeper layers of thought and dream, known rarely to the outer world at all.

The rush and glory of it all is more than my mind can deal with. I gather, though, O'Malley saw no definite forms, but rather knew "forces," powers, aspects of this Soul of Earth, facets she showed in long-forgotten days to men. Certainly, the very infusoria of his imagination were kindled and aflame when he spoke of them. Through the tangled thicket of his ordinary mind there shone this passion of an uncommon loveliness and splendour.

XXXVII

"The hours when the mind is absorbed by beauty are the only hours when we really live, so that the longer we can stay among these things, so much the more is snatched from inevitable time."

—RICHARD JEFFERIES

In the relationship that his everyday mind bore to his present state there lay, moreover, a wealth of pregnant suggestion. The bridge connecting his former "civilized" condition with this cosmic experience was a curious one. That outer, lesser state, it seemed, had known a foretaste sometimes of the greater. And it was hence had come those dreams of a Golden Age that used to haunt him. For he began now to recall the existence of that outer world of men and women, though by means of certain indefinite channels only. And the things he remembered were not what the world calls important. They were moments when he had known—beauty; beauty, however, not of the grandiose sort that holds the crowd, but of so simple and unadvertised a kind that most men overlook it altogether.

He understood now why the thrill had been so wonderful. He saw clearly why those moments of ecstasy he had often felt in Nature used to torture him with an inexpressible yearning that was rather pain than joy. For they were precisely what he now experienced when the viewless figure of a god passed by him. Down there, out there, below—in that cabined lesser state—they had been partial but were now complete. Those moments of worship he had known in woods, among mountains, by the shores of desolate seas, even in a London street, perhaps at the sight of a tree in spring or of a pathway of blue sky between the summer clouds,—these had been, one and all, tentative, partial revelations of the Consciousness of the Soul of Earth he now knew face to face.

These were his only memories of that outer world. Of people, cities, or of civilization apart from these, he had no single remembrance.

* * * * *

Certain of these little partial foretastes now came back to him, like fragments of dream that trouble the waking day.

He remembered, for instance, one definite picture: a hot autumn sun upon a field of stubble where the folded corn-sheaves stood; thistles waving by the hedges; a yellow field of mustard rising up the slope against the sky-line, and beyond a row of peering elms that rustled in the wind. The beauty of the little scene was somehow poignant. He recalled it vividly. It had flamed about him, transfiguring the world; he had trembled, yearning to see more, for just behind it he divined with an exulting passionate worship this gorgeous, splendid Earth-Being with whom at last he now actually moved. In that instant of a simple loveliness her consciousness had fringed his own—had bruised it. He had known it only by the partial channels of sight and smell and hearing, but had felt the greater thing beyond, without being able to explain it. And a portion of what he felt had burst in speech from his lips.

He was there, he remembered, with two persons, a man and woman whose name and face, however, he could not summon, and he recalled that the woman smiled incredulously when he spoke of the exquisite perfume of those folded corn-sheaves in the air. She told him he imagined it. He saw again the pretty woman's smile of incomprehension; he saw the puzzled expression in the eyes of the man; he heard him murmur something prosaic about the soul, about birds, too, and the prospects of killing hundreds later—sport! He even saw the woman picking her way with caution as though the touch of earth could stain or injure her. He especially recalled the silence that had followed on his words that sought to show them—Beauty.... He remembered, too, above all, the sense of loneliness among men that it induced in himself.

But the memory brought him a curious, sharp pain; and turning to that couple who were now his playmates in this Garden of the Earth, he called them with a singing cry and cantered over leagues of flowers, wind, and sunshine before he stopped again. They leaped and danced together, exulting in their spacious Urwelt freedom ... want of comprehension no longer possible.

* * * * *

The memory fled away. He shook himself free of it. Then others came in its place, another and another, not all with people, blind, deaf, and unreceptive, yet all of "common," simple scenes of beauty when something vast had surged upon him and broken through the barriers that stand between the heart and Nature. Such curious little scenes they were. In most of them he had evidently been alone. But one and all had touched his soul with a foretaste of this same nameless ecstasy that now he knew completely. In everyone the Consciousness of the Earth had "bruised" his own.

Utterly simple they had been, one and all, these partial moments of blinding beauty in that lesser, outer world:—A big, brown, clumsy bee he saw, blundering into the petals of a wildflower on which the dew lay sparkling.... A wisp of colored cloud driving loosely across the hills, dropping a purple shadow.... Deep, waving grass, plunging and shaking in the wind that drew out its underworld of blue and silver over the whole spread surface of a field.... A daisy closed for the night upon the lawn, eyes tightly shut, hands folded.... A south wind whispering through larches.... The pattering of summer rain upon young oak leaves in the dawn.... Fingers of long blue distance upon dreamy woods.... Anemones shaking their pale and starry little faces in the wind.... The columned stillness of a pine-wood in the dusk.... Young birch trees mid the velvet gloom of firs.... The new moon setting in a cloud of stars.... The hush of stars in many a summer night.... Sheep grazing idly down a sunbaked hill.... A path of moonlight on a lake.... A little wind through bare and wintry woods.... Oh! he recalled the wonder, loveliness, and passion of a thousand more!

They thronged and passed, and thronged again, crowding one another:—all golden moments of revelation when he had caught glimpses of the Earth, and her greater Moods had swept him up into herself. Moments in which a god had passed....

These were his only memories of that outer world he had left behind: flashes of simple beauty.

Was thus the thrill of beauty then explained? Was loveliness, as men know it, a revelation of the Earth-Soul behind? And were the blinding flash, the dazzling wonder, and the dream men seek to render permanent in music, color, line and language, a vision of her nakedness? Down there, the poets and those simple enough of heart to stand close to Nature, could catch these whispered fragments of the enormous message, told as in secret; but now, against her very heart he heard the thunder of the thing completely. Now, in the glory of all naked bodily forms,—of women, men and children, of swift animals, of flowers, trees, and running water, of mountains and of seas,—he understood these partial revelations of the great Earth-Soul that bore them, gave them life. For one and all there were channels for her loveliness. He saw the beauty of the "natural" instincts, the passion of motherhood and fatherhood—Earth's seeking to project herself in endless forms and variety. He understood why love increased the heart and made it feel at one with all the world.

* * * * *

Moreover, in some amazing fashion he was aware that others from that outer world beside himself had access here, and that from this Garden of the Earth's deep central personality came all the inspiration known to men. He divined that others were even now drawing upon it like himself. The thoughts of the poets went past him like thin flames; the dreams of millions—mute, inexpressible yearnings like those he had himself once known—streamed by in pale white light, to shoot forward with a little nesting rush into some great Figure ... and then return in double volume to the dreaming heart whence first they issued. Shadows, too, he saw, by myriads—faint, feeble groping's of men and women seeking it eagerly, yet hardly knowing what they sought; but, above all, long, singing, beautiful tongues of colored flame that were the instincts of divining children and of the pure in heart. These came in rippling floods unerringly to their goal, lingered for long periods before returning. And all, he knew, were currents of the great Earth Life, moods, thoughts, dreams—expressions of her various Consciousness with which she mothered, fed, and blessed all whom it was possible to reach. Their passionate yearning, their worship, made access possible. Along the tenderest portions of her personality these latter came, as by a spread network of infinitely delicate filaments that extended from herself, deliciously inviting....

* * * * *

The thing, however, that remained with him long after his return to the normal state of lesser consciousness was the memory of those blinding moments when a god went past him, or, as he phrased it in another way, when he caught glimpses of the Earth—naked. For these were instantaneous flashes of a gleaming whiteness, a dazzling and supreme loveliness that staggered thought and arrested feeling, while yet of a radiant simplicity that brought—for a second at least—a measure of comprehension.

He then knew not mere partial projections. He saw beyond—deep down into the flaming center that gave them birth. The blending of his being with the Cosmic Consciousness was complete enough for this. He describes it as a spectacle of sheer glory, stupendous, even terrifying. The refulgent majesty of it utterly possessed him. The shock of its magnificence came, moreover, upon his entire being, and was not really of course a "sight" at all. The message came not through any small division of a single sense. With a massed yet soaring power it shook him free of all known categories. He then fringed a region of yet greater being wherein he tasted for a moment some secret comprehension of a true "divinity." The deliverance into ecstasy was complete.

In these flashing moments, when a second seemed a thousand years, he further understood the splendor of the stage beyond. Earth in her turn was but a Mood in the Consciousness of the Universe, that Universe again was mothered by another vaster one ... and the total that included them all was not the gods—but God.

XXXVIII

The litter of disordered notebooks filled to the covers with fragments of such beauty that they almost seem to burn with a light of their own, lies at this moment before me on my desk. I still hear the rushing torrent of his language across the spotted table-cloth in that dark restaurant corner. But the incoherence seems only to increase with my best efforts to combine the two.

"Go home and dream it," as he said at last when I ventured a question here and there toward the end of the recital. "You'll see it best that way—in sleep. Get clear away from *me*, and my surface physical consciousness. Perhaps it will come to you then."

There remains, however, to record the manner of his exit from that great Garden of the Earth's fair youth. And he tells it more simply. Or, perhaps, it is that I understand it better.

For suddenly, in the midst of all the joy and splendor that he tasted, there came unbidden a strengthening of the tie that held him to his "outer," lesser state. A wave of pity and compassion surged in upon him from the depths. He saw the struggling millions in the prisons and cages civilization builds. He felt *with* them. No happiness, he understood, could be complete that did not also include them all; and—he longed to tell them. The thought and the desire tore across him burningly.

"If only I can get this back to them!" passed through him, like a flame. "I'll save the world by bringing it again to simple things! I've only got to tell it, and all will understand at once—and follow!"

And with the birth of the desire there ran a deep convulsive sound like music through the greater Consciousness that held him close. Those Moods that were the gods, thronged gloriously about him, almost pressing forwards into actual sight.... He might have lingered where he was for centuries, or forever; but this thought pulled him back—the desire to share his knowledge with the world, the passion to heal and save and rescue.

And instantly, in the twinkling of an eyelid, the Urwelt closed its gates of horn and ivory behind him. An immense dark shutter dropped noiselessly with a speed of lightning across his mind. He stood without....

He found himself near the tumbled-down stone huts of a hamlet that he recognized. He staggered, rubbed his eyes, and stared. A forest of beech trees shook below him in a violent wind. He saw the branches tossing. A Caucasian saddle-horse beside him nosed a sack that spilt its flour on the ground at his feet, he heard the animal's noisy breathing; he noted the sliding movement of the spilt flour before it finally settled; and some fifty yards beyond him, down the slopes, he saw a human figure—running.

It was his Georgian guide. The man, half stooping, caught the woolen bashlik that had fallen from his head.

O'Malley watched the man complete the gesture. Still running, he replaced the cap upon his head.

And coming up to his ears upon the wind were the words of a broken French sentence that he also recognized. Disjointed by terror, it completed an interrupted phrase:—

"... one of them is close upon us. Hide your eyes! Save yourself!. They come from the mountains. They are old as the stones ... run...!"

No other living being was in sight.

XXXIX

The extraordinary abruptness of the transition produced no bewilderment, it seems. Realizing that without Rostom he would be in a position of helplessness that might be serious, the Irishman put his hands to his lips and called out with authority to the running figure of his frightened guide. He shouted to him to stop.

"There is nothing to fear. Come back! Are you afraid of a gust of wind?"

And in his face and voice, perhaps too in his manner, was something he had brought back from the vision, for the man stopped at once in his headlong course, paused a moment to stare and question, and then, though still looking over his shoulder and making occasional signs of his religion, came slowly back to his employer's side again.

"It has passed," said O'Malley in a voice that seemed to crumble in his mouth. "It is gone again into the mountains whence it came. We are safe. With me," he added, not without a secret sense of humor stirring in him, "you will always be safe. I can protect both." He felt as normal as a British officer giving orders to his soldiers. And the Georgian slowly recovered his composure, yet for a long time keeping close to the other's side.

The transition, thus, had been as sudden and complete as anything well could be. O'Malley described it as the instantaneous dropping of a shutter across his mind. The entire vision had lasted but a fraction of a second, and in a fraction of a second, too, he had returned to his state of everyday lesser consciousness. That blending with the Earth's great Consciousness was but a flashing glimpse after all. The extension of personality had been momentary.

So absolute, moreover, was the return that at first, remembering nothing, he took up life again exactly where he had left it. The guide completed the gesture and the sentence which the vision had interrupted, and O'Malley, similarly, resumed his own thread of thought and action.

Only a hint remained. That, and a curious sense of interval, alone were left to witness this flash of an immense vision,—of cosmic consciousness—that apparently had filled so many days and nights.

"It was like waking suddenly in the night out of deep sleep," he said; "not of one's own accord, or gradually, but as when someone shakes you out of slumber and you are wide awake at once. You have been dreaming vigorously—thick, lively, crowded dreams, and they all vanish on the instant. You catch the tail-end of the procession just as it's diving out of sight. In less than a second all is gone."

For this was the hint that remained. He caught the flying tail-end of the vision. He knew he *had* seen something. But, for the moment, that was all.

Then, by degrees and afterwards, the details re-emerged. In the days that followed, while with Rostom he completed the journey already planned, the deeper consciousness gave back its memory piece by piece; and piece by piece he set it down in notebooks as best he could. The memory was on deposit deep within him, and at intervals he tapped it. Hence, of course, is due the confused and fragmentary character of those bewildering entries; hence, at the same time, too, their truth and value. For here was no imaginative dream concocted in a mood of high invention. The parts were disjointed, incomplete, just as they came. The lesser consciousness, it seems, could not contain the thing complete; nor to the last, I judge, did he ever know complete recapture.

* * * * *

They wandered for two weeks and more about the mountains, meeting various adventure by the way, reported duly in his letters of travel. But these concerned the outer man and have no proper place in this strange record … and by the middle of July he found himself once more in—civilization. At Michaelevo, he said good-bye to Rostom and took the train.

And it was with the return to the conditions of modern life that the reaction set in and stirred the deeper layers of consciousness to reproduce their store of magic. For this return to what seemed the paltry activities of an age of machinery, physical luxury, and superficial contrivances brought him a sense of pain that was acute and trenchant, more—a deep and poignant sense of loss. The yearnings, no longer satisfied, began again to reassert themselves. It was not the actual things the world seemed so busy about that pained him, but rather the point of view from which the world approached them—those that it deemed with one consent "important," and those, with rare exceptions, it obviously deemed worth no consideration at all and ignored. For him these values stood exactly reversed.

The Vision then came back to him, rose from the depths, blinded his eyes with maddening beauty, sang in his ears, possessed his heart and mind. He burned to tell it. The world of tired, restless men, he felt, must equally burn to hear it. Some vision of a simple life lived close to Nature came before his inner eye as the remedy for the vast disease of restless self-seeking of the age, the medicine that should cure the entire world. A return to Nature was the first step toward the great Deliverance men sought. And, most of all, he yearned to tell it first to Heinrich Stahl.

To hear him talk about it, as he talked perhaps to me alone, was genuinely pathetic, for here, in Terence O'Malley, I thought to see the essential futility of all dreamers nakedly revealed. His vision was so fine, sincere, and noble; his difficulty in imparting it so painful; and its marriage with practical action so ludicrously impracticable. At any rate that combination of vision and action, called sometimes genius, which can shake the world, assuredly was not his. For his was no constructive mind; he was not "intellectual"; he *saw*, but with the heart; he could not build. To plan a new Utopia was as impossible to him as to shape even in words the splendor he had known and lived. Bricks and straw could only smother him before he laid what most would deem foundations.

At first, too, in those days while waiting for the steamer in Batoum, he kept strangely silent. Even in his own thoughts was silence. He could not speak of what he knew. Even paper refused it. But all the time this glorious, winged thing, that yet was simple as the sunlight or the rain, went by his side, while his soul knew the relief of some divine, proud utterance that, he felt, could never know complete confession in speech or writing. Later he stammered over it—to his notebooks and to me, and partially also to Dr. Stahl. But at first it dwelt alone and hidden, contained in this deep silence.

The days of waiting he filled with walks about the streets, watching the world with new eyes. He took the Russian steamer to Poti and tramped with a knapsack up the Tchourokh gorge beyond Bourtchka, regardless of the Turkish gypsies and encampments of wild peoples on the banks. The sense of personal danger was impossible; he felt the whole world kin. That sense protected him. Pistol and cartridges lay in his bag, forgotten at the hotel.

Delight and pain lay oddly mingled in him. The pain he recognized of old, but this great radiant happiness was new. The nightmare of modern cheap-jack life was all explained; unjustified, of course, as he had always dimly felt, symptom of deep disorder; all due, this feverish, external business, to an odd misunderstanding with the Earth. Humanity had somehow quarreled with her, claiming an independence that could not really last. For her the centuries of this estrangement were but a little thing perhaps—a moment or two in that huge life which counted a million years to lay a narrow bed of chalk. They would come back in time. Meanwhile she ever called. A few, perhaps, already dreamed of return. Movements, he had heard, were afoot—a tentative endeavor here and there. They heard, these few, the splendid whisper that, sweetly calling, ever passed about the world.

For her voice in the last resort was more potent than all others—an enchantment that never wholly faded; men had but temporarily left her mighty sides and gone astray, eating of trees of knowledge that brought them deceptive illusions of a mad self-intoxication; fallen away into the pains of separateness and death. Loss of direction and central control was the result; the Babel of many tongues so clumsily invented, by which all turned one against another. Insubordinate, artificial centers had assumed disastrous command. Each struggled for himself against his neighbors. Even religions fought to the blood. A single sect could damn the rest of humanity, yet in the same breath sing complaisantly of its own Heaven.

Meanwhile She smiled in love and patience, letting them learn their lesson; meanwhile She watched and waited while, like foolish children, they toiled and sweated after futile transient things that brought no single letter of content. She let them coin their millions from her fairest thoughts, the gold and silver in her veins; and let them turn it into engines of destruction, knowing that each "life lost," returned into her arms and heart, crying with the pain of its wayward foolishness, the lesson learned; She watched their tears and struggling just outside the open nursery door, knowing they must at length return for food; and while thus waiting, watching, She heard all prayers that reached her; She answered them with love and forgiveness ever ready; and to the few who realized their folly—naughtiness, perhaps, at worst it was—this side of "death," She brought full measure of peace and joy and beauty.

Not permanently could they hurt themselves, for evil was but distance from her side, the ignorance of those who had wandered furthest into the little dark labyrinth of a separated self. The "intellect" they were so proud of had misled them.

And sometimes, here and there across the ages, with a glory that refused utterly to be denied, She thundered forth her old sweet message of deliverance. Through poet, priest, or child she called her children home. The summons rang like magic across the wastes of this dreary separated existence. Some heard and listened, some turned back, some wondered and were strangely thrilled; some, thinking it too simple to be true, were puzzled by the yearning and the tears and went back to seek for a more difficult way; while most, denying the secret glory in their hearts, sought to persuade themselves they loved the strife and hurrying fever best.

At other times, again, she chose quite different ways, and sent the amazing message in a flower, a breath of evening air, a shell upon the shore; though oftenest, perhaps, it hid in a strain of music, a patch of color on the sea or hills, a rustle of branches in a little twilight wind, a whisper in the dusk or in the dawn. He remembered his own first visions of it....

Only never could the summons come to her children through the intellect, for this it was that led them first away. Her message enters ever by the heart.

The simple life! He smiled as he thought of the bald Utopias here and there devised by men, for he had seen a truth whose brilliance smote his eyes too dazzlingly to permit of the smallest corner of darkness. Remote, no doubt, in time that day when the lion shall lie down with the lamb and men shall live together in peace and gentleness; when the inner life shall be admitted as the Reality, strife, gain, and loss unknown because possessions undesired, and petty selfhood merged in the larger life—remote, of course, yet surely not impossible. He had seen the Face of Nature, heard her Call, tasted her joy and peace; and the rest of the tired world might do the same. It only waited to be shown the way. The truth he now saw so dazzling was that all who heard the call might know it for themselves at once, cuirassed with shining love that makes the whole world kin, the Earth a mother literally divine. Each soul might thus provide a channel along which the summons home should pass across the world. To live with Nature and share her greater consciousness, *en route* for states yet greater, nearer to the eternal home—this was the beginning of the truth, the life, the way.

He saw "religion" all explained: and those hard sayings that make men turn away:—the imagined dread of losing life to find it; the counsel of perfection that the neighbor shall be loved as self; the fancied injury and outrage that made it hard for rich men to enter the kingdom. Of these, as of a hundred other sayings, he saw the necessary truth. It all seemed easy now. The world would see it with him; it must; it could not help itself. Simplicity as of a little child, and selflessness as of the mystic—these were the splendid clues.

Death and the grave, indeed, had lost their victory. For in the stages of wider consciousness beyond this transient physical phase he saw all loved ones joined and safe, as separate words upgathered each to each in the parent sentence that explains them, the sentence in the paragraph, the paragraph in the whole grand story all achieved—and so at length into the eternal library of God that consummates the whole.

He saw the glorious series, timeless and serene, advancing to the climax, and somehow understood that individuality at each stage was never lost but rather extended and magnified. Love of the Earth, life close to Nature, and denial of so-called civilization was the first step upwards. In the Simple Life, in this return to Nature, lay the opening of the little path that climbed to the stars and heaven.

XL

At the end of the week the little steamer dropped her anchor in the harbor and the Irishman booked his passage home. He was standing on the wharf to watch the unloading when a hand tapped him on the shoulder, and he heard a well-known voice. His heart leaped with pleasure. There were no preliminaries between these two.

"I am glad to see you safe. You did not find your friend, then?"

O'Malley looked at the bronzed face beside him, noted the ragged tobacco-stained beard, and saw the look of genuine welcome in the twinkling brown eyes. He watched him lift his cap and mop that familiar dome of bald head.

"I'm safe," was all he answered, "because I found him."

For a moment Dr. Stahl looked puzzled. He dropped the hand he held so tightly and led him down the wharf.

"We'll get out of this devilish sun," he said, leading the way among the tangle of merchandise and bales, "it's enough to boil our brains." They passed through the crowd of swarthy, dripping Turks, Georgians, Persians, and Armenians who labored half naked in the heat, and moved toward the town. A Russian gunboat lay in the Bay, side by side with freight and passenger vessels. An oil-tank steamer took on cargo. The scene was drenched in sunshine. The Black Sea gleamed like molten metal. Beyond, the wooded spurs of the Caucasus climbed through haze into cloudless blue.

"It's beautiful," remarked the German, pointing to the distant coastline, "but hardly with the beauty of those Grecian Isles we passed together. Eh?" He watched him closely. "You're coming back on our steamer?" he asked in the same breath.

"It's beautiful," O'Malley answered ignoring the question, "because it lives. But there is dust upon its outer loveliness, dust that has gathered through long ages of neglect, dust that I would sweep away—I've learnt how to do it. He taught me."

Stahl did not even look at him, though the words were wild enough. He walked at his side in silence. Perhaps he partly understood. For this first link with the outer world of appearances was difficult for him to pick up. The person of Stahl, thick-coated with the civilization whence he came, had brought it, and out of the ocean of glorious vision in his soul, O'Malley took at random the first phrases he could find.

"Yes, I've booked a passage on your steamer," he added presently, remembering the question. It did not seem strange to him that his companion ignored both clues he offered. He knew the man too well for that. It was only that he waited for more before he spoke.

They went to the little table outside the hotel pavement where several weeks ago they had drunk Kakhetian wine together and talked of deeper things. The German called for a bottle, mineral water, ice, and cigarettes. And while they sipped the cooling golden liquid, hats off and coats on the backs of their chairs, Stahl gave him the news of the world of men and events that had transpired meanwhile. O'Malley listened vaguely as he smoked. It seemed remote, unreal, almost fantastic, this long string of ugly, frantic happenings, all symptoms of some disordered state that was like illness. The scream of politics, the roar and rattle of flying-machines, financial crashes, furious labor upheavals, rumors of war, the death of kings and magnates, awful accidents and strange turmoil in enormous cities. Details of some sad prison life, it almost seemed, pain and distress and strife the note that bound them all together. Men were mastered by these things instead of mastering them. These unimportant things they thought would make them free only imprisoned them.

They lunched there at the little table in the shade, and in turn the Irishman gave an outline of his travels. Stahl had asked for it and listened attentively. The pictures interested him.

"You've done your letters for the papers," he questioned him, "and now, perhaps, you'll write a book as well?"

"Something may force its way out—come blundering, thundering out in fragments, yes."

"You mean you'd rather not—?"

"I mean it's all too big and overwhelming. He showed me such blinding splendors. I might tell it, but as to writing—!" He shrugged his shoulders.

And this time Dr. Stahl ignored no longer. He took him up. But not with any expected words or questions. He merely said, "My friend, there's something that I have to tell you—or, rather, I should say, to show you." He looked most keenly at him, and in the old familiar way he placed a hand upon his shoulder. His voice grew soft. "It may upset you; it may unsettle—prove a shock perhaps. But if you are prepared, we'll go—"

"What kind of shock?" O'Malley asked, startled a moment by the gravity of manner.

"The shock of death," was the answer, gently spoken.

The Irishman only knew a swift rush of joy and wonder as he heard it.

"But there is no such thing!" he cried, almost with laughter. "He taught me that above all else. There is no death!"

"There is 'going away,' though," came the rejoinder, spoken low; "there is earth to earth and dust to dust—"

"That's of the body—!"

"That's of the body, yes," the older man repeated darkly.

"There is only 'going home,' escape and freedom. I tell you there's only that. It's nothing but joy and splendor when you really understand."

But Dr. Stahl made no immediate answer, nor any comment. He paid the bill and led him down the street. They took the shady side. Passing beyond the skirts of the town they walked in silence. The barracks where the soldiers sang, the railway line to Tiflis and Baku, the dome and minarets of the church, were left behind in turn, and presently they reached the hot, straight dusty road that fringed the sea. They heard the crashing of the little waves and saw the foam creamily white against the dark grey pebbles of the beach.

And when they reached a small enclosure where thin trees were planted among sparse grass all brown and withered by the sun, they paused, and Stahl pointed to a mound, marked at either end by rough stone boulder. A date was on it, but no name. O'Malley calculated the difference between the Russian Calendar and the one he was accustomed to. Stahl checked him.

"The fifteenth of June," the German said.

"The fifteenth of June, yes," said O'Malley very slowly, but with wonder and excitement in his heart. "That was the day that Rostom tried to run away—the day I saw him come to me from the trees—the day we started off together … to the Garden…."

He turned to his companion questioningly. For a moment the rush of memory was quite bewildering.

"He never left Batoum at all, you see," Stahl continued, without looking up. "He went straight to the hospital the day we came into port. I was summoned to him in the night—that last night while you slept so deeply. His old strange fever was upon him then, and I took him ashore before the other passengers were astir. I brought him to the hospital myself. And he never left his bed." He pointed down to the little nameless grave at their feet where a wandering wind from the sea just stirred the grasses. "That was the date on which he died."

"He went away in the early morning," he added in a low voice that held both sadness and sympathy.

"He went home," said the Irishman, a tide of joy rising tumultuously through his heart as he remembered. The secret of that complete and absolute Leadership was out. He understood it all. It had been a spiritual adventure to the last.

Then followed a pause.

In silence they stood there for some minutes. There grew no flowers on that grave, but O'Malley stooped down and picked a strand of the withered grass. He put it carefully between the pages of his notebook; and then, lying flat against the ground where the sunshine fell in a patch of white and burning glory, he pressed his lips to the crumbling soil. He kissed the Earth. Oblivious of Stahl's presence, or at least ignoring it, he worshipped.

And while he did so he heard that little sound he loved so well—which more than any words or music brought peace and joy, because it told his Passion all complete. With his ears close to the earth, he heard it, yet at the same time heard it everywhere. For it came with the falling of the waves upon the shore, through the murmur of the rustling branches overhead, and even across the whispering of the withered grass about him. Deep down in the center of the mothering Earth he heard it too in faintly rising pulse. It was the exquisite little piping on a reed—the ancient fluting of the everlasting Pan....

And when he rose he found that Stahl had turned away and was gazing at the sea, as though he had not noticed.

"Doctor," he cried, yet so softly it was a whisper rather than a call, "I heard it then again; it's everywhere! Oh, tell me that you hear it too!"

Stahl turned and looked at him in silence. There was a moisture in his eyes, and on his face a look of softness that a woman might have worn.

"I've brought it back, you see, I've brought it back. For that's the message—that's the sound and music I must give to all the world. No words, no book can tell it." His hat was off, his eyes were shining, his voice broke with the passion of joy he yearned to share yet knew so little how to impart. "If I can pipe upon the flutes of Pan the millions all will listen, will understand, and—follow. Tell me, oh, tell me, that you heard it too!"

"My friend, my dear young friend," the German murmured in a voice of real tenderness, "you heard it truly—but you heard it in your heart. Few hear the Pipes of Pan as you do. Few care to listen. Today the world is full of other sounds that drown it. And even of those who hear," he shrugged his shoulders as he led him away toward the sea,—"how few will care to follow—how fewer still will dare."

And while they lay upon the beach and watched the line of foam against their feet and saw the seagulls curving idly in the blue and shining air, he added underneath his breath—O'Malley hardly caught the murmur of his words so low he murmured them:—

"The simple life is lost forever. It lies asleep in the Golden Age, and only those who sleep and dream can ever find it. If you would keep your joy, dream on, my friend! Dream on but dream alone!"

XLI

Summer blazed everywhere and the sea lay like a blue pool of melted sky and sunshine. The summits of the Caucasus soon faded to the east and north, and to the south the wooded hills of the Black Sea coast accompanied the ship in a line of wavy blue that joined the water and the sky indistinguishably.

The first-class passengers were few; O'Malley hardly noticed their existence even. An American engineer, building a railway in Turkey, came on board at Trebizond; there were one or two light women on their way home from Baku, and the attaché of a foreign embassy from Teheran. But the Irishman felt more in touch with the hundred peasant-folk who joined the ship at Ineboli from the interior of Asia Minor and were bound as third-class emigrants for Marseilles and far America. Dark-skinned, wild-eyed, ragged, very dirty, they had never seen the sea before, and the sight of a porpoise held them spellbound. They lived on the after-deck, mostly cooking their own food, the women and children sleeping beneath a large tarpaulin that the sailors stretched for them across the width of deck. At night they played their pipes and danced, singing, shouting, and waving their arms—always the same tune over and over again.

O'Malley watched them for hours together. He also watched the engineer, the over-dressed women, the attaché. He understood the difference between them as he had never understood it before. He understood the difficulty of his task as well. How in the world could he ever explain a single syllable of his message to these latter or waken in them the faintest echo of desire to know and listen. The peasants, though all unconscious of the blinding glory at their elbows, stood far nearer to the truth.

"Been further east, I suppose?" the engineer observed, one afternoon as the steamer lay off Broussa, taking on a little extra cargo of walnut logs. He looked admiringly at the Irishman's bronzed skin. "Take a better sun than this to put that on!"

He laughed in his breezy, vigorous way, and the other laughed with him. Previous conversations had already paved the way to a traveler's friendship, and the American had taken to him.

"Up in the mountains," he replied, "camping out and sleeping in the sun did it."

"The Caucasus! Ah, I'd like to get up there myself a bit. I'm told they're a wonderful thing in the mountain line."

Scenery for him was evidently a commercial commodity, or it was nothing. It was the most up-to-date nation in the world that spoke—

in the van of civilization—representing the last word in progress due to triumph over Nature.

O'Malley said he had never seen anything like them. He described the trees, the flowers, the tribes, the scenery in general; he dwelt upon the vast uncultivated spaces, the amazing fruitfulness of the soil, the gorgeous beauty above all. "I'd like to get the overcrowded cities of England and Europe spread all over it," he said with enthusiasm. "There is room for thousands there to lead a simple life close to Nature, in health and peace and happiness. Even your tired millionaires could escape their restless, feverish worries, lay down their weary burden of possessions, and enjoy the earth at last. The poor would cease to be with us; life become true and beautiful again—" He let it pour out of him, building the scaffolding of his dream before him in the air and filling it in with beauty.

The American listened in patience, watching the walnut logs being towed through the water to the side of the ship. From time to time, he spat on them or into the sea. He let the beauty go completely past him.

"Great idea, that!" he interrupted at length. "You're interested, I see, in socialism and communistic schemes. There's money in them somewhere right enough, if a man only could hit the right note at the first go off. Take a bit of doing, though!"

One of the women from Baku came up and leaned upon the rails a little beyond them. The sickly odor of artificial scent wafted down. The attaché strolled along the deck and ogled her.

"Get a few of that sort to draw the millionaires in, eh?" he added vulgarly.

"Even those would come, yes," said the Irishman softly, realizing for the first time within his memory that his gorge did not rise, "for they too would change, grow clean and sweet and beautiful."

The engineer looked sharply into his face, uncertain whether he had not missed a clever witticism of his own kind. But O'Malley did not meet his glance. His eyes were far away upon the snowy summit of Olympus where a flock of fleecy clouds hung hovering like the hair of the eternal gods.

"They say there's timber going to waste that you could get to the coast merely for the cost of drawing it—Caucasian walnut, too, to burn," the other continued, getting on to safer ground, "and labor's dirt cheap. There's every sort of mineral too God ever made. You could build light railways and run the show by electricity. And water-power for the asking. You'd have to get a Concession from Russia first though," he added, spitting down upon a huge floating log in the clear sea underneath, "and Russia's got palms that want a lot of greasing. I guess the natives, too, would take a bit of managing."

The woman beyond had shifted several feet nearer, and after a pause the Irishman found no words to fill, his companion turned to address a remark to her. O'Malley took the opening and moved away.

"Here's my card, anyway," the American added, handing him an over-printed bit of large pasteboard from a fat pocket-book that bore his name and address in silver on the outside. "If you develop the scheme and want a bit of money, count me in."

He went to the other side of the vessel and watched the peasants on the lower deck. Their dirt seemed nothing by comparison. It was only on their clothes and bodies. The odor of this unwashed humanity was almost sweet and wholesome. It cleansed the sickly taint of that other scent from his palate; it washed his mind of thoughts as well.

He stood there long in dreaming silence, while the sunlight on Olympus turned from gold to rose, and the sea took on the colors of the fading sky. He watched a dark Kurd baby sliding down the tarpaulin. A kitten was playing with a loose end of rope too heavy for it to move. Further off a huge fellow with bared chest and the hands of a colossus sat on a pile of canvas playing softly on his wooden pipes. The dark hair fell across his eyes, and a group of women listened idly while they busied themselves with the cooking of the evening meal. Immediately beneath him a splendid-eyed young woman crammed a baby to her naked breast. The kitten left the rope and played with the tassel of her scarlet shawl.

And as he heard those pipes and watched the grave, untamed, strong faces of those wild peasant men and women, he understood that low though they might be in scale of evolution, there was yet absent from them the touch of that deteriorating something which civilization painted into those other countenances. But whether the word he sought was degradation or whether it was shame, he could not tell. In all they did, the way they moved, their dignity and independence, there was this something, he felt, that bordered on being impressive. Their wants were few, their worldly possessions in a bundle, yet they had this thing that set them in a place apart, if not above, these others:—beyond that simpering attaché for all his worldly diplomacy, that engineer with brains and skill, those painted women with their clever playing upon the feelings and desires of their kind. There was this difference that set the ragged dirty crew in a proud and quiet atmosphere that made them seem almost distinguished by comparison, and certainly more desirable. Rough and untutored though they doubtless were, they still possessed unspoiled that deeper and more elemental nature that bound them closer to the Earth. It needed training, guidance, purifying; yes; but, in the last resort, was it not of greater spiritual significance and value than the mode of comparatively recently-developed reason by which Civilization had produced these other types?

He watched them long. The sun sank out of sight, the sea turned dark, ten thousand stars shone softly in the sky, and while the steamer swung about and made for peaked Andros and the coast of Greece, he still stood on in reverie and wonder. The wings of his great Dream stirred mightily … and he saw pale millions of men and women trooping through the gates of horn and ivory into that Garden where they should find peace and happiness in clean simplicity close to the Earth….

XLII

There followed four days then of sea, Greece left behind, Messina and the Lipari Islands past; and the blue outline of Sardinia and Corsica began to keep pace with them as they neared the narrow straits of Bonifacio between them. The passengers came up to watch the rocky desolate shores slip by so close, and Captain Burgenfelder was on the bridge.

Grey-headed rocks rose everywhere close about the ship; overhead the seagulls cried and circled; no vegetation was visible on either shore, no houses, no abode of man—nothing but the lighthouses, then miles of deserted rock dressed in those splendors of the sun's good-night. The dinner-gong had sounded but the sight was too magnificent to leave, for the setting sun floated on an emblazoned sea and stared straight against them in level glory down the narrow passage. Unimaginable colors painted sky and wave. The ruddy cliffs of bleak loneliness rose from a bed of flame. Soft airs fanned the cheeks with welcome coolness after the fierce heat of the day. There was a scent of wild honey in the air borne from the purple uplands far, far away.

"I wonder, oh, I wonder, if they realized that a god is passing close...!" the Irishman murmured with a rising of the heart, "and that here is a great mood of the Earth Consciousness inviting them to peace! Or do they merely see a yellow sun that dips beneath a violet sea...?"

The washing of the water past the steamer's sides caught away the rest of the half-whispered words. He remembered that host of many thousand heads that bowed in silence while a god swept by.... It was almost a shock to hear a voice replying close beside him:—

"Come to my cabin when you're ready. My windows open to the west. We can be alone together. We can have there what food we need. You would prefer it perhaps?"

He felt the touch of that sympathetic hand upon his shoulder and bent his head to signify agreement.

For a moment, face to face with that superb sunset, he had known a deep and utter peace in the vast bosom of this greater soul about him. Her consciousness again had bruised and fringed his own. Across that delicately divided threshold the beauty and the power of the gods had poured in a flood into his being. And only there was peace, only there was joy, only there was the death of those ancient yearnings that tortured his little personal and separate existence. The return to the world was aching pain again. The old loneliness that seemed more than he could bear swept icily through him, contracting life and freezing every spring of joy. For in that single instant of return he felt pass into him a loneliness of the whole travailing world, the loneliness of countless centuries, the loneliness of all the races of the Earth who were exiled and had lost the way.

Too deep it lay for words or tears or sighs. The doctor's invitation came most opportunely. And presently in silence he turned his back upon that opal sky of dream from which the sun had gone and walked slowly down the deck toward Stahl's cabin.

"If only I can share it with them," he thought as he went; "if only men will listen, if only they will come. To keep it all to myself, to dream alone, will kill me."

And as he stood before the door it seemed he heard wild rushing through the sky, the tramping of a thousand hoofs, a roaring of the wind, the joy of that free, torrential passage with the Earth. He turned the handle and entered the cozy room where weeks before they held the inquest on the little empty tenement of flesh, remembering how that other figure had once stood where he now stood—part of the sunrise, part of the sea, part of the morning winds.

* * * * *

They had their meal almost in silence, while the glow of sunset filled the cabin through the western row of port-holes, and when it was over Stahl made the coffee as of old and lit the familiar black cigar. Slowly O'Malley's pain and restlessness gave way before the other's soothing quiet. He had never known him before so calm and gentle, so sympathetic, almost tender. The usual sarcasm seemed veiled in sadness; there was no irony in the voice, nor mockery in the eyes.

Then to the Irishman it came suddenly that all these days while he had been lost in dreaming the doctor had kept him as of old under close observation. The completeness of his reverie had concealed from him this steady scrutiny. He had been oblivious to the fact that Stahl had all the time been watching, investigating, keenly examining. Abruptly he now realized it.

And then Stahl spoke. His tone was winning, his manner frank and inviting. But it was the sadness about him that won O'Malley's confidence so wholly.

"I can guess," he said, "something of the dream you've brought with you from those mountains. I can understand—more, perhaps, than you imagine, and I can sympathize—more than you think possible. Tell me about it fully—if you can. I see your heart is very full, and in the telling you will find relief. I am not hostile, as you sometimes feel. Tell me, my dear, young clear-eyed friend. Tell me your vision and your hope. Perhaps I might even help ... for there may be things that I could also tell you in return."

Something in the choice of words, none of which offended; in the atmosphere and setting, no detail of which jarred; and in the degree of balance between utterance and silence his world of inner forces just then knew, combined to make the invitation irresistible. Moreover, he had wanted to tell it all these days. Stahl was already half convinced. Stahl would surely understand and help him. It was the psychological moment for confession. The two men rose in the same moment, Stahl to lock the cabin doors against interruption, O'Malley to set their chairs more closely side by side so that talking should be easiest.

And then without demur or hesitation he opened his heart to this other and let the floodgates of his soul swing wide. He told the vision, and he told the dream; he told his hope as well. And the story of his passion, filled in with pages from those notebooks he ever carried in his pocket, still lasted when the western glow had faded from the sky and the thick-sown stars shone down upon the gliding steamer. The hush of night lay soft upon the world before he finished.

He told the thing completely, much, I imagine, as he told it all to me upon the roof of that apartment building and in the dingy Soho restaurant. He told it without reservations—his life-long yearnings: the explanation brought by the presence of the silent stranger upon the outward voyage: the journey to the Garden: the vision that all life—from gods to flowers, from men to mountains—lay contained in the conscious Being of the Earth, that Beauty was but glimpses of her essential nakedness; and that salvation of the world's disease of modern life was to be found in a general return to the simplicity of Nature close against her mothering heart. He told it all—in words that his passionate joy chose faultlessly.

And Heinrich Stahl in silence listened. He asked no single question. He made no movement in his chair. His black cigar went out before the half of it was smoked. The darkness hid his face impenetrably.

And no one came to interrupt. The murmur of the speeding steamer, and occasional footsteps on the deck as passengers passed to and fro in the cool of the night, were the only sounds that broke the music of that incurable idealist's impassioned story.

XLIII

And then at length there came a change of voice across the cabin. The Irishman had finished. He sank back in the deep leather chair, exhausted physically, but with the exultation of his mighty hope still pouring at full strength through his heart. For he had ventured further than ever before and had spoken of a possible crusade—a crusade that should preach peace and happiness to every living creature.

And Dr. Stahl, in a voice that showed how deeply he was moved, asked quietly:—

"By leading the nations back to Nature, you think they shall advance to Truth at last?"

"With time," was the reply. "The first step lies there:—in changing the direction of the world's activities, changing it from the transient Outer to the eternal Inner. In the simple life, external possessions unnecessary and recognized as vain, the soul would turn within and seek Reality. Only a tiny section of humanity has time to do it now. There is no leisure. Civilization means acquirement for the body: it ought to mean development for the soul. Once sweep aside the trash and rubbish men seek outside themselves today, and the wings of their smothered souls would stir again. Consciousness would expand. Nature would draw them first. They would come to feel the Earth as I did. Self would disappear, and with it this false sense of separateness. The greater consciousness would waken in them. The peace and joy and blessedness of inner growth would fill their lives. But, first, this childish battling to the death for external things must cease, and Civilization stand revealed for the bleak and empty desolate thing it really is. It leads away from God and from the things that are eternal."

The German made no answer; O'Malley ceased to speak; a long silence fell between them. Then, presently, Stahl relighted his cigar, and lapsing into his native tongue—always a sign with him of deepest seriousness—he began to talk.

"You've honored me," he said, "with a great confidence; and I am deeply, deeply grateful. You have told your inmost dream—the thing men find it hardest of all to speak about." He felt in the darkness for his companion's hand and held it tightly for a moment. He made no other comment upon what he had heard. "And in return—in some small way of return," he continued, "I may ask you to listen to something of my own, something of possible interest. No one has ever known it from my lips. Only, in our earlier conversations on the outward voyage, I hinted at it once or twice. I sometimes warned you—"

"I remember. You said he'd 'get' me, 'win' me over—'appropriation' was the word you used."

"I suggested caution, yes; urged you not to let yourself go too completely; told you he represented danger to yourself, and to humanity as it is organized today—"

"And all the rest," put in O'Malley a shade impatiently. "I remember perfectly."

"Because I knew what I was talking about." The doctor's voice came across the darkness somewhat ominously. And then he added in a louder tone, evidently sitting forward as he said it: "For the thing that has happened to yourself as I foresaw it would, had already *almost* happened to me too!"

"To you, doctor, too?" exclaimed the Irishman in the moment's pause that followed.

"I saved myself just in time—by getting rid of the cause."

"You discharged him from the hospital, because you were afraid!" He said it sharply as though are instant of the old resentment had flashed up.

By way of answer Stahl rose from his chair and abruptly turned up the electric lamp upon the desk that faced them across the cabin. Evidently he preferred the light. O'Malley saw that his face was white and very grave. He grasped for the first time that the man was speaking professionally. The truth came driving next behind it—that Stahl regarded him as a patient.

* * * * *

"Please go on, doctor," he said, keenly on the watch. "I'm deeply interested." The wings of his great dream still bore him too far aloft for him to feel more than the merest passing annoyance at his discovery. Resentment had gone too. Sadness and disappointment for an instant touched him perhaps, but momentarily. In the end he felt sure that Stahl would stand at his side, completely won over and convinced.

"You had a similar experience to my own, you say," he urged him. "I am all eagerness and sympathy to hear."

"We'll talk in the open air," the doctor answered, and ringing the bell for the steward to clear away, he drew his companion out to the deserted decks. They moved toward the bows, past the sleeping peasants. The stars were mirrored in a glassy sea and toward the north the hills of Corsica stood faintly outlined in the sky. It was already long after midnight.

"Yes, a similar thing nearly happened to me," he resumed as they settled themselves against a coil of rope where only the murmur of the washing sea could reach them, "and might have happened to others too. Inmates of that big *Krankenhaus* were variously affected. My action, tardy I must admit, saved myself and them."

And the German then told his story as a man might tell of his escape from some grave disaster. In the emphatic sentences of his native language, he told it, congratulating himself all through. The Russian had almost won him over, gained possession of his heart and mind, persuaded him, but in the end had failed—because the other ran away. It was like hearing a man describe an attempt to draw him into Heaven, then boast of his escape. His caution and his judgment, as he put it, saved him, but to the listening Celt it rather seemed that his compromise it was that damned him. The Kingdom of Heaven is hard to enter, for Stahl had possessions not of the wood and metal order, but possessions of the brain and reason he was too proud to forego completely. They kept him out.

With increasing sadness, too, he heard it; for here he realized was the mental attitude of an educated, highly civilized man today—a representative type regarded by the world as highest. It was this he had to face. Moreover, Stahl was more than merely educated, he was understandingly sympathetic, meeting the great dream halfway; seeing in it possibilities; admitting its high beauty, and even sometimes speaking of it with hope and a touch of enthusiasm. Its originator nonetheless he regarded as a reactionary dreamer, an unsettling and disordered influence, a patient, if not even something worse!

Stahl's voice and manner were singular while he told it all, revealing one moment the critical mind that analyzed and judged, and the next an enthusiasm almost of the mystic. Alternately, like the man and woman of those quaint old weather-glasses, each peered out and showed a face, the reins of compromise yet ever seeking to hold them well in leash and drive them together.

Hardly, it seems, had the strange Russian been under his care a week before he passed beneath the sway of his curious personality and experienced the attack of singular emotions upon his heart and mind.

He described at first the man's arrival, telling it with the calm and balanced phrases a doctor uses when speaking merely of a patient who had stirred his interest. He first detailed the method of suggestion he had used to revive the lapsed memory—and its utter failure. Then he passed on to speak of him more generally: but briefly and condensed.

"The man," he said, "was so engaging, so docile, his personality altogether so attractive and mysterious, that I took the case myself instead of delegating it to my assistants. All efforts to trace his past collapsed. It was as if he had drifted into that little hotel out of the night of time. Of madness there was no evidence whatever. The association of ideas in his mind, though limited, was logical and rigid. His health was perfect, barring strange, sudden fever; his vitality tremendous; yet he ate most sparingly and the only food he touched was fruit and milk and vegetables. Meat made him sick, the huge frame shuddered when he saw it. And from all the human beings in the place with whom he came in contact he shrank with a kind of puzzled dismay. With animals, most oddly it seemed, he sought companionship; he would run to the window if a dog barked, or to hear a horse's hoofs; a Persian cat belonging to one of the nurses never left his side, and I have seen the trees in the yard outside his window thick with birds, and even found them in the room and on the sill, flitting about his very person, unafraid and singing.

"With me, as with the attendants, his speech was almost nil—laconic words in various languages, clipped phrases that sometimes-combined Russian, French, or German, other tongues as well.

"But, strangest of all, with animal life he seemed to hold this kind of communication that was Intelligible both to himself and them. Animals certainly were 'aware' of him. It was not speech. It ran in a deep, continuous murmur like a droning, humming sound of wind. I took the hint thus faintly offered. I gave him his freedom in the yards and gardens. The open air and intercourse with natural life was what he craved. The sadness and the air of puzzled fretting then left his face, his eyes grew bright, his whole presentment happier; he ran and laughed and even sang. The fever that had troubled him all vanished. Often myself I took the place of nurse or orderly to watch him, for the man's presence more than interested me: it gave me a renewed sense of life that was exhilarating, invigorating, delightful. And in his appearance, meanwhile, something that was not size or physical measurement, turned—tremendous.

"A part of me that was not mind—a sort of forgotten instinct blindly groping—came of its own accord to regard him as some loose fragment of a natural, cosmic life that had somehow blundered down into a human organism it sought to use....

"And then it was for the first time I recognized the spell he had cast upon me; for, when the Committee decided there was no reason to keep him longer, I urged that he should stay. Making a special plea, I took him as a private patient of my own. I kept him under closer personal observation than ever before. I needed him. Something deep within me, something undivined hitherto, called out into life by his presence, could not do without him. This new craving, breakingly wild and sweet, awoke in my blood and cried for him. His presence nourished it in me. Most insidiously it attacked me. It stirred deep down among the roots of my being. It 'threatened my personality' seems the best way I can put it; for, turning a critical analysis upon it, I discovered that it was an undermining and revolutionary change going steadily forward in my character. Its growth had hitherto been secret. When I first recognized its presence, the thing was already strong. For a long time, it had been building.

"And the change in a word—you will grasp my meaning from the shortest description of essentials—was this: that ambition left me, ordinary desire crumbled, the outer world men value so began to fade."

"And in their place?" cried O'Malley breathlessly, interrupting for the first time.

"Came a rushing, passionate desire to escape from cities and live for beauty and simplicity 'in the wilderness'; to taste the life *he* seemed to know; to go out blindly with him into woods and desolate places and be mixed and blended with the loveliness of Earth and Nature. This was the first thing I knew. It was like an expansion of my normal world—almost an extension of consciousness. It somehow threatened my sense of personal identity. And—it made me hesitate."

O'Malley caught the tremor in his voice. Even in the telling of it the passion plucked at him, for here, as ever, he stood on the border-line of compromise, his heart tempting him toward salvation, his brain and reason tugging at the brakes.

"The sham and emptiness or modern life, its drab vulgarity, the unworthiness of its very ideals stood appallingly revealed before some inner eye just opening. I felt shaken to the core of what had seemed hitherto my very solid and estimable self. How the man thus so powerfully affected me lies beyond all intelligible explanation. To use the obvious catchword 'hypnotism' is to use a toy and stop a leak with paper. For his influence was *unconsciously* exerted. He cast no net of clever, persuasive words about my thought. Out of that deep, strange silence of the man it somehow came. His actions and his simple happiness of face and manner—both in some sense the raw material of speech perhaps—may have operated as potently suggestive agents; but no adequate causes to justify the result, apart from the fantastic theories I have mentioned, have ever yet come within the range of my understanding. I can only give you the undeniable effects."

"Your sense of extended consciousness," asked his listener, "was this continuous, once it had begun?"

"It came in patches," Stahl continued. "My normal, everyday self was thus able to check it. While it derided, commiserated this everyday self, the latter stood in dread of it and even awe. My training, you see, regarded it as symptom of disorder, a beginning of unbalance that might end in insanity, the thin wedge of a dissociation of the personality Morton Prince and others have described."

His speech grew more and more jerky, even incoherent; evidently the material had not even now been fully reduced to order in his mind.

"Among other curious symptoms I soon established that this subtle spreading of my consciousness grew upon me especially during sleep. The business of the day distracted, scattered it. On waking in the morning, as with the physical fatigue that comes toward the closing of the day, it was strongest.

"And so, in order to examine it closely when in fullest manifestation, I came to spend the nights with him. I would creep in while he slept and stay till morning, alternately sleeping and waking myself. I watched the two of us together. I also watched the 'two' in me. And thus, it was made the further strange discovery that the influence he exerted on me was strongest while he slept. It is best described by saying that in his sleep I was conscious that he sought to draw me with him—away somewhere into his own wonderful world—the state or region, that is, where he manifested completely instead of partially as I knew him here. His personality was a channel somewhere out into a living, conscious Nature...."

"Only," interrupted O'Malley, "you felt that to yield and go involved some nameless inner catastrophe, and so resisted?" He chose his phrase with purpose.

"Because I discovered," was the pregnant answer, given steadily while he watched his listener closely through the darkness, "that this desire for escape the man had wakened in me was nothing more or less than the desire to leave the world, to leave the conditions that prevented—

in fact to leave the body. My discontent with modern life had gone as far as that. It was the birth of the suicidal mania."

* * * * *

The pause that followed the words, on the part of Dr. Stahl at any rate, was intentional. O'Malley held his peace. The men shifted their places oil the coil of rope, for both were cramped and stiff with the lengthy session. For a minute or two they leaned over the bulwarks and watched the phosphorescent foam in silence. The blue mountainous shores slipped past in shadowy line against the stars. But when they sat down again their relative positions were not what they had been before. Dr. Stahl had placed himself between his listener and the sea. And O'Malley did not let the manoeuvre escape him. Smiling to himself he noticed it. Just as surely he noticed, too, that the whole recital was being told him with a purpose.

"You really need not be afraid," he could not resist saying. "The idea of escape *that* way has never even come to me at all. And, anyhow, I've far too much on hand first in telling the world my message." He laughed in the silence that took his words, for Stahl said nothing and made as though he had not heard. But the Irishman understood that it was in the spirit of feeble compromise that danger lay—if danger there was at all, and he himself was far beyond such weakness. His eye was single and his body full of light, and the faith that plays with mountains had made him whole. Return to Nature for him involved no denial of human life, nor depreciation of human interests, but only a revolutionary shifting of values.

"And it was one night while he slept and I watched him in the little room," resumed the German as though there had been no interruption, "I noticed first so decisively this growing of a singular size about him I have already mentioned and grasped its meaning. For the bulk of the man while growing—emerging, rather, I should say—assumed another shape than his own. It was not my eyes that saw it. I saw him as *he felt himself to be*. The creature's personality, his essential inner being, was acting directly upon my own. His influence was at me from another point or angle. First the emotions, then the senses you see. It was a finely organized attack.

"I definitely understood at last that my mind was affected—and proved it too, for the instant effort I made at recovery resulted in my seeing him normal again. The size and shape retreated the moment I denied them."

O'Malley noticed how the speaker's voice lingered over the phrase. Again, he knew the intention of the pause that followed. He held his peace, however, and waited.

"Nor was sight the only sense affected," Stahl continued, "for smell and hearing also brought their testimony. Through all but touch, indeed, the hallucination attacked me. For sometimes at night while I sat up watching in the little room, there rose outside the open window in the yards and gardens a sound of tramping, a distant roaring as of voices in a rising wind, a rushing, hollow murmur, confused and deep like that of forests, or the swift passage of a host of big birds across the sky. I heard it, both in the air and on the ground—this tramping on the lawns, this curious shaking of the atmosphere. And with it at the same time a sharp and mingled perfume that made me think of earth and leaves, of flowers after rain, of plains and open spaces, most singular of all—of animals and horses.

"Before the firm denial of my mind, they vanished, just as the change of form had vanished. But both left me weaker than they found me, more tender to attack. Moreover, I understood most plainly, that they emanated all from him. These 'emanations' came, too, chiefly, as I mentioned, whilst he slept. In sleep, it seemed, he set them free. The slumber of the body disengaged them. And then the instinct came to warn me—presenting itself with the authority of an unanswerable intuition—the realization, namely, that if, for a single moment in his presence, I slept, the changes would leap forward in my own being, and I should join him."

"Escape! Know freedom in a larger consciousness!" cried the other.

"And for a man of my point of view and training to have permitted such a conviction at all," he went on, the interruption utterly ignored again, "proves how far along the road I had already traveled without knowing it. Only at the time I was not aware of this. It was the shock of full discovery later that brought me to my senses, when, seeking to withdraw,—I found I could not."

"And so, you ran away." It came out bluntly enough, with a touch of scorn but ill-concealed.

"We discharged him. But before that came there was more I have to tell you—if you still care to hear it."

"I'm not tired, if that's what you mean. I could listen all night, as far as that goes."

He rose to stretch his legs a moment, and Stahl rose too—instantly. Together they leaned over the bulwarks. The German's hat was off, and the air made by the steamer's passage drew his beard out. The warm soft wind brought odors of sea and shore. It caressed their faces, then passed on across those sleeping peasants on the lower deck. The masts and rigging swung steadily against the host of stars.

"Before I thus knew myself half caught," continued the doctor, standing now close enough beside him for actual contact, "and found it difficult to get away, other things had happened, things that confirmed the change so singularly begun in me. They happened everywhere; confirmation came from many quarters; though slight enough, they filled in all the gaps and crevices, strengthened the joints, and built the huge illusion round me all complete until it held me like a prison.

"And they are difficult to tell. Only, indeed, to yourself who underwent a similar experience up there in the mountains, could they bring much meaning. You had the same temptation and you—weathered the same storm." He caught O'Malley's arm a moment and held it. "You escaped this madness just as I did, and you will realize what I mean when I say that the sensation of losing my sense of personal identity became so dangerously, so seductively strong. The feeling of extended consciousness became delicious—too delicious to resist. A kind of pagan joy and exultation known to some in early youth, but put away with the things of youth, possessed me. In the presence of this other's soul, so strangely powerful in its silence and simplicity, I felt as though I touched new sources of life. I tapped them. They poured down and flooded me—with dreams—dreams that could really haunt—with unsettling thoughts of glory and delight beyond the body. I got clean away into Nature. I felt as though some portion of me just awakening reached out across him into rain and sunshine, far up into the sweet and starry sky—as a tree growing out of a thicket that chokes its lower part finds light and freedom at the top."

"It caught you badly, doctor," O'Malley murmured. "The gods came close!"

"So badly that I loathed the prisoned darkness that held me so thickly in the body. I longed to know my being all dispersed through Nature, scattered with dew and wind, shining with the star-light and the sun. And the manner of escape I hinted to you a little while ago came to seem right and necessary. Lawful it seemed, and obvious. The mania literally obsessed me, though still I tried to hide it even from myself ... and struggled in resistance."

"You spoke just now of other things that came to confirm it," the Irishman said while the other paused to take breath. All this he knew. He grew weary of Stahl's clever laboring the point that it was madness. A little knowledge is ever dangerous, and he saw so clearly why the hesitation of the merely intellectual man had led him into error. "Did you mean that others acknowledged this influence as well as yourself?"

"You shall read that for yourself tomorrow," came the answer, "in the detailed report I drew up afterwards; it is far too long to tell you now. But I may mention something of it. That breaking out of patients was a curious thing, their trying to escape, their dreams and singing, their efforts sometimes to approach his room, their longing for the open and the gardens; the deep, prolonged entrancing of a few; the sounds of rushing, tramping that they, too, heard, the violence of some, the silent ecstasy of others. The thing may find its parallel, perhaps, in the collective mania that sometimes afflicts religious communities, in monasteries or convents. Only here there was no preacher and eloquent leader to induce hysteria—nothing but that silent dynamo of power, gentle and winning as a little child, a being who could not put a phrase together, exerting his potent spell unconsciously, and chiefly while he slept.

"For the phenomena almost without exception came in the night, and often at their fullest strength, as afterwards reported to me, while I dozed in his room and watched beside his motionless and slumbering form. Oh, and there was more as well, much more, as you shall read.

The stories my assistants brought me, the tales of frightened nurse and warder, the amazing yarns the porter stammered out, of strangers who had rung the bell at dawn, trying to push past him through the door, saying they were messengers and had been summoned, sent for, had to come,—large, curious, windy figures, or, as he sometimes called them with unconscious humor, 'like creatures out of fairy books or circuses' that always vanished as suddenly as they came. Making every allowance for excitement and exaggeration, the tales were strange enough, I can assure you, and the way many of the patients knew their visions intensified, their illusions doubly strengthened, their efforts even to destroy themselves in many cases almost more than the staff could deal with—all this brought the matter to a climax and made my duty very plain at last."

"And the effect upon yourself—at its worst?" asked his listener quietly.

Stahl sighed wearily a little as he answered with a new-found sadness in his tone.

"I've told you briefly that," he said; "repetition cannot strengthen it. The worthlessness of the majority of human aims today expresses it Best—what you have called yourself the 'horror of civilization.' The vanity of all life's modern, so-called up-to-date tendencies for outer, mechanical developments. A wild, mad beauty streaming from that man's personality overran the whole place and caught the lot of us, myself especially, with a lust for simple, natural things, and with a passion for spiritual beauty to accompany them. Fame, wealth, position seemed the shadows then, and something else it's hard to name announced itself as the substance.... I wanted to clear out and live with Nature, to know simplicity, unselfish purposes, a golden state of childlike existence close to dawns and dew and running water, cared for by woods and blessed by all the winds...." He paused again for breath, then added:—

"And that's just where the mania caught at me so cunningly—till I saw it and called a halt."

"Ah!"

"For the thing I sought, the thing *he* knew, and perhaps remembered, was not possible *in the body*. It was a spiritual state—"

"Or to be known subjectively!" O'Malley checked him.

"I am no lotus-eater by nature," he went on with energy, "and so I fought and conquered it. But first, I tell you, it came upon me like a tempest—a hurricane of wonder and delight. I've always held, like yourself perhaps, that civilization brings its own army of diseases, and that the few illnesses known to ruder savage races can be cured by simple means the earth herself supplies. And along this line of thought the thing swept into me—the line of my own head-learning. This was natural enough; natural enough, too, that it thus at first deceived me.

"For the quack cures of history come to this—herb simples and the rest; only we know them now as sun-cure, water-cure, open-air cure, old Kneipp, sea-water, and a hundred others. Doctors have never swarmed before as they do now, and these artificial diseases civilization brings in such quantity seemed all at once to mean the abeyance of some central life or power men ought to share with—Nature.... You shall read it all in my written report. I merely wish to show you now, how the insidious thing got at me along the line of my special knowledge. I saw the truth that priests and doctors are the only possible and necessary 'professions' in the world, and—that they should be really but a single profession...."

XLIV

He drew suddenly back with a kind of jerk. It was as though he realized abruptly that he had said too much—had overdone it. He took his companion by the arm and led him down the decks.

As they passed the bridge the Captain called out a word of welcome to them; and his jolly, boisterous laugh ran down the wind. The American engineer came from behind a dark corner, almost running into them; his face was flushed. "It's like a furnace below," he said in his nasal familiar manner; "too hot to sleep. I've run up for a gulp of air." He made as though he would join them.

"The wind's behind us, yes," replied the doctor in a different tone, "and there's no draught." With a gesture, half bow, half dismissal, he made even this thick-skinned member of "the greatest civilization on earth" understand he was not wanted. And they turned at the cabin door, O'Malley a moment wondering at the admirable dignity with which the "little" man had managed the polite dismissal.

Himself, perhaps, he would not have minded the diversion. He was a little weary of the German's long recital. The confession had not been complete, he felt. Much had been held back. It was not altogether straightforward. The dishonesty which hides in compromise peeped through it everywhere.

And the incoherence of the latter part had almost bored him. For it was, he easily divined, a studied incoherence. It was meant to touch a similar weakness in himself—if there. But it was *not* there. He saw through the whole manoeuvre. Stahl wished to warn and save him by showing that the experience they had partly shared was nothing but a strange mental disorder. He wished to force in this subtle way his own interpretation of it upon his friend. Yet at the same time the intuitive Irishman discerned that other tendency in the man which would so gladly perhaps have welcomed a different explanation, and even in some fashion did actually accept it.

O'Malley smiled inwardly as he watched him prepare the coffee as of old. And patiently he waited for the rest that was to come. In a certain sense it all was useful. It would be helpful later. This was an attitude he would often have to face when he returned to civilized life and tried to tell his Message to the thinking, educated men of today—the men he must win over somehow to his dream—the men, without whose backing, no Movement could hope to meet with even a measure of success.

"So, like myself," said Stahl, as he carefully tended the flame of the spirit-lamp between them, "you have escaped by the skin of your teeth, as it were. And I congratulate you—heartily."

"I thank you," said the other dryly.

"You write your version now, and I'll write mine—indeed it is already almost finished—then we'll compare notes. Perhaps we might even publish them together."

He poured out the fragrant coffee. They faced each other across the little table. But O'Malley did not take the bait. He wished to hear the balance his companion still might tell.

And presently he asked for it.

"With the discharge of your patient the trouble ceased at once, then?"

"Comparatively soon. It gradually subsided, yes."

"And as regards yourself?"

"I came back to my senses. I recovered my control. The insubordinate impulses I had known retired." He smiled as he sipped his coffee. "You see me now," he added, looking his companion steadily in the eyes, "a sane and commonplace ship's doctor."

"I congratulate you—"

"*Vielen Dank.*" He bowed.

"On what you missed, yet almost accomplished," the other finished. "You might have known, like me, the cosmic consciousness! You might have met the gods!"

"In a strait-waistcoat," the doctor added with a snap.

They laughed at one another across their coffee cups as once before they had laughed across their glasses of Kakhetian wine—two eternally antagonistic types that will exist as long as life itself.

But, contrary to his expectations, the German had little more to tell. He mentioned how the experience had led his mind into strange and novel reading in his desire to know what other minds might have to offer by way of explanation, even the most fanciful and far-fetched. He told, though very briefly, how he had picked up Fechner among others, and carefully studied his "poetic theories," and read besides the best accounts of "spiritistic" phenomena, as also of the rarer states of hysteria, double-consciousness, multiple personality, and even those looser theories which suggest that a portion of the human constitution called "astral" or "etheric" may escape from the parent center and, carrying with it the subtler forces of desire and yearning, construct a vivid subjective state of mind which is practically its Heaven of hope and longing all fulfilled.

He did not, however, betray the results upon himself of all this curious reading and study, nor mention what he found of truth or probability in it all. He merely quoted books and authors, in at least three languages, that stretched in a singular and catholic array from Plato and the Neo-Platonists across the ages to Myers, Du Prel, Flournoy, Lodge, and Morton Prince.

Out of the lot, perhaps,—O'Malley gathered it by inference rather than from actual statement, from fragments of their talks upon the outward voyage more than from anything let fall just then—Fechner had proved the most persuasive to this man's contradictory and original mind. It certainly seemed, at least, as if he knew some secret sympathetic leaning toward the idea that consciousness and matter were inseparable, and that a Cosmic Consciousness "of sorts" might pertain to the Earth as, equally, to all the other stars and planets. The *Urwelt* idea he so often referred to had seized a part of his imagination—that, at least, was clear.

The Irishman drank it all in, but he was too exhausted now to argue, and too full besides to ask questions. His natural volubility forsook him. He let the doctor have his say without interruptions. He took the warnings with the rest of it. Nothing the other said had changed him.

It was not the first sunrise they had watched together, and as they took the morning air on deck once more, Corsica rising like a dream the night had left behind her on the sea, he listened with fainter interest to the German's concluding sentences.

"At any rate you now understand why on that other voyage I was so eager to watch you with your friend, so keen to separate you, to prevent your sleeping with him, and at the same time so desirous to see his influence upon you at close quarters; and also—why I always understood so well what was going on both outwardly and within."

O'Malley quietly reiterated the belief he still held in the power of his own dream.

"I shall go home and give my message to the world," was what he said quietly. "I think it's true."

"It's better to keep silent," was the answer, "for, even if true, the world is not ready yet to listen. It will evaporate, you'll find, in the telling. You'll find there's nothing to tell. Besides, a dream like yours must dawn on all at once, and not on merely one. No one will understand you."

"I can but try."

"You will reach no men of action; and few of intellect. You will merely stuff the dreamers who are already stuffed enough. What is the use, I ask you? What is the use?"

"It will set the world on fire for simplicity," the other murmured, knowing the great sweet passion flame within him as he watched the sun come slowly out of the rosy sea. "All the use in the world."

"None," was the laconic answer.

"They might know the gods!" cried O'Malley, using the phrase that symbolized for him the entire Vision.

Stahl looked at him for some time before he spoke. Again, that expression of wistful, almost longing admiration shone in the brown eyes.

"My friend," he answered gravely, "men do not want to know the gods. They prefer their delights less subtle. They crave the cruder physical sensations that bang them toward excitement—"

"Of disease, of pain, of separateness," put in the other.

The German shrugged his shoulders. "It's the stage they're at," he said. "You, if you have success, will merely make a few uncomfortable. The majority will hardly turn their heads. To one in a million you may bring peace and happiness."

"It's worth it," cried the Irishman, "even for that one!"

Stahl answered very gently, smiling with his new expression of tenderness and sympathy. "Dream your great dream if you will, but dream it, my friend, alone—in peace and silence. That 'one' I speak of is yourself."

The doctor pressed his hand and turned toward his cabin. O'Malley stood a little longer to share the sunrise. Neither spoke another word. He heard the door shut softly behind him. The unspoken answer in his mind was in two words—two common little adjectives: "Coward and selfish!"

But Stahl, once in the privacy of his cabin, judging by the glance visible on his face ere he closed the door, may probably have known a very different thought. And possibly he uttered it below his breath. A sigh most certainly escaped his lips, a sigh half sadness, half relief. For O'Malley remembered it afterwards.

"Beautiful, foolish dreamer among men! But thank God, harmless—to others and—himself."

And soon afterwards O'Malley also went to his cabin. Before sleep took him he lay deep in a mood of sadness—almost as though he had heard his friend's unspoken thought. He realized the insuperable difficulties that lay before him. The world would think him "mad but harmless."

Then, with full sleep, he slipped across that sunrise and found the old-world Garden. He held the eternal password.

"I can but try…!"

XLV

And here the crowded, muddled notebooks come to an end. The rest was action—and inevitable disaster.

The brief history of O'Malley's mad campaign may be imagined. To a writer who found interest in the study of forlorn hopes and their leaders, a detailed record of this particular one might seem worthwhile. For me personally it is too sad and too pathetic. I cannot bring myself to tell, much less to analyze the story of a broken heart, when that heart and story are those of a close and deeply admired intimate, a man who gave me genuine love and held my own.

Besides, although a curious chapter in uncommon human nature, it is not by any means a new one. It is the true story of many a poet and dreamer since the world began, though perhaps not often told nor even guessed. And only the poets themselves, especially the little poets who cannot utter half the fire that consumes them, may know the searing pain and passion and the true inwardness of it all.

Most of those months it chanced I was away, and only fragments of the foolish enterprise could reach me. But nothing, I think, could have stopped him, nor any worldly selfish wisdom made him even pause. The thing possessed him utterly; it had to flame its way out as best it could. To high and low, he preached by every means in his power the Simple Life; he preached the mystical life as well—that the true knowledge and the true progress are within, that they both pertain to the inner being and have no chief concern with external things. He preached it wildly, lopsidedly, in or out of season, knowing no half measures. His enthusiasm obscured his sense of proportion, and the extravagance hid the germ of truth that undeniably lay in his message.

To put the movement on its feet at first he realized every possession that he had. It left him penniless, if he was not almost so already, and in the end it left him smothered beneath the glory of his blinding and unutterable Dream. He never understood that suggestion is more effective than a sledge-hammer. His faith was no mere little seed of mustard, but a full-fledged forest singing its message in a wind of thunder. He shouted it aloud to the world.

I think the acid disappointment that lies beneath that trite old phrase "a broken heart" was never really his; for indeed it seemed that his cruel, ludicrous failure merely served to strengthen hope and purpose by making him seek for a better method of imparting what he had to say. In the end he learned the bitter lesson to the full. But faith never trailed a single feather. Those jeering audiences in the Park; those empty benches in many a public hall, those brief, ignoring paragraphs in the few newspapers that filled a vacant corner by labeling him crank and long-haired prophet; even the silence that greeted his pamphlets, his letters to the Press, and all the rest, hurt him for others rather than for himself. His pain was altruistic, never personal. His dream and motive, his huge, unwieldy compassion, his genuine love for humanity, all were big enough for that.

And so, I think, he missed the personal mortification that disappointment so deep might bring to dreamers with an aim less unadulteratedly pure. His eye was single to the end. He attributed only the highest motives to all who offered help. The very quacks and fools who flocked to his banner, eager to exploit their smaller fads by joining them to his own, he welcomed, only regretting that, as Stahl had warned him, he could not attract a better class of mind. He did not even see through the manoeuvres of the occasional women of wealth and title who sought to conceal their own mediocrity by advertising in their drawing-rooms the eccentricities of men like himself. And to the end he had the courage of his glorious convictions.

The change of method that he learned at last, moreover, was characteristic of this faith and courage.

"I've begun at the wrong end," he said; "I shall never reach men through their intellects. Their brains today are occupied by the machine-made gods of civilization. I cannot change the direction of their thoughts and lusts from outside; the momentum is too great to stop that way. I must get at them from within. To reach their hearts, the new ideas must rise up *from within*. I see the truer way. I must do it *from the other side*. It must come to them—in Beauty."

For he was to the last convinced that death would merge him in the being of the Earth's Collective Consciousness, and that, lost in her deep eternal beauty, he thus might reach the hearts of men in some stray glimpse of nature's loveliness and register his flaming message. He loved to quote from Adonais:

"He is made one with Nature: there is heard
His voice in all her music, from the moan
Of thunder, to the song of night's sweet bird;
He is a presence to be felt and known
In darkness and in light, from herb and stone,
Spreading itself where'er that Power may move
Which has withdrawn his being to its own.
He is a portion of the loveliness
Which once he made more lovely: he doth bear
His part, while the one Spirit's plastic stress
Sweeps through the dull dense world..."

And this thought, phrased in a dozen different ways, was always on his lips. To dream was right and useful, even to dream alone, because the beauty of the dream must add to the beauty of the Whole of which it is a part and an interpretation. It was not really lost or vain. All must come back in time to feed the world. He had known gracious thoughts of Earth too big to utter, almost too big to hold. Such thoughts could not ever be really told; they were incommunicable. For the mystical revelation is incommunicable. It has authority only for him who feels it. A corporate revelation is impossible. Only those among men could know, in whose hearts it rose intuitively and made its presence felt as innate ideas. Inspiration brings it, and beauty is the vehicle. Their hearts must change before their minds could be reached.

"I can work it better from the other side—from that old, old Garden which is the Mother's heart. In this way I can help at any rate...!"

XLVI

It was at the close of a wet and foggy autumn that we met again, winter in the air, all London desolate; and his wasted, forlorn appearance told me the truth at once. Only the passionate eagerness of voice and manner were there to prove that the spirit had not weakened. There glowed within a fire that showed itself in the translucent shining of the eyes and face.

"I've made one great discovery, old man," he exclaimed with old, familiar, high enthusiasm, "one great discovery at least."

"You've made so many," I answered cheerfully, while my real thoughts were busy with his bodily state of health. For his appearance shocked me. He stood among a litter of papers, books, neckties, nailed boots, knapsacks, maps and what-not, that rolled upon the floor from the mouth of the Willesden canvas sack. His old grey flannel suit hung literally upon a bag of bones; all the life there had seemed concentrated in his face and eyes—those far-seeing, light blue eyes. They were darker than usual now, eyes like the sea, I thought. His hair, long and disordered, tumbled over his forehead. He was pale, and at the same time flushed. It was almost a disembodied spirit that I saw.

"You've made so many. I love to hear them. Is this one finer than the others?"

He looked a moment at me through and through, almost uncannily. He looked in reality beyond me. It was something else he saw, and in the dusk I turned involuntarily.

"Simpler," he said quickly, "much simpler."

He moved up close beside me, whispering. Was it all imagination that a breath of flowers came with him? There was certainly a curious fragrance in the air, wild and sweet like orchards in the spring.

"And it is—?"

"That the Garden's everywhere! You needn't go to the distant Caucasus to find it. It's all about this old London town, and in these foggy streets and dingy pavements. It's even in this cramped, undusted room. Now at this moment, while that lamp flickers and the thousands go to sleep. The gates of horn and ivory are here," he tapped his breast. "And here the flowers, the long, clean open hills, the giant herd, the nymphs, the sunshine and the gods!"

So attached was he now to that little room in Paddington where his books and papers lay, that when the curious illness that had caught him grew so much worse, and the attacks of the nameless fever that afflicted him turned serious, I hired a bedroom for him in the same house. And it was in that poky, cage-like den he breathed his last.

His illness I called curious, his fever nameless, because they really were so and puzzled everyone. He simply faded out of life, it seemed; there was no pain, no sleeplessness, no suffering of any physical kind. He uttered no complaint, nor were there symptoms of any known disorder.

"Your friend is sound organically," the doctor told me when I pressed him for the truth there on the stairs, "sound as a bell. He wants the open air and plenty of wholesome food, that's all. His body is ill-nourished. His trouble is mental—some deep and heavy disappointment doubtless. If you can change the current of his thoughts, awaken interest in common things, and give him change of scene, perhaps—" He shrugged his shoulders and looked very grave.

"You think he's dying?"

"I think, yes, he is dying."

"From—?"

"From lack of living pure and simple," was the answer. "He has lost all hold on life."

"He has abundant vitality still."

"Full of it. But it all goes—elsewhere. The physical organism gets none of it."

"Yet mentally," I asked, "there's nothing actually wrong?"

"Not in the ordinary sense. The mind is clear and active. So far as I can test it, the process of thought is healthy and undamaged. It seems to me—"

He hesitated a moment on the doorstep while the driver wound the motor handle. I waited with a sinking heart for the rest of the sentence.

"...like certain cases of nostalgia, I have known—very rare and very difficult to deal with. Acute and vehement nostalgia, yes, sometimes called a broken heart," he added, pausing another instant at the carriage door, "in which the entire stream of a man's inner life flows to some distant place, or person, or—or to some imagined yearning that he craves to satisfy."

"To a dream?"

"It might be even that," he answered slowly, stepping in. "It might be spiritual. The religious and poetic temperament are most open to it, *and* the most difficult to deal with when afflicted." He emphasized the little word as though the doubt he felt was far less strong than the conviction he only half concealed. "If you would save him, try to change the direction of his thoughts. There is nothing—in all honesty I must say it—nothing that I can do to help."

And then, pulling at the grey tuft on his chin and looking keenly at me a moment over his glasses,—"Those flowers," he said hesitatingly, "you might move those flowers from the room, perhaps. Their perfume is a trifle strong ... It might be better." Again, he looked sharply at me. There was an odd expression in his eyes. And in my heart there was an odd sensation too, so odd that I found myself bereft a moment of any speech at all, and when my tongue became untied, the carriage was already disappearing down the street. For in that dingy sick-room there were no flowers at all, yet the perfume of woods and fields and open spaces had reached the doctor too, and obviously perplexed him.

"Change the direction of his thoughts!" I went indoors, wondering how any honest and even half-unselfish friend, knowing what I knew, could follow such advice. With what but the lowest motive, of keeping him alive for my own happiness, could I seek to change his thoughts of some imagined joy and peace to the pain and sordid facts of an earthly existence that he loathed?

But when I turned I saw the tousled yellow-headed landlady standing in the breach. Mrs. Heath stopped me in the hall to inquire whether I could say "anythink abart the rent perhaps?" Her manner was defiant. I found three months were owing.

"It's no good arsking 'im," she said, though not unkindly on the whole. "I'm sick and tired of always being put off. He talks about the gawds and a Mr. Pan, or some such gentleman who he says will look after it all. But I never sees 'im—not this Mr. Pan. And his stuff up there," jerking her head toward the little room, "ain't worth a Sankey-moody 'ymn-book, take the lot of it at cost!"

I reassured her. It was impossible to help smiling. For some minds, I reflected, a Sankey hymn-book might hold dreams that were every bit as potent as his own, and far less troublesome. But that "Mr. Pan, or some such gentleman" should serve as a "reference" between lodger and landlady was an unwitting comment on the modern point of view that made me want to cry rather than to laugh. O'Malley and Mrs. Heath between them had made a profounder criticism than they knew.

* * * * *

And so, by slow degrees he went, leaving the outer fury for the inner peace. The center of consciousness gradually shifted from the transient form, which is the true ghost, to the deeper, permanent state which is the eternal reality. For this was how he phrased it to me in one of our last, strange talks. He watched his own withdrawal.

In bed he would lie for hours with fixed and happy eyes, staring apparently at nothing, the expression on his face quite radiant. The pulse sank often dangerously low; he scarcely seemed to breathe; yet it was never complete unconsciousness or trance. My voice, when I found the heart to try and coax his own for speech, would win him back. The eyes would then grow dimmer, losing their happier light, as he turned to the outer world to look at me.

"The pull is so tremendous now," he whispered; "I was far, so far away, in the deep life of Earth. Why do you bring me back to all these little pains? I can do nothing here; there I am of use..."

He spoke so low I had to bend my head to catch the words. It was very late at night and for hours I had been watching by his side. Outside an ugly yellow fog oppressed the town, but about him like an atmosphere I caught again that fragrance as of trees and flowers. It was too faint for any name—that fugitive, mild perfume one meets upon bare hills and round the skirts of forests. It was somehow, I fancied, in the very breath.

"Each time the effort to return is greater. In there I am complete and full of power. I can work and send my message back so splendidly. Here," he glanced down at his wasted body with a curious smile, "I am only on the fringe—it's pain and failure. All so ineffective."

That other look came back into the eyes, more swiftly than before.

"I thought you might like to speak, to tell me—something," I said, keeping the tears with difficulty from my voice. "Is there no one you would like to see?"

He shook his head slowly, and gave the peculiar answer:

"They're all in there."

"But Stahl, perhaps—if I could get him here?"

An expression of gentle disapproval crossed his face, then melted softly into a wistful tenderness as of a child.

"He's not there—yet" he whispered, "but he will come too in the end. In sleep, I think, he goes there even now."

"Where are you really then?" I ventured, "And where is it you go to?"

The answer came unhesitatingly; there was no doubt or searching.

"Into myself, my real and deeper self, and so beyond it into her—the Earth. Where all the others are—all, all, all."

And then he frightened me by sitting up in bed abruptly. His eyes stared past me—out beyond the close confining walls. The movement was so startling with its suddenness and vigor that I shrank back a moment. The head was sideways. He was intently listening.

"Hark!" he whispered. "They are calling me! Do you hear…?"

The look of joy that broke over the face like sunshine made me hold my breath. Something in his low voice thrilled me beyond all I have ever known. I listened too. Only the rumble of the traffic down the distant main street broke the silence, the rattle of a nearer cart, and the footsteps of a few pedestrians. No other noises came across the night. There was no wind. Thick yellow fog muffled everything.

"I hear nothing," I answered softly. "What is it that *you* hear?"

And, making no reply, he presently lay down again among the pillows, that look of joy and glory still upon his face. It lay there to the end like sunrise.

The fog came in so thickly through the window that I rose to close it. He never closed that window, and I hoped he would not notice. For a sound of wretched street-music was coming nearer—some beggar playing dismally upon a penny whistle—and I feared it would disturb him. But in a flash he was up again.

"No, no!" he cried, raising his voice for the first time that night. "Do not shut it. I shan't be able to hear then. Let all the air come in. Open it wider… wider! I love that sound!"

"The fog—"

"There is no fog. It's only sun and flowers and music. Let them in. Don't you hear it now?" he added. And more to bring him peace than anything else, I bowed my head to signify agreement. For the last confusion of the mind, I saw, was upon him, and he made the outer world confirm some imagined detail of his inner dream. I drew the sash down lower, covering his body closely with the blankets. He flung them off impatiently at once. The damp and freezing night rushed in upon us like a presence. It made me shudder, but O'Malley only raised himself upon one elbow to taste it better, and—to listen.

Then, waiting patiently for the return of the quiet, trance-like state when I might cover him again, I moved toward the window and looked out. The street was empty, save for that beggar playing vilely on his penny whistle. The wretch came to a standstill immediately before the house. The lamplight fell from the room upon his tattered, broken figure. I could not see his face. He groped and felt his way.

Outside that homeless wanderer played his penny pipe in the night of cold and darkness.

Inside the Dreamer listened, dreaming of his gods and garden, his great Earth Mother, his visioned life of peace and simple things with a living Nature...

And I felt somehow that player watched us. I made an angry sign to him to go. But it was the sudden touch upon my arm that made me turn round with such a sudden start that I almost cried aloud. O'Malley in his night-clothes stood close against me on the floor, slight as a spirit, eyes a-shine, lips moving faintly into speech through the most wonderful smile a human face has ever shown me.

"Do not send him away," he whispered, joy breaking from him like a light, "but tell him that I love it. Go out and thank him. Tell him I hear and understand and say that I am coming. Will you...?"

Something within me whirled. It seemed that I was lifted from my feet a moment. Some tide of power rushed from his person to my own. The room was filled with blinding light. But in my heart there rose a great emotion that combined tears and joy and laughter all at once.

"The moment you are back in bed," I heard my voice like one speaking from a distance, "I'll go—"

The momentary, wild confusion passed as suddenly as it came. I remember he obeyed at once. As I bent down to tuck the clothes about him, that fragrance as of flowers and open spaces rose about my bending face like incense—bewilderingly sweet.

And the next second I was standing in the street. The man who played upon the pipe, I saw, was blind. His hand and fingers were curiously large.

I was already close, ready to press all that my pockets held into his hand—ay, and far more than merely pockets held because O'Malley said he loved the music—when something made me turn my head away. I cannot say precisely what it was, for first it seemed a tapping at the window of his room behind me, and then a little noise within the room itself, and next—more curious than either,—a feeling that something came out rushing past me through the air. It whirled and shouted as it went...

I only remember clearly that in the very act of turning, and while my look still held that beggar's face within the field of vision, I saw the sightless eyes turn bright a moment as though he opened them and saw. He did most certainly smile; to that I swear.

But when I turned again the street immediately about me was empty. The beggar-man was gone.

And down the pavement, moving swiftly through the curtain of fog, I saw his vanishing figure. It was large and spreading. In the fringe of light, the lamp-post gave, its upper edges seemed far above the ground. Someone else was with him. There were two figures.

I heard that sound of piping far away. It sounded faint and almost flute-like in the air. And in the mud at my feet the money lay—spurned utterly. I heard the last coins ring upon the pavement as they settled. But in the room, when I got back, the body of Terence O'Malley had ceased to breathe.

***** END *****